7

Contents

Yui Yuigahama

Yukino Yukinoshita

MY YOUTH R♥MANTIC C☺MEDY iS WRØNG, AS I EXPECTED

Wataru Watari
Illustration **Ponkan⑧**

VOLUME
7

YEN
ON
NEW YORK

MY YOUTH ROMANTIC COMEDY IS WRONG, AS I EXPECTED Vol. 7

WATARU WATARI

Illustration by Ponkan⑧

Translation by Jennifer Ward

Cover art by Ponkan⑧

YAHARI ORE NO SEISHUN LOVE COME WA MACHIGATTEIRU.

Vol. 7 by Wataru WATARI

© 2011 Wataru WATARI

Illustration by PONKAN⑧

All rights reserved.

Original Japanese edition published by SHOGAKUKAN.

English translation rights arranged with SHOGAKUKAN through Tuttle-Mori Agency, Inc., Tokyo.

English translation © 2019 by Yen Press, LLC

Yen On

1290 Avenue of the Americas

New York, NY 10104

Visit us at yenpress.com

facebook.com/yenpress

twitter.com/yenpress

yenpress.tumblr.com

instagram.com/yenpress

First Yen On Edition: February 2019

Yen On is an imprint of Yen Press, LLC.

The Yen On name and logo are trademarks of Yen Press, LLC.

Library of Congress Cataloging-in-Publication Data

Names: Watari, Wataru, author. | Ponkan 8, illustrator.

Title: My youth romantic comedy is wrong, as I expected / Wataru Watari ; illustration by Ponkan 8.

Other titles: Yahari ore no seishun love come wa machigatteiru. English

Description: New York : Yen On, 2016–

Identifiers: LCCN 2016005816 | ISBN 9780316312295 (v. 1 : pbk.) | ISBN 9780316396011 (v. 2 : pbk.) | ISBN 9780316318068 (v. 3 : pbk.) | ISBN 9780316318075 (v. 4 : pbk.) | ISBN 9780316318082 (v. 5 : pbk.) | ISBN 9780316411868 (v. 6 : pbk.) | ISBN 9781975384128 (v. 7 : pbk.)

Subjects: | CYAC: Optimism—Fiction. | School—Fiction.

Classification: LCC PZ7.1.W396 My 2016 | DDC [Fic]—dc23

LC record available at http://lccn.loc.gov/2016005816

ISBN: 978-1-9753-8412-8

10 9 8 7 6 5 4 3 2 1

LSC-C

Printed in the United States of America

MY YOUTH R♥MANTIC C☺MEDY iS WRØNG, AS I EXPECTED

seven

Cast of Characters

Hachiman Hikigaya.......... The main character. High school second-year. Twisted personality.

Yukino Yukinoshita.......... Captain of the Service Club. Perfectionist.

Yui Yuigahama.................. Hachiman's classmate. Tends to worry about what other people think.

Yoshiteru Zaimokuza......... Nerd. Ambition is to become a light novel author.

Saika Totsuka.................. In tennis club. Very cute. A boy, though.

Hayato Hayama.................. Hachiman's classmate. Popular. In the soccer club.

Kakeru Tobe..................... Hachiman's classmate. An excitable character and member of Hayama's clique.

Yumiko Miura................... Hachiman's classmate. Reigns over the girls in class as queen bee.

Hina Ebina........................ Hachiman's classmate. Part of Miura's clique, but a slash fangirl.

Shizuka Hiratsuka............. Japanese teacher. Guidance counselor.

Haruno Yukinoshita.......... Yukino's older sister. In university.

Komachi Hikigaya............. Hachiman's little sister. In her third year in middle school.

SOUBU HIGH SCHOOL

Hachiman Hikigaya

Topic: Yasaka Shrine and Belief in Goryou

The spirit enshrined in Yasaka Shrine is Gozu Tennou. Believed to bring about plague and disaster, he would typically be loathed and avoided, but at Yasaka Shrine, he is hallowed as a god.

The reason for this is belief in goryou. Simply put, this is the belief that enshrining a harmful and malicious god as an honored spirit—a goryou—to appease it will enable the people to avoid its curse. By worshiping, deifying, and placating this god, they attempt to avoid disaster.

This hatred and fear will lead to persecution and utter loathing. Eventually, this treatment will become so intense that it becomes its own form of reverence. It's quite common in this country for those who were once abhorred as vengeful spirits to be later venerated as gods. Even the divine Sugawara no Michizane was one of these, feared so much that people began to worship him.

In other words, the hated are the closest to the divine. So then isn't that proof that such people are in fact to be admired?

I see—so I was a god after all...

Hachiman Hikigaya's life at school is, in fact, extremely peaceful.

It was that season again—the one that makes me think girls are actually more attractive in additional clothes rather than fewer. The cultural festival was over, the athletic festival had come and gone without any major hiccups, and the year would conclude in less than two months. The weather had suddenly got colder, and the wind had turned from cool breezes to wintry chills.

The world around me was colder and bleaker, too.

My seat in the middle of the classroom was like the eye of a hurricane, a vacuum no one dared approach. Everyone seemed to like the edges and corners—perhaps this is a custom of the Japanese. On the train or the bus, people always choose the sides and corners first. If you turned them into cute girls, I'm sure Wall-chan and Corner-chan would be super-popular.

And so there was no one around my spot in the center. It had always been like this.

What was different now was how they looked at me.

They weren't oblivious to me. They were deliberately going out of their way to tell me they were ignoring me. Their eyes would flick toward me for just an instant, as if they were smothering snickers.

When I'd look to see where the sound was coming from, our eyes would lock. Meeting such looks is the way of the Hikigaya.

So it would be normal for them to look away again, and indeed, that's what they used to do.

But when they had the upper hand, that didn't always happen. In fact, after we'd stared at each other for two full seconds, they would giggle about it with their friends and begin their witty repartee interwoven with tasteful jokes such as *Like, he's looking at us (lol)* and *What's with that guy? (lol)* and *Ew (lol)*.

I felt a bit like a panda— No, that's an exaggeration. More like an axolotl or a sea monkey or something. *Oh man, what the heck? Am I the lovable type?* "Gross-cute," I think they call it.

I had to encourage myself, or it'd break me a little.

There was already a slight chip on one of my edges, and I'd even cried a little in bed at night. I pride myself in my Diamond-level hardness (according to the Superhuman Hardness scale), but diamond is just strong against scratches, and they actually break right apart if you give one a good whack with a hammer. You said diamond is unbreakable, didn't you? You lied.

But fortunately, it was no longer the whole grade year that was anti-Hikigaya—partly because people weren't paying much attention to me in the first place, so their attention went elsewhere quickly. They say rumors last seventy-five days, and basically, that's how it works. They're like the new *waifus* you get every season. Since they never treated me like a person in the first place, that period was condensed, and now they were so disinterested in me that I wouldn't even get a bit on *Where Are They Now?*

The world isn't concerned with me. There are plenty of other amusements out there.

That day, the classroom was filled with the same old lighthearted conversations.

The back of the class was abuzz with noisy conversation. It was just like gorillas drumming: an attempt to emphasize their existence. By the way, "drumming" in Japanese is translated *taiko*-ing.

Within this melting pot of conversation, the chatter of these kids making their mark on the world often reached my ears. Glancing over, I saw the Tobe-Ooka-Yamato trio sitting on desks. *There are chairs. Why don't you sit on those?*

"Man, what're we gonna do on the field trip?" Tobe brought up the topic, and Ooka raised his hand up high to reply.

"It's Kyoto, right? So we gotta go to USJ. USJ! USJ!"

"Ain't that in Osaka?" Yamato quipped, strangely calm and quiet.

"Whoo! A punchline from the home o' comedy, y'all!" Tobe, meanwhile, was hysterical.

…Eugh.

Frankly, I couldn't stand listening to their bad accents. *If someone from Kansai were here, these guys would probably get hit with an ashtray.* One of the defining traits of a Kansai local is their fury at crappy imitations of their accent. I reckon Conan said somethin' 'bout that.

There's nothing more dubious than a Kanto person's attempt at a Kansai accent. Should my crimes on that front be forgiven? Probably not.

With no way of knowing what was going on in my head, the three boys continued their exuberant conversation. The way they'd glance over at the girls to see if anyone noticed how much fun they were having was shallow but adorable.

"But, like, going all the way to Osaka'd be a pain in the ass," Tobe said while tugging at the hair at the back of his neck.

"Darn tootin'." The smugness radiated off Ooka.

But then in came calm, cool, and slow-on-the-uptake Yamato. He ignored the opportunity for a quip, contemplating silently before taking careful aim and saying, "…Why don't you just go by yourself, Tobe?"

"Whoa! You wanna leave me out? That's Whassis-tani, though."

They all burst into laughter.

Nearby, Oda and Tahara had been showing each other their phones, but I could see their shoulders shaking with little *snerk*s of suppressed laughter if I looked.

Yeah, yeah, laugh it up. So funny. What a riot; better call the cops.

Well, this was how they'd been treating me these days. They made me the butt of all their jokes as they all found their own ways to probe the boundary line of how much they could say and how far they could go.

By the way, there's no such thing as bullying at my school, and all these things are just jokes. Just playing around. Not bullying at *aaaaaall*. They were just *teeeeasing*. The usual. No matter how cruel their words or behavior, they can blow it all off by claiming it was just a joke. It's superconvenient. Say that to anyone, and you're Cell telling Vegeta to laugh. They have no choice.

But why do they do it? Well, it's just the conventional method of making something accepted.

When something difficult to accept is allowed into a group, a compromise is made. The only way it can be done is to make it funny. It's a necessary step to introduce something foreign into a group.

For a certain period of time, there had also been some passionate lobbying for Sagami in Class 2-F, and you might have been witness to all the disgust directed my way and a lovely sense of friendship and consideration for Sagami. But time flies when you're in high school. By the time the athletic festival was over, the "poor Sagamin" fad had ended, and now we were in the midst of a "let's make jokes about Hikitani" fad. I'm the star of the times.

They had already forgotten about Sagami and how everything started with her, and only the dregs remained—the part about treating Hachiman Hikigaya like crap—and it was now a custom. This concept of a ritual reduced to a formality is easy to understand if you imagine some religious ceremony, a historied set of behaviors that once had reasons behind it, losing its original meaning. Take the Bon Odori, or Christmas. People enjoy it and accept it without really knowing where it came from.

These things eventually become part of the group identity, a unified culture, and are performed to reaffirm group solidarity.

They'll probably get tired of this soon enough, though.

But now that the whole class was getting excited for the field trip, it was at its peak. These rituals become necessary especially at the times when everyone has to exercise their strength as a unit: when they're putting together cliques and talking about where they'll go and what they'll do.

As Tobe and his friends went on about *Whassis-tani, Whassis-tani*, gradually, the topic of conversation shifted. *And hey, my name isn't even Hikitani in the first place.*

Stroking his crew cut, Ooka said, "Anyway, this field trip, though. Sick."

"Sick," Yamato agreed. He didn't ask what was sick. What's sick is sick. What's so sick? It's real sick. If you point out the circular logic, you lose. Sick.

"So anyway, hey, Tobe, like, what're you gonna do about the thing?" Ooka brought up this subject nervously, as if he wanted so badly to ask he just couldn't help himself.

Tobe got kinda shy and bashful. "Wait, you're asking me? I guess you are. Well, y'know, isn't it obvious?" He cleared his throat lightly and paused for emphasis. "…I mean, I'm gonna do it."

The other guys *ohh*'d in admiration of his pointlessly determined expression. *Do what, I wonder. Drugs? It sure seems like he's done enough to damage the speech center of his brain already, though.*

Tobe and the guys did a one-eighty, suddenly quiet. It seemed this was something they really didn't want others to be hearing about.

Since everyone in the classroom, including the trio themselves, was now absorbed in their own conversations, attention had moved away from me. If they glanced over to check on me, they would find me staring blankly at the ceiling.

It's nice sitting on the edge of your chair, slouching into it with all your weight on the back. Sighing, I slowly closed my eyes. The classroom was abuzz with excited chattering about the approaching field trip. This meant I was freed from uncomfortable looks and sneers.

Suddenly, a shadow fell over me. *What?* I thought, and I opened my eyes to see a familiar chest—er, face. "Yahallo." Yuigahama was peering down on me from above.

"Uhhh…" I felt like I was about to fall out of my chair, but I endeavored to reply calmly.

"You're coming to club today, right?"

"Yeah."

"Okay. Then see you in the clubroom," she said quietly. This consideration was a big deal. She had apparently chosen a moment when everyone wasn't looking. With an air of secrecy, she gave a little wave in front of her chest, then returned to Miura, who gave me a questioning look but immediately dropped her gaze to her phone again.

As expected of the Queen of Fire. She walked her own path, and it seemed she wasn't much interested in the lives of the common people. She was neither an enemy nor a friend, but she also wasn't a neutral party. Her noninvolvement was something to be thankful for.

That look just now had probably not been really about me, but rather her showing concern for Yuigahama. Talking to me under the current circumstances was a fairly risky thing to do, but Yuigahama had a knack for reading the room and keeping everyone uncomfortable. I'm sure a desire for self-preservation was a major factor in her behavior, but the heaviest implication was that she was trying to avoid making me a target.

When everyone hates you but you nevertheless must associate yourself with a group, the first thing you must do is remove the targets of attack to the best of your ability. The three keys are not making mistakes, not showing fault, and avoiding errors. Wait…those are all functionally the same thing.

But even saying that, pride in your own perfection can also be an opening to attack. So first of all, the trick is to do nothing. If you don't do anything, you'll never fail.

Also, don't get involved with anyone.

Involvement with other people inevitably brings about friction—and not just between the two relevant parties. You also have to account for anyone watching. You have to be especially careful about making contact with those who tend to attract attention.

I should be somewhat careful myself. I don't want to drag anyone else into this.

Yuigahama was always considerate enough to be aware of her position in the upper caste when she spoke to me, and that's why she chose an inconspicuous moment to come talk to me, but I doubted I should rely too heavily on her for that.

Until now, just avoiding attention had been enough, but from here on out, it might be better to make myself physically scarce, like by leaving the classroom and doing something with my phone. I could pretend like I'd gotten a phone call... No, they'd catch on immediately. They would know right away that nobody would ever call me.

In the end, I was left with nothing to do, and so I lay back down on my desk.

Around the time when the break was almost over, the traffic through the classroom door reached a fever pitch. Everyone who had gone to hang out in other classrooms or to the washroom or to buy drinks was filtering back in.

I opened my eyelids a crack and saw a long ponytail out of the corner of my eye.

Her blue-tinged black hair was tied up in a scrunchie, and when she closed her phone, her beaming smile suddenly turned bored.

That girl with the brother complex. She's been texting him again? I've got to be careful when I text Komachi, too, or they'll call me a siscon. In fact, they'll even call me a sispuri. Or not.

Saki Kawa-something—I'll call her Sakikawa for short—was looking all around the room warily. It seemed she was worried someone might have seen her grinning just now.

Her gaze hit mine.

"Yeep!" She jumped a little with a strange, quiet yelp. Her face reddened visibly, and then she looked down and swiftly headed to her own seat. She'd been like that ever since the cultural festival. She avoided getting anywhere near me, and whenever she met my eyes, she was extremely obvious about turning away.

Yes, yes, that's best. There's an appropriate distance to be kept if we're both to live our lives in comfort.

Some might make the impertinent claim that only we humans kill our own species, but that's not quite true. Wild animals will make serious attempts to kill one another if their territories collide. There are all kinds of territorial overlaps at school, so of course there's gonna be conflict.

Most of all, in high school, we each have our own social groups, our own castes, and we're all of different types.

Each person really is unique.

Case in point, the one trotting up to me right that minute.

"Hachiman." A voice of heavenly music, the gait of one who walks atop the clouds themselves, and the form of a divine messenger.

Totsuka's seriously an angel.

Totsuka was so angelic, he wasn't bothered by the air coming from us foul humans, and so he came to talk to me. "They said we're going to decide on groups for the field trip in the next long homeroom." Totsuka passed along the news he'd heard somewhere.

The field trip was looming; it would be a three-night stay the following week. On the first day, we'd all be in class groups; on the second day, we'd split into smaller groups with other classmates; and on the third day, we were all free to do what we wanted. Only the first day had a fixed schedule; from the second day onward, we could all go where we wanted, which meant the hot topic for discussion in the classroom now was the second and third days.

In other words, the groups that would be decided in the next long homeroom were like the prelims that would decide about two-thirds of the field trip.

Not that it had much to do with me, since I'd be paired up with whoever was left over and follow along behind them.

"...Oh, well, everyone's basically decided already, right?"

"I dunno... I haven't decided yet," Totsuka muttered quietly, looking down. Maybe he was embarrassed he still didn't have a place to go when most everyone else had decided on their groups.

"..."

There was an uncomfortable pause, and noticing the silence, Totsuka lifted his head to cover the awkwardness with a warm expression.

I want to protect this smile.

I'm generally not disposed to invite other people to things, but this was the long-awaited school field trip. Maybe I could give it a shot this time. *But, like, giving it a shot with a guy... How did I get here?*

"...Well, we could be a group."

"Yeah!" He seized onto the favorable reply and broke into a grin, and the sight left me content. If I'd been a wandering ghost, that would have sent me peacefully on to the next life. If the JSDF had canvassed me then, I would probably have joined. "So then we need two others, right? What should we do?"

"A group of four, huh...? Well, I guess we need to find another couple of people without a full group yet and dock with them." Of the ones left over, whoever left the most vivid impression would carry out the operation with us.

"Yeah! And then we have to think about where we're going."

"Sure, we can just go wherever."

It looked like class was about to start. Totsuka seemed ready to dive straight into thinking up ideas, but I gently sent him back to his seat. I didn't forget to give him a light, casual touch on the shoulder as he went, either.

Totsuka nodded, waved at me, and returned to his seat.

The eyes around us turned to Totsuka for an instant, but I couldn't sense any distaste for him.

Maybe it was his androgynous appearance. I figure his position is a little different from most.

But I didn't want to give him undue attention just in case, for the future.

I'd never been the one to go talk to him, and I probably never would. I wouldn't go out of my way to approach him, either. Things would be fine as long as I maintained an appropriate and reasonable distance. And the responsibility for taking care on that front lay on my shoulders.

I would spend my time as I always had.

Today, like every day, I committed myself to pretending to sleep. At times like these, it's particularly important to stay in control and maintain your normal pattern of behavior. With my left arm as a pillow, I put my face down on the desk, and in the right side of my field of vision, I spotted a rare duo.

It was right before class.

Hayama and Ebina were coming back. I'd seen them together as part of the same social clique, but I'd basically never seen them talking alone together before.

Oh, now that I think of it, I didn't see them in the classroom earlier.

The two of them exchanged a few whispered words—secrets, perhaps—and then quickly separated.

"Hey, hey, hey!" Ebina called, an offhand and lighthearted greeting, as she headed toward Miura and Yuigahama. She was cheerful, as always, and they received her with the same reaction they always did.

But unlike theirs, Hayama's expression was solemn.

Unusually for him, his smile seemed somehow grim. It almost seemed sad to me, like he was laughing at his own expense. It was noticeable enough that even I could pick up on it, and I wasn't close to him. So of course, the others could tell, too.

Of the three guys, the first to talk to him was Tobe. "Hey, Hayato. Did you go somewhere? Pulling a Whassis-tani and going off by yourself?"

"It wasn't anything important. Let me go to the bathroom alone, at least. And you really like that joke, don't you? You're overusing it." Still smiling, Hayama poked Tobe in the head.

"Geh!" The sound from Tobe fell somewhere between an exhalation and a word.

Yamato and Ooka followed in Hayama's footsteps. "Oof, you got told."

"You mean he got Tobe'd?"

"I'm the joke now?! Come on, man, gimme a break!"

The laughter grew and spread.

As it did, jokes about Tobe-ing and getting Tobe'd ripped out across the whole room, and now Tobe was the trend.

The clique of Hayama the thought leader was a force to be reckoned with. Hikitani jokes were now a relic of the past.

Thanks to that, my days were peaceful once again.

Glorious lonerdom, just as before.

In fact, I even got the feeling that everyone was acting even more distant than they had before. My existence had been buried in the darkness.

Now, I was kind of like a ninja. *Domo*, greetings, it is I, the ninja Hikigaya.

I'm looking forward to going to Kinkaku-ji Temple in Kyoto...

Nobody knows why **they** came to the Service Club.

Someone must have brought in an electric kettle at some point, because I could hear one whistling. Yukinoshita noticed the water was boiling and carefully folded over the corner of her magazine: the "dog-ear." Though since she loves cats, she might argue it isn't a dog ear but the ear of a Scottish fold. If you don't know, the Scottish fold is a popular breed of cat with characteristic "dog-eared" bent ears, which is unusual for a cat.

She set her magazine on the desk and got up to fetch the kettle.

Yuigahama had been lazily toying with the cell phone in her hand until she called out to Yukinoshita, eyes sparkling with anticipation. "Yay! Snack time!" As Yukinoshita prepared the cups and tea leaves, Yuigahama fished through her bag for some treats to go with the drinks.

On the desktop was a pretty cup and a saucer, plus a mug printed with an unmotivated-looking dog lying in a slump.

I'd been seeing them a lot lately, now that we were deeper into fall and you could hear the footsteps of the coming winter. Out of the corner of my eye, I could see Yukinoshita making tea as I read my paperback.

She poured hot water into the glass pot, and the leaves slowly rose in a dance. The way they fluttered up only to quietly drift down again was reminiscent of the little flecks in a snow globe.

Yukinoshita poured first into the cup, then in the mug, and then, teapot still in hand, she froze. Putting her hand on her chin, she seemed to consider something a moment before reaching out to the paper cups that were always kept in the clubroom and pouring the liquid into one of those, too. She gave the paper cup a cold and dissatisfied glare, even though she was the one responsible for it, then transferred the rest of the tea into a ceramic pot and put a cozy on it to keep it warm.

Then she took her cup and saucer and returned to her seat. Still clacking away on her cell phone, Yuigahama followed suit with her mug.

With no one claiming it, the paper cup was left all alone. The steam rising from it wavered, unsure where to go.

"The tea...will get cold."

"...My tongue burns easily." It had taken me a few moments to understand that the cup was for me. But I wasn't enough of a contrarian that I couldn't accept something someone went to the effort of leaving for me. When I figured the tea had cooled a bit, I reached out for it.

As I sipped at my drink, Yuigahama was holding her own mug in both hands and blowing on it to cool it down. "Oh yeah, so it's about time for the field trip, huh?"

The term made Yukinoshita's eyebrows twitch. Lately, our class had been talking about nothing else. It seemed those ripples had reached the Service Club, too.

"Have you guys already decided where you're going and stuff?" Yuigahama asked.

"I'm about to," Yukinoshita replied.

"Depends on where the people in my group go," I said. To me, a field trip is basically just forcible displacement. The other members of my group would stand in front of me and come up with a plan that included none of my opinions and act like I wasn't there, and I would silently follow after them. I wasn't particularly dissatisfied with this arrangement; I liked that it was easy, though it wasn't quite what I'd call fun.

A chummy group will be considerate and take my opinions into account sometimes, but a foreign body is still a foreign body. Something to be eliminated.

As someone with a long history of being that particular alien element, I take this fact for granted. This should also be the same for Yukinoshita, who would have similarly been treated this way.

"Oh yeah, so, Yukinoshita, what do you do for field trips and events and stuff?" I asked her, suddenly curious.

Teacup in one hand, Yukinoshita tilted her head slightly. "? What do you mean?"

"You don't have any friends in your class, right?"

To a stranger, it would sound like a pretty mean question, but Yukinoshita didn't seem bothered by it. She replied matter-of-factly, "No. So?"

"I was just wondering what you do about groups and stuff," I said.

Yukinoshita must have finally grasped the intentions behind my question, as she put down her teacup and spoke with understanding. "—Oh, if that's what you mean, I simply go with whoever invites me."

"What? You get i-invited?" I asked in surprise. That was unexpected.

Yukinoshita looked a little sullen as she replied, "I don't know what sort of impression you have of me, but I've never had trouble finding a group. Usually, some girls will come talk to me." She swept her hair off her shoulder.

Yuigahama was listening to us off to the side, and she touched her cup to her mouth as she looked up. "Oh, I think I kinda get that. Class J is mostly girls, so I think they'd be into someone as cool and calm as Yukinon."

"Huh. I see... In Class J, huh?"

Yukinoshita was in Class J, the international curriculum. Since Class J was 90 percent girls, the vibe there was a little different from all the other, normal classes, almost like a girls' school. If you're close enough when you walk by them, they smell nice—well, it's a mix of a lot of smells, and it makes me feel a little sick. Also, in winter, they tend to wear their gym pants under their skirts and fool around by rolling up one another's skirts, which is pretty entertaining to watch from afar.

I'm sure Yukinoshita's class shares a sense of comfort, familiarity, or ease, since it's all the same sex. Or maybe you could say it's easier to form cliques. That's one plus of not having the eyes of the opposite sex on you.

Guys are so worried about how girls see them, it tends to make them act weird. Like Tobe and friends and their gorilla drumming in the classroom the other day, or the bad-boy act. You might also be able to include M-2 types in that category. Oh, of course, this includes me. And I'm sure it's probably similar for girls.

In fact, Yukinoshita must have experienced this plenty in her life. When you put pubescent boys and girls together in one classroom, stuff happens—between boys and girls, and among the boys and the girls, too. Stuff happens in life. Which is why we have pensions.

"Agh. Man, I wish our school could've gone to Okinawa or something," Yuigahama said, sitting on the edge of her seat and looking at the ceiling.

"I don't know about going at this time of year... I wouldn't really recommend it," Yukinoshita replied, turning to gaze out the window. The cold wind made everything sound bleak. Even on the southern island of Okinawa, you couldn't expect to have fun in the ocean, or *shii* or *marin* or whatever they call it in English, at this time of year.

"Really? But there's nothing to do in Kyoto, y'know? All they have there is temples and shrines. We have that stuff in our neighborhood... Like, we can go to the Inage Sengen shrine whenever..."

Classic Yuigahama. The remark made my head hurt. Yukinoshita must have felt the same way, as she was lightly pressing her temples. "You have absolutely no sense of the weight of history or cultural value, do you?" she muttered, then sighed.

Yuigahama immediately went on the defensive. "I mean, I don't even know what we would do at a temple..."

Well, it's not like I didn't get at all what she was saying. If you don't have any interest in temples or shrines, it must be boring as hell. Most teenagers probably don't find themselves interacting with any of that stuff aside from major life events like weddings or New Year's.

"There are plenty of things to do. And more importantly, this trip isn't for fun. Of course, there's the history, and we also have the opportunity to see and touch our nation's culture directly—"

"I don't think that's what these trips are about," I interrupted Yukinoshita's opining.

"Oh. Well then, what exactly is their purpose?" Yukinoshita shot me a belligerent look, suggesting she was irritated by the interruption.

That's a little scary, ma'am. But unflinchingly, I continued, "In my opinion...it's a chance to practice life as adults in society."

"...I see. True, we do use the Shinkansen and other public transportation, and stay at hotels..." Yukinoshita folded her arms, her eyes shifting up and to the right in thought.

But I wasn't done yet. "You're forced to go on a business trip you don't want to go on, and at your destination, you're forced to meet some higher-ups you don't want to see. You're not the one choosing where you stay or what you eat for dinner, either. On top of that, when you go sightseeing, you've got to appease people, smother your own opinions, and conform in all sorts of little ways. You have to make do with the money you've got as you consider all the little compulsory details, like, *Well, I'll get a souvenir around this price for that one person, but I don't have to get anything for that other guy, I guess.* Field trips teach you all these lessons. It's like training for how to deceive yourself into thinking the world can be fun in its own way when you compromise, even though it will never go how you want," I finished.

Yuigahama gave me the most pitiful look. "Whoa, your field trips sound miserable..."

"I sincerely doubt the organizers are putting together the travel itinerary from such a pessimistic perspective," Yukinoshita said with some bafflement.

"Oh!" Yuigahama said, as if she'd hit on something. "B-but you know, even if you're right about that, Hikki, it's still up to us how we enjoy it, right?"

"Uh, well, I guess..." It's true; no matter what sort of curriculum or quota is levied upon you, how you take it is a matter of individual choice.

I was on my way to being convinced by Yuigahama's counterargument when suddenly, Yukinoshita smiled. "Indeed. I'm sure even you're looking forward to something, aren't you, Hikigaya?"

"I guess…" *Like sharing a room with Totsuka, or a bath with Totsuka, or eating with Totsuka…* Yeah, okay, there were some things I was looking forward to a little bit.

"Hikki, is there anything you're excited about?" Yuigahama asked.

"Oh, well, I do like Kyoto to begin with, you know," I replied.

Yukinoshita's eyes widened. "That's surprising. I assumed you were all about throwing tradition and formality in the trash."

…What an awful way to phrase it. Whatever. I've gotten used to all that.

"To humanities types who enjoy Japanese history and language, it's a holy land." If we're talking historical novels, you have the works of Ryotaro Shiba, and in more recent general literature, there's *The Tatami Galaxy*. When you're into those things, you do develop some interest in the city of Kyoto.

"Anyway," I continued, "being unable to go where you want is a defining feature of field trips. Eventually, I'll go on my own."

"Isn't traveling by yourself kinda lonely?" Yuigahama murmured.

Naw, I think traveling solo is pretty fun. You're not forced to accommodate others, which is enough to make it more comfortable all on its own.

I wasn't the only one thinking along these lines. Yukinoshita dipped her head in acknowledgment. "Not at all. If you go alone, you can take your time sightseeing. I think it would be enjoyable."

"Yeah, yeah. And the best part is that you can really bask in the feel of everything. If you try to watch the rock garden in Ryouan-ji Temple with a crowd of loud high school kids in the background, you might just pick up one of the rocks to smash open some heads."

"Obviously, I wouldn't do that… It's a World Heritage site after all." Yukinoshita was disgusted—for relatively academic reasons. Not much of a humanist, this one.

"What about you guys?" I asked. "Anywhere you want to go, or things you want to do?"

"I haven't looked into it at all yet, but I'm thinking I might wanna see Kiyomizu-dera Temple. It's famous and stuff."

"Someone sure likes bandwagons..."

Yuigahama was just being Yuigahama, and I replied before I even thought about it. She pouted a little, puffing up her cheeks.

"What's wrong with that? Oh, and I wanna see Kyoto Tower."

"We have basically the same thing in Chiba."

"That's the Port Tower!"

They've got similar names, don't they? Though actually, the names are about all that's similar about them.

You really do end up more attached to your home region. I love the Port Tower. Though they don't do fireworks shows there anymore, so there aren't many opportunities to check it out.

But then Yukinoshita had to put a damper on my local loyalties. "If we're talking Port Towers, the one in Kobe is more famous, though."

"That's fine. Chiba's is taller."

"I have no idea what you mean by *fine*..." Yukinoshita gently touched her temple as if to push back a headache.

"So, Yukinoshita. What about you?" I asked her.

She paused a moment to consider. "Me...? Well, you already mentioned the rock garden in Ryouan-ji Temple, and Yuigahama brought up Kiyomizu-dera Temple, but I'd also like to visit some other famous spots like Rokuon-ji and Jishou-ji Temples."

I think that was a string of unfamiliar words to Yuigahama. She just blinked. "Rokuonji Anjishouji...?"

"Don't mix them all together... Oh, hey, it kinda makes for a cool character name!" Rokuonji Anjishouji. He'd probably be a monk character with superpowers—that's how it feels anyway.

"The names Kinkaku-ji and Ginkaku-ji might be more well-known, generally."

"Y-you coulda just said that!" said Yuigahama. "Oh, but I'm going to the Kinkaku-ji Temple. Yumiko wants to go see it."

"Yeah, that temple sure suits her perfectly..." It fit my mental image of the glamorous Miura to a T.

As I was imagining the queen bee jangling with golden decorations, Yukinoshita continued, "And the Philosopher's Walk, too. It's supposed to be nice during cherry blossom season, but I think it would be lovely when the leaves are changing as well. Also, some temples and shrines allow special nighttime visits, so if the schedule permits, I'd like to go... but it may not be possible to go out at night on a school field trip." Yukinoshita was gushing.

Yuigahama gave her a questioning look. "You know a lot about this..."

"What are you, a travel magazine?" *She's really too excited about this...*

"It's nothing, really... This information about Kyoto is within the scope of common knowledge." Yukinoshita jerked her face away grumpily and reached out to her magazine. Wait, now that I got a good look at it, her reading material was, in fact, the travel magazine *Jalan*.

It was unusual to see Yukinoshita so innocently looking forward to something, though.

Right as I quietly turned away in an effort to smother my smile before it escaped, my eyes met with Yuigahama's, and she had the exact same look. That just made it funnier, and I couldn't suppress a little snicker.

"...What's the matter?"

"Nothing at all!"

As Yukinoshita glowered icily, Yuigahama frantically waved her hands in an attempt to distract her. But that wasn't enough for Yukinoshita to let it drop, and the frigid glare remained.

"Ah...ah-ha-ha-ha..." Yuigahama laughed pathetically until something occurred to her. "So anyway, Yukinon, let's go look at stuff together on the last day."

Yukinoshita tilted her head. "Together?"

"Yeah, together!" Yuigahama flashed her a bright smile.

However, Yukinoshita was still thinking. Quietly, she began to speak, and I could predict what she was about to say. "But…"

"She's not in our class." I beat her to the punch.

But Yuigahama nodded carelessly. "I know. But the third day is a free day, so I can call you up, and we can hang out in Kyoto!"

"I'm not certain it's *that* free…," said Yukinoshita.

"Huh? It'll be fine, won't it? I don't really know, though."

She doesn't even think about these things…

But maybe on the third day I could just drift wherever my whims took me and say I was making the most of my free day. *I've always wanted to go to the ruins of the Shinsengumi headquarters or the Ikedaya Inn. Though I hear the Ikedaya isn't there anymore, and now it's a pub. If I went on a tour of the historical sites, I'd be the only one getting excited.*

As I was ruminating, Yuigahama moved the conversation along without me. "Of course, only if it fits your schedule. How 'bout it?"

"…I don't mind."

"All right! Then we're set!"

Yukinoshita quietly looked away, while Yuigahama beamed and scooched her chair closer to Yukinoshita's.

Friendship is beautiful, I guess. Well, if they could enjoy themselves on this field trip even though they're in different classes, I suppose I couldn't complain.

"And you too, Hikki! Let's go someplace together!"

"Hmm, uh…" Yuigahama large eyes flicked my way for an instant. I wasn't expecting to hear that right then, and I found myself unable to reply.

As I considered how exactly to respond, the silence was broken by a knock on the door.

"Come in," Yukinoshita responded, and the door opened.

Our visitors were not who you'd expect. Actually, the only people who ever came to this clubroom were people you didn't expect, or people I didn't want to be here at all… People who'd fit in here, or whose presence would seem right, or who would otherwise fall within the category of those I'd expect, never seemed to come.

But this time, it was fair to say that even among the unexpected, these were some of the least expected.

It was Hayama, and behind him, Tobe, Yamato, and Ooka.

A very surprising quartet. I don't know if they're actually close, but they appeared to be a friendly foursome.

Hayama had come here a few times before, so he acted like he knew how this whole thing went, but the other three were looking around the clubroom with curiosity.

Then their eyes stopped on me.

They didn't have to bother with saying anything aloud for me to tell what they were thinking. All of them were wearing the same baffled expression. They all looked at one another, then back at me again.

But I couldn't take them to task for their rude looks—I'm sure I was staring back at them in just the same way. *Why the hell are these guys here?*

Of course, I wasn't the only one with that question. It seemed Yukinoshita and Yuigahama were equally baffled. "Do you need something?" Yukinoshita said in a mildly chilly tone, and Yuigahama gave a couple of nods in agreement.

Hayama glanced at Tobe as if to check with him. For some reason, Tobe kept fidgeting with his hair, brushing it up at the back of his neck and tugging at it. Kinda gross.

"Yes, I brought the guys because we have a consultation for you…" Hayama sounded like he was distancing himself from the situation—basically, he wasn't doing the consulting himself, but one of his lackeys had some issue.

"Go on, Tobe."

"Out with it!"

Prompted by the two guys beside him, Tobe opened his mouth, but all that came out was a groan as he contemplated. "Mmrrgh…"

Huh? What? Myrrh? Are you planning on embalming someone?

After what seemed to be some deep thought, by Tobe standards, he shook his head. Thanks to his long hair, the gesture reminded me of a sopping-wet stray dog. "Uh, actually, forget it! I'm not gonna ask Hikitani for anything!"

…Huh? The hell? Are you tryin' to pick out a brand-new fight from the Hikitani rack here, eh?

Though my heart is a peaceful one, I felt as if the rage was about to give me an awakening, but with a few deep breaths, I stealthily let it out. After calming myself somewhat, I glanced around to see Yamato and Ooka with little smiles that said, *Oh, you're so hopeless,* while Hayama was breathing a short sigh. Yuigahama's mouth hung open, while Yukinoshita's was in a tight line.

A moment of silence.

The silence felt strange, like a creepy-crawly feeling in your butt that makes it impossible to sit still, and the one to break it was Hayama. "Tobe. We're the ones who came here with a request."

"Well, I mean, y'know, I can't talk about this sorta thing to Hikitani. Trust score zero, man!"

I found myself discovering an unexpected drawback to being recognized—which in my case meant being hated.

The person who was supposed to have come with a request wasn't saying anything, which created more silence. So when Yuigahama spoke, though it was quiet, I could hear her just fine.

"Geez…"

Thank you for going to the trouble to voice my inner feelings out loud. But, Yuigahama, hearing that from you feels so unsettling. What's up?

"Do you have to say it like that, Tobecchi? You could at least be nicer about it," she said.

"I mean, but, like…"

I was grateful she was telling him off, but getting into conflict here wasn't gonna help her any.

I wondered what I should do now, but Yukinoshita came up with

the answer first. "I see. Well, the problem is with Hikigaya, so there's no way around that. Why am I not surprised...? So, I'm sorry, but could you leave?"

Well, she was right. If Tobe was saying he couldn't talk with me around, it was best for me to go. "All right, once you've done your stuff, call me or whatever." I started to get up.

But Yukinoshita stopped me. "Wait. Where are you going?"

"Huh? You just said..." I looked at her and saw her eyes were shifting slowly from me over to Tobe and the others.

"*They're* the ones who will be leaving."

"Huh?" Tobe squawked. He and his friends were now just as frozen as I was.

But Yukinoshita didn't care one bit as she continued, "There's no need for us to listen to a request from people with no manners and no sense for common courtesy. You may leave at your earliest convenience." Her tone was the same as always, that Yukinoshita-like extreme composure. But her expression was somewhat colder than usual, and her frozen gaze pierced Tobe.

"This is kinda awkward..." Yuigahama's stinging remark just made it even more agonizing.

I was stuck getting halfway out of my seat during that whole frozen moment, and it was starting to make my back sore.

I sort of wanted them to make up their minds about who would leave.

Could everyone just leave instead, and we'd all call it a day? No?

"...Well, this is our fault. Tobe, let's come back another time. Or maybe we should just resolve this ourselves," Hayama said with some resignation, breathing a sigh of relief.

Yeah, yeah, just keep your mouth shut and leave.

But Hayama's remark became the trigger that unfroze Tobe. Once he was moving again, he started combing up the hair at the back of his neck again. "Come on, I can't back out now... Besides, I told Hikitani about it before, during summer vacation, so I should just come out and say it."

"…All right." Seeing Tobe's determination, Hayama backed down.

I was a little surprised Tobe didn't listen to Hayama's attempt to stop him, but this was kind, noble, righteous Hayama here. He might have just done it to gauge how serious Tobe was. At his core, Hayama was the sort who would support his friends and push them along, so of course he would do something like that. I guess. I couldn't understand the guy.

I don't know whether Hayama was doing this to be considerate or not, but either way, it hadn't worked on Tobe. He still seemed to be having a hard time spitting it out, though.

Agh, if you're not gonna say it, you can leave, you know?

"Um…" Finally able to spit something out, Tobe wavered. There wasn't much to be curious about here, but everyone was quietly listening.

"Um…"

You're still not gonna say it? You're really dragging this out. Are we on a variety show?

Why *do* they always have to stick multiple commercial breaks in these moments? And once you think the ads are finally done, it's starts up again from right before the reveal. Are they time leaping? This is why I hardly watch anything but anime anymore.

"Um, actually…" After taking his sweet time, Tobe finally started talking. "I think…Ebina's…pretty cool, you know? And, well, I kinda wanna clinch it during this trip."

About half of that was code—actually, he was talking almost entirely in implications.

"For real?!" Yuigahama's eyes sparkled. My reaction was a little like hers.

Oh-ho, so he was serious about what he said during the summer camp in Chiba Village. Because of this prior information I had, I got what Tobe was trying to say even though he was speaking in allusions, but Yukinoshita tilted her head in a questioning gesture.

She appeared to have no idea what this was about, so Yuigahama whispered into her ear. Yukinoshita made listening noises as Yuigahama told her, but then she stopped suddenly. And then, with a complicated expression on her face, she tilted her head.

Might as well summarize the gist of it myself, then. "So you mean, like...you're saying you want to tell her how you feel and start dating her?" I asked Tobe, putting it in terms that might be a little embarrassing for a pubescent boy.

Tobe swept up his hair again, turned to me, and pointed at me. "Yeah, yeah, basically. But it'd be pretty harsh to get rejected. Glad you get my drift, Hikitani."

Well, he changed his tune quickly... Oh well, that's the kind of guy he is. He had told me about this stuff during the summer camp after all.

But still...

"Hmph. So you don't wanna get rejected, huh?"

Don't be so naive. Being rejected, rebuffed, and dumped is a part of life. Once you enter the workforce, you'll have jobs with no apparent meaning dumped on you, and some of them will make you go, *Is this even my job?* So yeah, get used to dumping now.

This is so lame, I thought, putting my face down on my desk with my right arm as my pillow.

Yukinoshita, who was within my field of vision, was slightly nonplussed. She put her hand to her mouth, pondering.

Just one person there seemed ready to bite: Yuigahama.

Her chair scraped as she hopped up and leaned forward on her desk with deep interest. Her eyes were sparkling with enthusiasm for this juicy bit of romantic gossip that had fallen so suddenly into her lap. "Come on! Like, this stuff is really nice! I'll cheer you on!"

Meanwhile, Yukinoshita seemed to have fallen into thought. "What does one do, specifically, for a date...?"

You don't even know that? I thought, but I guess I didn't really know, either. Glaze them with syrup, maybe?

It seemed the other two already meant to accept the request, but I wasn't really into it.

Trying to get people to help you with this is a mistake to begin with.

You hear about it everywhere from elementary school to high school, but I've never witnessed a single instance of other people helping that actually worked out. Generally, they get some laughs out of it, and then it's over. If you try to talk to someone about it, they'll very often turn it into a joke. Or into leverage the moment you have some minor fight, even if that wasn't their initial intent, or a bargaining chip to find out someone else's crush. You really can't underestimate elementary school–level information warfare.

That was why I really didn't want to engage in any cooperation or support. I mean, it kinda reminds me of a painful past, you know.

When my reluctance started to show, Hayama turned the discussion to me, wearing a similarly wry smile. "I guess it's not that simple after all."

"Well…" Not knowing how to react, I quietly looked away. And my eyes met with Yukinoshita's.

She was tilting her head as if to say, *What do you think?*

I gave a little shake of my head with a double helping of rottenness in my eyes to reply, *No way…*

Yukinoshita gave a little nod of recognition and said, "Sorry, but it doesn't seem we can help you."

"Nope," I agreed.

And so it was over.

"…Okay. Well, of course." Hayama nodded in acceptance, his gaze coming to a halt at his feet.

It would be conceited to believe we could help with anything and everything. After all, our position isn't so different from those who come to consult with us. Hayama might feel the same way.

The realm of impossibility is greater than that of possibility; it's the way of the world. *Indeed, it is truly regrettable, but we cannot be of any use. Yes, um, truly regrettable. I mean, I'm not in possession of a girlfriend myself, so, well, uh, I think it's a rather difficult problem.*

But one of us wasn't convinced of this, so…

"Huh?! Why not? Let's help him!" Yuigahama persisted, tugging at Yukinoshita's blazer. At a loss, Yukinoshita glanced at me, and Yuigahama followed suit. Now both of them were staring at me.

Hold on here. Don't try to force the decision on me… I just said we can't!

Tobe must have realized what those looks meant, as he took a step forward and grinned at me. "Hikitani… No—Hikitani, sir! Do me a solid!"

Hey, hey, hey, the politeness fix just makes it even ruder. And you're still getting my name wrong.

"Look, he's asking you!"

"C'mon."

Ooka and Yamato served as Tobe's smiling reinforcements. *I always end up in the minority position every time, don't I?*

"It does look like Tobecchi needs help, Yukinon."

"…Well, if you insist, I suppose we can consider it."

Yuigahama implored with moist eyes, and Yukinoshita capitulated.

Pardon me, Miss Yukinoshita, but you're being too easy on her these days.

So now, I could be the squeaky wheel going *No, I don't wanna*, but it wasn't gonna do anything. No matter when, no matter where, once you're outvoted, you're done for. Though the opinions of the minority might be respected, they can never make the decisions. I learned that as a member of elementary school society. I'd be forced to give in now, too.

"Then I guess we do it…"

"Yuss! Thanks a bunch! Major thanks, Yui, Yukinoshita!" Tobe crowed.

Hey. And me. There's me… What about me?

Oh, whatever. It wasn't like I was doing it because I wanted to be thanked. I was just doing it because it was my job.

And my policy was that if I was going to do something, I'd try to do it at least kinda right. I wouldn't put in 100 percent, but I'd exert enough effort for a passing grade. I'd recently gained the spirit of the corporate slave after being on the committee for the last cultural festival. I'd try hard enough that I wouldn't be fired.

"Okay, so," I said, "what do you want us to do, specifically?"

"Well, like I said, I'm gonna be confessing, right? So, like, you basically play wingman?"

The moment he said the word *confessing*, Yuigahama put her hand to her mouth and let out a breathy "Yeek!" I was sorry to be thinking this when she was getting all excited about it, but I did not think this would end well. *And also, I said* specifically. *Give me a specific reply.*

"Well, I get how you feel," I said. "Actually, it's all I get. But listen, Tobe. Maybe it's mean to say this, but isn't this a *risukii* thing to do?" I said, using the English word.

Tobe momentarily stopped tugging at his hair. "*Risukii*? Oh, yeah, yeah. It's *risukii*. *Risukii*."

Does he actually understand what that means? It's not cat food, you know? It wasn't the nickname for Littbarski when he was playing for JEF, either.

I wasn't sure how much Tobe understood, but I was even more dubious about Yuigahama. She spun around toward me to ask, "What do you mean, *risukii*?"

"*Risuku*. Risk. English for danger, the possibility of suffering loss," Yukinoshita explained like a Pokédex.

"I get what it means, you know! I'm asking what sort of risks there are!"

Yukinoshita was unfazed by Yuigahama's huffing outburst. Perhaps she knew Yuigahama knew and was teasing her…

Well, like they say, you teach me, and I'll teach you—I had to explain this from square one. "Well, first of all, you're confessing, right? Then you get rejected, right?"

"You're assuming she's gonna say no?!"

"You fool. That's not all. What comes next is already set in stone."

Yuigahama's yelp of surprise came too early. The rejection would just be the beginning. There's more that comes after. You might think you're at rock bottom right now, but in life, there's always another bottom beneath rock bottom. Yes, you can fall forever...

"The day after your confession, the whole class will inevitably know about it. That wouldn't be so bad, if it ended there. But you know... you'll hear them talking, here and there:

"*I hear Hikigaya confessed to Kaori yesterday.*'

"*Whoa, poor Kaori.*' (Like, why poor Kaori?)

"*And via text, too!*'

"*Whaaat? Someone's got no guts. Geez, via text? Who does that?*'

"*Right?*'

"*I'm glad I never gave him my number.*'

"*Nobody's gonna confess to you, so you'll be okay (lol).*'

"*Whaaat? That's so mean! (lol).*'

"...People will throw it into their pleasant little conversations, and then you'll feel the sting when you happen to overhear it. That's the risk," I finished. That's what gets you while you're down. Right when you're suffering from a broken heart, you get social assassination, too.

"This was about you again, Hikki...," Yuigahama muttered quietly.

Why even bother saying that at this point? I wouldn't know anything about other people. When I talk, it's generally about myself.

Oh, this is no good. When I start talking about myself, I can't help going on and on. Phew~. I'm tired (lol).

Perhaps my fervent speech was too much. The entire room had gone silent.

"...Do you get it?" I asked, for emphasis.

Yukinoshita put her hand to her forehead and sighed. "That was because it was you, Hikigaya."

"Hey, personally, I think it's a common experience for middle schoolers."

But apparently, it was not for Tobe. My explanation was in vain, and indeed, the fine gentleman did not take what I had to say seriously, no, not in the least.

"Okay, okay, then I'm fine as long as I don't confess via text, right? Besides, guys like me don't care what other people say. It doesn't bother me." Tobe jerked his thumb firmly at himself, and Ooka and Yamato piggybacked on that.

"Man, you're so cool, Tobe. Gonna tell her face-to-face!"

"Like a man."

"Come on, a guy's gotta do it that way!" Tobe said, but he was blushing a bit, too.

Could you please not…?

Sorry to butt in when you're acting all shy, Tobe, but the so-called risks go beyond the aforementioned. "…Well, it's not only that."

"There's more…?" Yuigahama cut in, sounding like she'd just about had it.

"Of course. There's lots of other risks. For example, when you confess your love for a friend, you're risking your ongoing relationship."

"Come on, now, we already knew that." Hayama dropped a hand on my shoulder to cut me off, like he was trying to console me. "…I get it, so we'll manage that part," he said.

All I could do in response was nod in silence. I was sure Hayama had always handled himself socially way better than someone like me did. So then I figured I didn't have to worry about it.

But looking up at his face, he didn't have his usual smile. He was watching the three idiots with an expression that had a somehow sorrowful edge to it.

"Well, I have practice, so sorry, but I'm counting on you to handle the rest… Don't stay too late, Tobe," Hayama said, leaving the clubroom.

"Oh, I'm going, too."

"I have club, too."

Ooka and Yamato followed after him. It seemed they'd simply come to accompany Tobe and weren't planning to help us come up with ideas. This is what you call "dumping it on someone else."

"Roger, roger, I'll come soon!" Tobe replied to the three of them casually and then turned back to face me. "So, let's rock this."

And what exactly do you want me to rock? This town? Your world? Around the clock?

"Okay, but what should we even do about this...?" Yukinoshita muttered, at a loss.

Indeed, we had basically no know-how in the realm of the lovey-dovey. Maybe he just picked the wrong people here. There had to be any number of others who would be better suited for the job.

"Tobe, why are you coming to us about this?" I asked.

"Huh? Oh, well, you know. You guys are Hayato's top rec, right?"

"Not really... Isn't this sort of Hayama's area of expertise?" I said.

Tobe's head drooped a little. "Oh, well, it's like, y'know. He's a really good guy... And he's good-looking, right? So he doesn't really have problems with this stuff..."

I understood what Tobe was trying to say. Just as people crack jokes about what hot guys can get away with, you can assume from appearances that Hayama has not, in fact, ever worried about this. It might be difficult for Tobe to share his distress with a classy babe magnet when you can just feel the effort they're putting in to actually win girls over.

Hayama is an attractive guy, the kind anyone would recognize whether they wanted to or not. I think he's so attractive, you can't help but say *Whoa!*

And I'm not just talking about his face or looks. He's upbeat and considerate, and it seems as if basically nobody hates him.

But that's exactly why. That inability to hate him might be the reason you want to distance yourself from him. When someone is so inarguably perfect, their existence itself is a deadly weapon.

Maybe Yukinoshita was on that dimension, too, as someone fundamentally equal to Hayama. But for better or for worse, she's a jerk. She says and does things that ruin her utterly perfect qualities.

However, it's fair to call Hayama perfect in personality as well. He's not only good-looking, he's sociable, he's smart, and he's expressive. He has too many positive traits to count.

That's why he brings with him a form of torture.

Because when someone is excellent and amazing compared with anyone, that includes you. You don't have a choice; you're forced to recognize where you're inferior and flawed.

That's why, if you were to try to come up with a flaw of his, that would be it.

Even watching him from afar, you can tell. Maybe people who have seen him up close would feel it even more strongly.

Yuigahama put on a bit of a wry smile, too. "Hmm... It's true Hayato doesn't seem like he'd have these problems."

"Right?" Tobe agreed.

Yukinoshita nodded in response, too, and then gave me a brilliant, beaming smile. "I see. So that's why you came to consult with Hikigaya."

"Hey, you're making it sound like I'm having some massive struggle with relationships," I snapped back. She said that with such a sweet look on her face.

But Yukinoshita and Yuigahama both looked away.

"...Pff."

"Agh..."

Yukinoshita breathed a short, pitying sigh, while Yuigahama agreed with a deploring sigh of her own. And then the two of them went silent.

"Don't go quiet and look away. You're just making it seem even worse."

As my mood spiraled steadily downward, Tobe patted me on the shoulder. "Well, so anyway, glad to have your help, Hikitani."

...*Still getting my name wrong.*

Kakeru Tobe is just hopelessly shallow.

The day after Tobe came to consult with us, we decided to analyze his request in detail and discuss how we would deal with it.

Frankly, I wasn't really enthusiastic.

I mean, other peoples' problems—relationship-wise—are just stupid to me, and the one to come in with this request was Tobe, besides. So of course it'd be hard for me to get excited.

In brief, here's what he was asking:

He was going to tell Ebina he had a crush on her, so he wanted us backing him up.

Come on... Right from the get-go, his request was flaky and thin, kinda like an ad for some new kind of pastry.

And so, after hearing his request the day before, we were now at the next stage, considering what we should do.

Yukinoshita rapped the edge of a stack of some nearby papers on her desk a couple of times to even them out, then turned back to us.

"Right, then. For now, let's begin by reviewing our situation. Then we'll gather information and consider how to handle this."

Hmm, a Yukinoshita-like approach. But I was a little uneasy. I mean, in sports manga, the data-collection character always looks good at first but ends up losing.

"First, I suppose we'll start with what we know about Tobe," she continued.

"Yeah, all right," I said. "As the ancients said, know thine enemy, know thyself, and you'll give up on a hundred battles."

"So you're giving up...?" said Yuigahama.

I mean, I do actually think we should... I mean, I doubt this is gonna work for him. Half sighing, I glanced over at the guy sitting beside me.

"Well then, a simple self-introduction," Yukinoshita prompted, and Tobe grinned.

"Yeah. Kakeru Tobe, Class 2-F. I'm in the soccer club." Tobe, who'd come to the Service Club room all excited, was now slouching in his chair as he joined our conversation. Well, if we were going to be gathering information about him, it was fastest to ask the guy in question.

"You don't have to go to club?" I inquired.

"It's totally fine. The old captain's already retired, so now the club captain's Hayato. I'm good."

Taking a lot of things for granted there, aren't you? Eh-heh-heh.

"Let's look for some positive qualities you can emphasize," said Yukinoshita. "If you can communicate them in a more effective way, I think Ebina will take notice."

Tick, tick, tick, tick, tick, ding. Time's up.

In silence, we all used up our thinking time, when Tobe went "Ah!" and raised his hand.

Yes, Tobe. Please tell us.

"...I'm friends with Hayato."

"Aaand he immediately piggybacks on someone else...," Yuigahama muttered, sounding somewhat exasperated.

Well, it's hard to come up with your own positive attributes on the spot—unless you're amazing like me, with just so many virtues.

In that case, it would be best to ask someone who was pretty familiar with him. "Can't you come up with something, Yuigahama?" I asked.

Yuigahama folded her arms in a thinking pose and *hmm*'d. When she finally hit on something, she clapped her hands. "Um, like, how he's always so bright and sunshiny?"

"If shining was enough to make people like you, bald guys would be super-popular." Also, you'd expect people to be fond of light bulbs, too. But now that I think about it, Pikachu is super-popular, so maybe if you got a Shiny one and put it on your head, the masses would flock to you. Or maybe not.

But anyway, maybe sometimes things aren't apparent to you precisely because they're so close. So maybe next, it'd be best to delve into his finer qualities by examining how he was seen from afar instead. "What about you, Yukinoshita?" I asked.

"Hmm...," Yukinoshita considered, putting a hand to her chin. "Obnoxious...? No... Loud? He's loud, so...perhaps his liveliness." She gave a bright smile at the end, but she'd completely exposed her thought process in getting to that point.

"...Okay, I get it." I now knew she would never, ever give anyone a compliment.

She must have been unsatisfied with my reaction, as she then turned the question to me. "Why don't you think about it?"

"Hey, you can't squeeze out what isn't there."

"...What isn't there is your motivation."

I think what's really missing is an interest in Tobe, though. But I'd feel bad about saying that, so I decided to keep my mouth shut. In fact, I had quite a lot of confidence in my ability to maintain a lack of interest in things, so saying something would be just making trouble.

But, well, we wouldn't be getting anywhere if I simply said I wasn't interested. So I decided to consider the matter seriously for a moment—*consider* meaning "make shit up" or something similar in this context. I didn't really know much about Tobe in the first place. Heck, I'd only just learned that his given name was Kakeru.

Anyway, if I had to describe him, well, what you see is what you get.

If you were to ask Hayama, he would say, *He comes off like a tough guy, but he's actually really good at setting an upbeat mood. He's a good guy.*

But ask Yukinoshita, and he'd be a frivolous party-type who had no talents aside from being loud.

Well, my evaluation would be basically that. There were no stand-out incidents for me to bring up, and I couldn't detect any trait that would form the core of his personality. He was unquestionably a background NPC.

I'm sure the above impression is a superficial evaluation of his type.

But now I knew more about him—at least, more than I did at the beginning of second year, when I only saw him as one of Hayama's hangers-on—thanks to that hot summer night together under the same roof. Though putting it that way may invite some misunderstandings, we did go to summer camp together and stuff. Based on those experiences, I'd try to make a guess.

He'd show off because he wanted a girl to like him, he'd take steps toward accomplishing his goal of getting a girlfriend, and when he had a crush, he'd feel jealous of his friends.

That kinda guy.

That's not gonna be useful. That's just Basic Boy A. You can find him anywhere.

The fact of the matter was that of all the people I knew, the most normal, the most regular, the most ordinary and mediocre, might just be Tobe.

I do consider myself a fairly typical high school student with a healthy dose of common sense, possessed of enough good instincts that they call me (well, I call myself) the Conscience of Chiba. But Tobe reached a level of normalness that frightened even me.

Tl;dr—Tobe was worthless.

Even after comprehensive analysis, I couldn't think of any positive traits in him.

I had nothing, but Yukinoshita and Yuigahama were silently pressing me, and Tobe was eyeing me hopefully like this time I'd say something nice for sure.

"Tobe's positive traits…are not what I'd be looking for. Actually, I think it might be faster for him to fit Ebina's tastes. Like, I'm sure she has a type, probably."

I wasn't exactly in a position to be looking down upon the little people and describing their fortes, so I chose to nudge the conversation in a different direction. It was more constructive to think about this realistically instead of focusing on something that didn't exist, right?!

"Ohhh, okay," Yuigahama agreed—surprisingly, since I'd come up with that one out of desperation. *Good, good. I rather like simple souls.*

Yukinoshita nodded, indicating this sounded good to her, too. "You mean to target her weakness, hmm? Impressive as always. You are peerless when it comes to using underhanded methods."

"That's a really weird compliment…" I wasn't glad to hear that at all. In fact, the compliment was rather suspect.

"So then what is Ebina into?" I asked.

Ebina is also a young lady just beginning to bloom, and for such a girl, this is the age when they're in love with love. She should be just like a flower, a proper young lady. And of course, young women enjoy talking about crushes with one another.

I looked expectantly at Yuigahama, but she avoided my gaze. "Um…well, in Hina's case…it's less about what kind of guys she likes, and more that she likes guys together…"

…Well, you know, even a corpse flower is still a flower. And as they say, even if it's rotten, it's still good fish. Or actually, is it the rotting that makes her Ebina?

"Well, I guess I'd call that side of her, like…unique? Eccentric? It works for her, y'know?"

Ohhh, how admirable, Tobe. You really defended her. I guess this is why they say "love is blind."

But he did defend her, which must mean he had a real affection for her. I'd probably lose my mind with rage if someone were to speak badly of Totsuka or Komachi, too, so he must feel something close to that.

It seemed the others could get a vague sense of it, too, as Yukinoshita gave an approving nod. But then she tilted her head again. "Tobe's feelings aside…what does she think of you?"

"I—I dunno." Yuigahama seemed uncomfortable with Yukinoshita's direct question.

Whoops, and there's your answer. That question was so easy, I was mentally betting on Super Hitoshi.

"Oh man, I'm *uriouscay* as *ellhay* about that." Tobe suddenly leaned forward, ready to go.

"…Listen, Tobe," I said. "This is basically going to be like…the Final Judgment."

"Come on, I have to hear this, or I can't get anywhere, right?"

"O-okay…"

Right, then. The answer, please, Yuigahama.

She looked at us, and her words caught in her throat with an *ulp*. "…I think, maybe, she thinks of you as a good person," Yuigahama said, gently averting her eyes.

Ngh… The tears…

A good person.

When a girl calls you that, it basically always means "good to ignore," or at best, "good to use." In other words, it meant he essentially had zero chance.

But Tobe was the one person in the room smiling as if he were certain of his victory as he slowly muttered, "…That's a positive assessment, right?"

The only positive thing here is your mind-set. Or your test results for being clinically short a few screws. I came up with numerous remarks to lambaste him with but, unfortunately, absolutely no ideas.

Tobe is aggressively idiotic, far more than I imagined.

"B-but look, she doesn't hate you, so that's a good thing, right?" Yuigahama desperately attempted to support him, but resignation was already swirling in the air between me and Yukinoshita.

"There's a limit to our capabilities," Yukinoshita said.

"The barrier between Tobe and Ebina is just too big, you know?" I agreed.

As was apparent, Tobe was an excitable character, the frivolous type. Ebina, on the other hand, was a modest, sweet pervert.

But in this situation, the irregular individual was Ebina.

I think it's unusual for an out-and-out slash fangirl to be in the top caste. If a closeted one were in her position, I think she'd actually be pretty secretive about it. I hear there are more attractive, outgoing types at those sorts of events than you would think. Source: manga. I read it in *801-chan* and *Genshiken*, so you know it's true.

Normally, Tobe and Ebina would have occupied different levels in the hierarchy. The clique Tobe associated with was fundamentally the cool one, the focus of attention. Ebina did have a pretty face, and she was cute in a mousy sort of way, but I think that definition of *cute* is a little off if we're comparing her with Miura.

Typically, I think she would be the secret object of affection for boys one rank lower than the top group on the social ladder, or those from middle ranks, or even boys of the lowest category, who hold on to the hope that *maybe she would even go out with me?* They'd think of her as the supercute girl noticed by no one else. There was a possibility that middle school Hachiman could have gotten a crush on someone like her.

But what destroyed this typical idea was the indomitable Yumiko Miura.

Yumiko had quite thoroughly, mercilessly, and passionately gathered the cutest girls around her to compose her clique. She chose what she wanted without ever questioning the differences between what made them attractive. Well, it was a little baffling that Kawasaki wasn't included there. She was pretty, too. If only she would fix the grumpy attitude and the brother complex.

Miura, the one who had created this nonstandard social situation, was, in a way, bound to become a key factor in this matter.

The moment the thought hit me, Yuigahama mentioned Miura. "Maybe it'd be best to get someone else to help, like Yumiko."

"Yeah," I agreed. "It's like they always say. If you want to shoot the general, first, give up."

"You're still giving up?!"

I'd stunned Yuigahama again, but, well, I actually had a reason. "We *should* give up on that angle... I mean, I doubt Miura's going to help."

"H-hmm...but Yumiko's into this stuff."

"...Just drop it," I insisted, and Yuigahama looked at me with surprise.

I'd said it a little sharper than I'd meant to. I figured that in all probability, this request was not going to go well.

And when it went sour, it wasn't hard to imagine how Ebina would see it: Yuigahama and Miura would be the ones who pushed Tobe into it.

That's how it would end up, no matter what actually happened.

If Yuigahama was the only one involved, she could use the Service Club as her excuse. I figured the interference of outsiders like myself and Yukinoshita would be taken as an inevitability, providing cover for her. But if even Miura were to join in on this, the weak connection between her and the Service Club would place emphasis on Yuigahama's influence, and then Ebina might come to resent Yuigahama for it.

That would basically suck.

There was too little to be gained, and the risks weren't worth it.

"Well, anyway...just don't do it."

"Okay...then I won't." She didn't ask for an explanation. I was grateful for that. I didn't feel like I'd be able to present sound logic. It would have been stupid and annoying to spell out a detailed justification of what was nothing more than an emotional argument.

"But then we're at a complete stalemate." Yukinoshita breathed a short sigh, sounding a little tired.

Indeed, the indicators were pointing toward probable defeat. I couldn't see any positive signs. "Why don't you just give up?" I suggested to Tobe. I was sick of this.

In response, he flicked himself in the forehead and slumped his shoulders.

"Whoa! You're harsh, Hikitani. A real-deal nasty talker, just like Hayato says… But I know your game, y'know? You're just putting it on."

"Uh, I'm totally serious, though…"

But Tobe wasn't going to listen to what I said. He turned right back to me with no hesitation. "But, like, y'know what they always say. The opposite of love is indifference. So that means you're taking this real serious for me, right?"

E-eugh… He's so obnoxious… His brand of obnoxiousness was the polar opposite of Zaimokuza's.

I mean, *obviously* the opposite of love is hate.

Disinterest is just an inability to give an evaluation because you don't know someone, and once you know them, you're forced to categorize them as someone you like or hate. And once you categorized a person as hated, you'll pursue them and loathe them eternally for the purpose of their abuse. The opposites of love are loathing and the desire to kill.

Of course, Tobe couldn't tell what I was thinking, and he gazed out the window as he explained in fits and starts. "I'm…pretty serious… Yamato and Ooka are cheering me on, but I kinda feel like they're actually in it for the laughs…" He paused for a moment, then rubbed his nose like he was a little embarrassed. "So it actually feels kinda nice that you're seriously trying to stop me, y'know?"

"…"

That's not what's going on. You're not allowed to just decide this is positive, without any input from anyone else. Look, it's very much not like that. Could you not?

"And that's how Ebina can be, too. Sometimes she'll just randomly hit real deep. I guess you'd say she's not who she seems at first? That's the kinda thing that gets me. Agh, now that was an embarrassing thing to say! I'm being a creep!" Tobe fluffed up the hair at the back of his neck aggressively to cover his embarrassment.

Thank you for that gleeful and completely unasked-for explanation. Don't grin at me. Your hair is annoying. It's too long. Just get a damn haircut.

But…huh, he's actually been paying attention to what she's like.

I've spent many years observing people myself, which was why I'd gotten the vague inkling that Ebina wasn't just the cute girl she appeared to be.

She had something quietly hidden inside her, too.

Tobe hadn't yet reached the essence of that, but now I was sure he'd picked up on some things, since he'd been watching her all this time.

These are the thoughts that get you started, and then before you know it, you're following her with your eyes, which leads you to learn something new about her, and then your chest starts feeling hot. Anyone will have gone through that process…including me and Tobe.

Boys are so stupid. Even when they know it won't end well, that isn't enough reason for them to give up. Boys truly are dumb.

Exactly as I had once been, Tobe was a boy in love. He might have been a normie or top caste or whatever, but at his core, he was just a single-minded boy.

"Well, there's something to be said for giving it a shot, even if you know it won't work," I said. If he was going to make a serious go at this, I'd help. That was the founding idea for this club anyway.

"Hey, you gotta make it so it *does* work." Tobe put his hands together in a quick gesture of supplication.

I was shooing it away with a wave as if to say *I get it, I get it* when I heard the muffled vibration of a cell phone.

"Oh, that's mine. 'Sup… Huh? Oh, sorry, man! Coming now!" Tobe ended the call in a rush and snatched up his bag.

By the time Yuigahama asked, "What is it?" Tobe had already dashed to the door.

"Going to club now! The old captain said he was gonna come watch, so I gotta go, or I'm in trouble! See ya!" Before he even finished talking, he flung open the door and ran out.

Watching him go, Yukinoshita muttered, "He really is loud…"

Once Tobe was gone, suddenly, the clubroom was quiet.

Now that the scene had once again turned calm, we all ended up at loose ends. Each of us vaguely reached out to whatever was nearby. Yukinoshita started preparing tea, while I pulled the paperback on the desk closer to me. Yuigahama flipped through the magazine in front of her.

Then Yuigahama's hands stopped, and her eyes were fixed on the page. Curious about her unusually serious reaction, I popped my head around my book to peek. "What're you looking at? …Oh, matchmaking shrines."

"I figured divine help could be a thing…um, for Tobecchi," Yuigahama replied, her eyes never leaving the magazine.

Having finished making the tea, Yukinoshita joined in. "There are lots of temples and shrines in Kyoto where you can have your relationships blessed, enough that there are tours just for that purpose. But praying for it? That's going a little far…"

"Yeah, it's like that saying: 'Divine resignation in the darkest of times.'" Instead of divine supplication? Divine resignation: giving up in a godly manner. Ha-ha, look, I'm giving up again… It's pretty lonely when you set up the joke and nobody else goes for the punchline.

As I was mulling over this, I glanced over at Yuigahama to see that, for some reason, her eyes were sparkling. "…That's it!"

"That's it?"

Was my divine resignation bit that witty? I personally wasn't a fan. It sounded kinda forced.

"Not that. They could get closer by having a walk around Kyoto! He could, like, casually come up with little trivia facts about the city. Hina said she likes Kyoto, so I think it could work!"

Trivia. It comes from the word *trivial*. In other words, stuff that doesn't matter. There's some trivia for you.

In other words, since he wasn't getting anywhere when everything was normal at school, Tobe would have to count on the newness of the field trip to change things.

The field trip was going to be four days long. I think there's some American movie called, like, *How to Get a Girl in Four Days*. Starring Cameron Diaz and Hugh Grant.

But anyway, in that short period of time, we had to create a situation where Ebina would be attracted to Tobe... *Yeah, that's impossible.*

"So then first, wouldn't we have to make sure they end up somewhere together?" Yukinoshita said, pouring out tea for all of us.

Yuigahama took her mug, had a sip, and raised her head. "The first day, we're all together as a class, so that's no problem. And then for the group day, I'll be with Hina and Yumiko. We've basically decided already."

No doubt. Assuming that would happen, in order to create a group of four, someone else would have to join their group. But we didn't really have to take their influence into consideration...

So then I pondered what to do with Tobe, but Yuigahama cut off my train of thought. "So for the guys, you just have to be in Tobecchi's group, Hikki. Then if we choose the same places, on the second day they can be together, too."

"...Huh? Uh, I'm going to be in a group with Totsuka, though," I replied, waving my hands like, *I can't, I can't*, and Yukinoshita interjected in support of me.

"Won't Tobe and his friends have decided to be a group of four? There wouldn't be anything to gain by throwing Hikigaya in there, and I doubt it would make anyone happy."

I should have been thankful that Yukinoshita agreed with me. But I didn't feel grateful at all. I wonder why.

"Yeah, but if me and Hikki come up with a schedule for us, then we'll end up being together on the second day, too, and I think it's best to have two people there, for support." Yuigahama, coming up with a logical argument... My eyes widened in shock at this rare occurrence, and I missed my opportunity to present a counterargument.

And when I failed to say anything, Yukinoshita nodded with an *mm-hmm*. "I see. Well, Ooka and Yamato were both willing to accompany him to the clubroom, so I'm sure if we explain, they'll agree."

"Yeah, I'll try talking to them when we're deciding on groups."

Oh no. Things are moving along fast. At this rate, I'll end up in a group with Hayama and co. I have to avoid this! "Wait, hey, listen to me—," I began, but Yuigahama clapped her hands as if an idea had hit her.

"So then for the groups, we can split those four into two and have you and Sai-chan together in a group, Hikki?"

...That's fine. It's actually more than fine. Let's do that.

X   X   X

Class 2-F was typically pretty boisterous. I think the main reason for this was because Hayato Hayama and Yumiko Miura, who were probably top caste even relative to the whole grade, were the leaders of the clique that formed the nucleus of the class. When these animated personalities got together, naturally, laughter would ring out and bright smiles would blossom.

And that day, our class was a notch more boisterous than usual.

We were deciding on groups for the school field trip. One hour of long homeroom was set aside for this, but it wouldn't actually take that much time to decide, because the people who were friends to begin with could *schwoop* together instantly. So why did this take an hour? This was both a kindness toward and torture for loners. The purpose of this hour was to glance around and wonder who you should join.

But this time, I already had a group.

Yuigahama had talked with Ooka and Yamato and divided their pack of four in half, and I was placed with Totsuka, Hayama, and Tobe—the same people I'd been with for that summer camp.

Since a bunch of groups were sorted out already, those people now started enjoying a carefree chat time.

Nearby, Yuigahama and her friends were right in the final adjustment stage of group formation.

"We need one more person," Yuigahama said.

Miura's sausage curls boinged as she tugged at them and replied, "Can't we just go with three?"

The teacher told us to make groups of four...

As Miura blithely tried to break this rule, someone popped up from behind to bop her on the shoulder—Ebina. "Hey guys~. ♪" Her voice made both Yuigahama and me turn around.

"Oh, Hina. About the group of four," Yuigahama began.

It seemed Ebina had brought over someone unexpected. "How about Saki-Saki comes with us?"

What's with that nickname? I bet she'd be good at mah-jongg.

The nickname from Ebina made Kawasaki squirm in embarrassment. "I-I'm fine, really...and don't call me Saki-Saki."

"Why don't we go together? If you're interested... Oh, I think when we're traveling around Kyoto, those guys are gonna be with us, though, so if you don't mind that." Yuigahama glanced at us as she explained.

"Oh, is that right?" Ebina replied, instead of Kawasaki. She looked toward us. The glint in her eyes was terribly sharp. She was carefully scrutinizing our group.

"We're gonna be with the guys? Is that gonna work out?" Kawasaki asked.

Ebina reacted to that. Her previous look was gone, replaced with enthusiastic panting.

"It'll be great! Totally! I can watch Hayama/Hikitani up close all I want! I can see Hayahachi in Kyoto!"

That's why she's eyeing us?

"What are you talking about? And I mean, Hikitani is..." Kawasaki sounded exasperated, glancing over at me. And then at super-high-speed, her head jerked back again, and she grabbed Ebina. "Y-you mean H-Hikitani is…?!! N-no way, no way, no way!"

"Ah-ha! It's okay! At first it looks like a total crack ship, but then you start watching and realize it's the one *true* pairing! Hayato is actually hyperaware of him and sometimes gives him these despondent looks—"

"Who gives a damn about Hayato?!" Kawasaki yelled, and the moment she did, a chair scraped on the ground behind her.

"Huh? What did you just say?" Everything was tense all of a sudden. It seemed she had incurred the wrath of Queen Miura. Miura *click-click*ed her nails on her desk belligerently.

But Kawasaki also prepared for battle in her own way, flipping back her long ponytail as she turned her head to glare at her opponent. Kawasaki was capable of glaring at anyone straight in the eye, even Yukinoshita. "I said, Who gives a damn? Why don't you clean out your ears once in a while?"

"*What?*"

"What?"

Fight! Fight! Showdown time! This is really scary…

"H-hey, come on, guys! S-so anyway, we've got a group…" Yuigahama cut between them, trying her best to avoid a head-on collision.

Oh, I get it.

I understood why Kawasaki wasn't in Miura's clique, even though she was pretty. Kawasaki and Miura were too similar.

I don't wanna go on a field trip with these guys…

At the end of the day, **Hina Ebina** is rotten?

Finally, the field trip was the next day. We were having our last meeting before departure in the clubroom of the Service Club.

Since group formation had gone well the other day, it seemed one way or another we would be able to achieve our initial goal of making sure Ebina and Tobe would be together in Kyoto. Though I think it would have ended up like that naturally even if we didn't do anything, but, well, the difference here was my presence. Though it wasn't like anything was going to change anyway.

Our task now was the producer's job of making Tobe look attractive—somehow. Producing Tobe. We're producing, Producer!

And so we decided to carefully examine Kyoto hot spots with the help of travel magazines and even restaurant review apps.

"All right, let's plan this thing!" Yuigahama lined up a whole array of tourist guides and travel magazines on the desk.

"Where'd you get these from...?" I asked her.

"Huh? There's the stuff I got from Yukinon, the stuff I borrowed from the library, and some from Miss Hiratsuka."

I get the first two, but what about that last one? She's all gung ho about this trip, too? ... Well, whatever. I was actually looking forward to Kyoto myself. If this hadn't been a field trip, I'd have been even more excited.

For now, I flipped through a magazine at hand. Why do these

sorts of travel magazines use tons of feminine colors like red and pink anyway? Are there no cool travel magazines called manly things like *A Man's Journey Alone: The Kyoto Arc* or *The Ten Warrior Conspiracy Arc* or *Trust and Betrayal*?

For now, I flipped past the standard tourist spots and flipped past the dining information that frequently appeared between them. Just call me Flip Turner.

Generally, you'd do this schedule planning with your own group, but Yuigahama said she'd take care of the tour schedule for the girls, while I made the one for the boys, so that we'd inevitably stage something like fate: *"What a coincidence! We ended up on the same tour!"*

But, um, hey, I don't really think anyone is going to fall for this...

"If we just run into one another, it'll feel destined or something!" said Yuigahama.

Except it wasn't. *Just how much of a romantic are you? Stop it! Stop the romance!*

I mean, if you happen to run into a girl during your free day, you're gonna be like, *Oh crap, I have to make it look like I wasn't following her!* And then you have to deliberately shoot past them or end up turning down some side road you didn't plan to go on. Don't underestimate a boy's self-consciousness.

But Yuigahama didn't understand even a fraction of the pure feelings of high school boys as she flippity-flipped open the travel magazines. "I wonder where would be good...," she said, but she wasn't looking very closely at the details of any of the articles as she skimmed through page after page. I've seen that speed-reading technique before. Her method of reading travel magazines was to rely purely on feelings. Truly Yuigahama-like.

This contrasted with Yukinoshita's style, which involved drinking in every single letter as if she were reading a book. "Where indeed... The leaves will still be red around the time we go, so perhaps Arashi-yama or Toufuku-ji Temple would be nice. And if you're going all the way over there, Fushimi Inari Shrine is close by..."

"You even know the geography... Wait—have you been there?" I asked.

For some reason, Yukinoshita gave me a puzzled look. "No."

"So you looked up all that stuff?"

"The fact that I've never been is why I'm looking it up. And besides, we have an opportunity for all of us to go. It's best to enjoy it," Yukinoshita said, smiling.

Surprised by her positivity, the only reply I could muster was a weak "Uh-huh."

She'd softened from before. Yuigahama was probably a big part of that. I think those changes aren't a bad thing, though. I would just appreciate it if those gentler moments were clearer and more predictable. *You can still have a pretty sharp tongue sometimes, y'know.*

"Oh, look, look, Hikki," said Yuigahama. "I hear this spot has, like, mysterious energy!"

"That's just where *you* want to go, isn't it?" said Yukinoshita.

As the three of us were doing our research and engaging in asinine conversation, suddenly, there was a knock on the door. It was so tentative, we hadn't noticed it the first few times. Then another one: *tunk, tunk.*

"Come in," Yukinoshita, the master of this clubroom, called out.

"Per'n me!" came the bungled greeting as the door slowly slid open. A girl stepped into the room.

She had black shoulder-length hair and red-framed glasses, and the eyes behind her thin lenses were clear. She appeared somewhat dainty, thanks to the shape of her face and her build. If she were behind the counter at a library, she would make a wonderful picture.

"Oh, Hina." With a scrape of her chair, Yuigahama stood, and Ebina acknowledged her presence in return.

"Hey, Yui. Hallo-hallo!"

"Yahallo!"

...Huh? What's that? The greeting of some tribe? Miura must have suffered so much, being forced to deal with this.

"And Yukinoshita, and Hikitani. Hallo-hallo~."

"Hey," I responded, reminiscent of a certain NHK character.

Yukinoshita responded calmly. "I haven't seen you in some time. Please sit wherever you like," she prompted.

Ebina seated herself in the nearest chair and looked curiously around the clubroom.

During the summer camping trip, Ebina had spent time with us and helped us deal with an issue then, so she would have had at least a passing understanding of what the Service Club did.

"Hmm. So this is the Service Club, huh?" she muttered, then gently leaned forward, focusing on Yukinoshita directly ahead of her. "I came because I wanted to consult with you about something..."

So she's come with a request? I was curious as to what she needed help with. She sure didn't seem like the kind of person who'd have problems, at least, or maybe just not the type to rely on someone else when she did run into trouble. My impression was that her personality was hard to grasp.

I must not have been the only one thinking that, as Yukinoshita and Yuigahama both sat up a little straighter, too, listening seriously.

"U-um..." Ebina took a good look at us, then blushed and looked away in embarrassment. But still, her strong determination gave her the courage to speak. "I kinda wanted to talk to you about something—about Tobecchi..."

"About T-T-T-T-Tobecchi?! Wh-what, what?!"

No wonder Yuigahama was champing at the bit. Just a little while ago—well, actually, for the past few days, we'd been up in arms because of Tobe's issue. Specifically, his feelings for Ebina. Though I didn't let it show in my behavior, I was curious about how she felt about him.

With all our eyes focused on her, Ebina blushed even redder. "Um, i-it's hard to say it, but..." Her eyes kept flicking downward to the hem of her skirt as she twisted it around her fingers, searching for the right words.

U-um, i-it's hard to say it, I can't help staring at that gesture, so if possible, I would like you to not.

But that aside, just what was making the cheerful Ebina stutter so shyly?

…I-it couldn't be—was this a sweeping victory for Tobe? *Absolutely unforgivable.*

"So Tobecchi…"

"Yeah, Tobecchi?!" Yuigahama reacted intensely, urging her on.

This seemed to help Ebina muster her resolve at last: She took a little breath, opened her eyes wide, and shared her honest feelings with us.

"Tobecchi seems too friendly with Hayato and Hikitani lately, and Ooka and Yamato are so frustrated! But I wanted to see them cling to their passion! This will ruin the love triangle!!"

Angle! Angle! Angle! Angle…gle…gle…gle…gle…

Ebina's voice echoed in the quiet room. Nobody else could say anything. All we could do was stare into space.

We were completely dumbfounded. Not just astounded or confounded but dumbfounded… We had found all the dumb there was to find.

The first one to reboot was Yuigahama. As expected from someone who hung out with her regularly, she was swift at dealing with this. "Um…so what does that mean, exactly?" she asked.

Ebina nodded deeply. "Tobecchi's been talking with Hikitani a lot lately, right? And the groups we've set up for the trip seem weird, too. The two of them keep giving each other meaningful looks… Guh-heh-heh-heh-heh…"

This chortling mid-explanation is terrifying…

"Oh, bad Hina, bad Hina." Coming to her senses, Ebina wiped the trickle of drool from her mouth. It seemed that without Miura to stop her, she couldn't curb her fantasies. Miura was actually not entirely unlike a mom… And her tastes were a little out there, with Ebina and Yuigahama the idiot as her friends. I was starting to feel sorry for her lately. It was kinda cute.

But this wasn't the time to be avoiding reality with such thoughts. Ebina's explanation wasn't over. With a look, I prompted her to continue.

Catching my gaze, Ebina grinned. "I don't know why you're suddenly friends...but Tobecchi seems kinda distant from Ooka and Yamato, and it's been on my mind."

I understood that Ebina was concerned. Hayama's group of four splitting up to make way for me and Totsuka was a break from the norm. Ebina wouldn't be the only one who found it strange; our other classmates would have probably noticed, too.

"That's, uh, you know..." How would I talk my way out of this? We'd basically convinced Ooka and Yamato, but we couldn't explain the rationale for this to Ebina herself, so I found myself unsure how to proceed.

But Ebina shook her head as if to say I didn't have to finish for her to understand. "Hikitani, listen. If you're going to invite people, I want you to invite everyone. I want you to take all comers, with your deepest sincerity. Basically, I want you to take them all at once, right to the bottom...of your heart."

"I don't wanna... It's not gonna happen..." I instinctively shook my head violently as utter hopelessness descended on me. This was the feeling of overwhelming despair you get when there are still two more transformations left. I felt like I might even cry a little.

Ebina must have understood my shock, as her expression wilted into something meek. "I see... Of course."

So she understands...

"You're not a slutty bottom. You're a fail bottom. Sorry for asking too much."

"No, no, no, I'm not; that's absolutely not what's going on here." This was more than just a misunderstanding. My head sank into my hands. Of course, I wasn't the only one. Yuigahama softly sighed with the look of one who has given up.

The only one who was somehow keeping it together was Yukinoshita.

Closing her eyes, she pressed her temple and said, "Which means…? I would appreciate it if you would explain for us." Her expression utterly exhausted, Yukinoshita did her best to somehow interpret this. Girls who give it their all are great. I'd given up trying to understand Ebina, so I very much wanted Yukinoshita to make up the difference with her efforts.

"It's just… I get this feeling that maybe the group's kind of changed from how it used to be…" Ebina's voice shifted, hiding something more melancholy.

Yuigahama attempted to jump in and relieve her concern. "But you know, I think maybe Ooka and Yamato sometimes deal with complicated stuff, too, right? Guys in general. With relationships and stuff."

"Complicated relationships between boys… Oh, Yui, that's so dirty…"

"Did I say something weird?!"

"No, what *you* said was normal," I told her. "Don't worry." *The weird one here is Ebina. Why's she blushing?* "Well, everyone has their issues. You can't know what other people are feeling. Maybe they're close and just not showing it on the surface."

"You might be right. But I'm certain things are different from how they were before. And I don't really like that," Ebina said with a smile. "I want us all to get along, like we have been."

There was nothing rotten or naughty about that expression. It was an extremely natural smile.

It seemed Ebina liked the status quo with relationships in her class right now—and not as seen through slash goggles but including her own position, too.

Everyone getting along.

I hate those words, but of course, some people want that. But was that all she was saying? I couldn't really tell just who Hina Ebina was.

That made me want to guess at what she really meant.

…No, forget it. Always trying to read into what people say is a bad habit of mine.

Right when it seemed this bad habit would rear its head yet again,

Ebina seemed to suddenly rethink the matter and add, "Oh, but…I'd like it if you joined the boys' group and made friends with us, though, Hikitani. It'd be nice for my eyes anyway."

"I'm not gonna join their clique, so take care of your eyes yourself," I replied. "You should eat some fruits and berries."

And when she says "nice for my eyes," she doesn't mean me on my own. She wants me together with someone else, doesn't she…?

Ebina chuckled and stood. "Well, that's all, then. I'm expecting hot stuff out of this field trip!" Hastily slurping up the drool pooling in her mouth, Ebina winked at me. *No, I think you're expecting the wrong stuff.* "I'm counting on you, Hikitani," she called out to me as she left the room. I watched her go, and our eyes met.

"Whatever was that about…?" Yukinoshita asked the extremely obvious question.

"I dunno. Well, I guess we should make it so they can all be friends? I don't feel like we have to do anything, though. They get along well already." They'd put together groups with Tobe's romantic success in mind. You could say that act itself was proof of their friendship.

Yuigahama gave a couple of nods in apparent understanding. "Yeah. Besides, even if she does want the guys to be friendly, I wouldn't know anything about that… Hikki, how do guys become friends?" she asked.

But before I could reply, Yukinoshita patted Yuigahama on the shoulder, giving a rather sad smile. "I think it may be rather cruel to ask him that. Yuigahama, let's be a little more considerate. All right?"

"Yeah, exactly, be more considerate—*Yukinoshita*," I shot back.

Cruelty posing as kindness is way worse.

Anyway, the field trip would start tomorrow. The only unresolved matter for the Service Club was Tobe. In other words, there was nothing to worry about.

But the words meant for me alone were echoing in my ears.

×　×　×

I went home and started getting ready for the field trip the next day. Not like I had much to bring, except for a few changes of clothes. Wait, do you need anything else for a school field trip?

Thinking wasn't bringing up any ideas, so for the time being, I hovered in front of my dresser, pulling out clothes that seemed suitable. If you pack extra underwear and socks, you don't need to worry, even on heavy flow days.

Next, I'd grab toiletries... *Don't they have these where we're staying? Well, I guess I'll bring 'em, just in case.*

And that was everything. One bag was enough for my stuff.

Yeek! It's like I'm a seasoned traveler! I'm so cool! Everyone always struggles carrying so much junk with them, like Uno and cards and mah-jongg tiles. I hear some people even bring full game consoles, which is frankly awe-inspiring. But come on, in the modern world, you can get most things at your destination if you have any issues, and you can look up almost anything else with just your cell phone. Travel is convenient now but somehow bland.

With the packing completed, I brought my bag out into the living room and tossed it on the floor.

Now, since I'll be getting up early, let's go to bed early. We were meeting at Tokyo Station to go to Kyoto on the Shinkansen.

If I was late, I'd get left behind.

Technically, I could ride the Shinkansen by myself, and I could also contact the others with my cell phone. The cost of the ticket... would hurt, but couldn't you transfer that? And, like, why can't you pick whatever time you want when you're the one paying for it? What's the deal? Is there any love there?

In fact, wouldn't being late actually be better so I could experience the feeling of traveling alone at a leisurely pace, eating a lunchbox from the station? I thought, and my desire to wake up early suddenly deflated.

Throwing myself deep into the sofa, I was considering having a coffee (MAX Coffee), when I heard the *tappity-tappity* of Komachi trotting up to me. *Stop running in such a small house.*

"Bro, you forgot this," she said, dangling a certain device on its strap before me.

"...I don't need a camera."

There'd be no opportunity for me to use one. For scenery, there are tons of better photos already out there anyway.

"Then your Vita?" She'd taken the trouble of putting my darling little Vita in its special case and even attached a strap so she could swing it in front of me.

"Vita's staying home. You take care of her."

"Roger." Komachi nodded, seeming especially amenable to the idea, and softly tucked my sweet Vita into her pocket.

...Y-you'll give her back, right? I—I just lent her to you, okay? This isn't that thing where a brother lends his little sister an electronic dictionary or something and suddenly it belongs to her, right?

As I bit my tongue to keep from making sure, Komachi was poking her cheek with her finger in puzzlement, blissfully unaware of my turmoil. "But then what'll you be taking, Bro? Won't you have a hard time alone without anything to kill time with?"

I'm thankful for your concern, but you underestimate your big brother.

"E-books are a thing these days, so I won't be bored."

You really do underestimate me, Komachi. When you're at my level, with just one cell phone, you can kill time easily, and I can even do it with nothing at all. In class, your big brother can make a frog with his fingers. Ribbit, ribbit.

I could never, ever say this to my little sister.

"And anyway, it's not like I'm going out there to have fun," I said.

Komachi blinked, then asked me doubtfully, "...What are you going for, then?"

"Asceticism, I guess..." Unconsciously, I looked off into the distance. These school trips have never left me with any decent memories. Sometimes I even wonder if it's supposed to be a test of endurance, a seventy-two-hour no-talking contest. Of course, I've won.

As I was silently drifting into the past, Komachi slapped her fist into her palm as if she'd just thought of something. "I nearly forgot! Here."

She handed me something white. Underwear? No, a piece of paper. Well, I wouldn't have wanted underwear, though. Um, you know, I mean, like, in terms of how I'd have to react considerately and stuff.

But no matter how dumb my little sister was, she had enough sense for this, at least; what she handed me was actually a paper folded in that distinctly girly way.

This diamond shape, this box thing, that gets passed down in classes made me remember that one time in middle school when I passed one of those on without knowing what it said. It was nasty stuff about me, and when they were all giggling about it at the back of the class, I felt so hopeless. Don't fold your letters like this.

When I opened the paper, I discovered rounded characters written in vivid pink and yellow crawling all over the place. Crawling with love, I might hope.

Komachi's Recommended Souvenir List!

In third place! Nama yatsuhashi! *(Original sweets, or authentic ones from the flagship shop or main shop or whatever is good.)*

In second place! Youjiya's oil-absorbing sheets! (Please get some for Mom, too.)

In first place! See after these messages!

…What an irritating way to end it.

"What the hell is in first place?"

"The number-one souvenir is talking about your wonderful memories with you." Komachi gave me a sweet, sweet smile. Sly-cute… "I hear there's a ton of matchmaking shrines and stuff, so you should go get matched!"

"Don't worry about that junk. Just study."

"Okaaay! All righty, then. Say hi to everyone for me."

"Sure."

Now there were even more places I had to go. Well, I could buy *nama yatsuhashi* at the station...and the Youjiya oil sheets were so famous even I'd heard of them, so I bet they were selling them at the station, too.

So that meant the one place I had to go was...

...Maybe I'll go visit a god of academics.

As you can see,
Yui Yuigahama is doing her best.

'Sup! I'm Hachiman! I'm goin' to Tokyo!

And so I headed straight for Tokyo to get on the Shinkansen.

I woke up earlier than usual so I could leave early. When I saw my parents going off to work, they ended up tasking me with getting souvenirs for them, on top of Komachi's request.

But, Daddy, these days, minors can't buy alcohol, even if they're on an errand for an adult. I know you gave me this money to buy sake, but I'll just keep it, okay?

It's not that far from Chiba to Tokyo. In fact, it's fair to say Chiba is the prefecture closest to Tokyo. In other words, being the prefecture closest to the capital, it's nearly equal to the capital, so it's basically the capital, too, isn't it? *Great. Chiba is great.*

You can take just one slick rapid-service train to Tokyo station, or there's also the option of the Chiba Line. *Fast. Chiba is fast.*

But Tokyo Station doesn't exactly welcome anyone on the platform for the Sobu rapid service and the Keiyo Line platforms—the Chiba Line rapid service is so deep underground that you're like, *What the hell, are we going to dig for oil?* The Keiyo Line in particular is so far away that you can't even call it Tokyo Station at all… *Far. Chiba is far.*

And if you're taking the Shinkansen, Shinagawa is more convenient, even if it is farther away.

Just how much of a boondock is Tokyo, being so far away from Chiba? And Kyoto's even farther; must really be the middle of nowhere.

I leisurely took the local train from the station closest to my house to Tsudanuma, where I transferred to the Sobu Line rapid service.

I dashed over to transfer to the rapid train leaving right that moment, breathing a sigh when the doors closed behind me. *Good thing I made it*, I thought in relief, and when I lifted my head, my eyes met another pair that were clear and pale as ice.

"…"

"…"

Neither of us said anything.

With a restless swish of her bluish-black ponytail, she glanced outside.

Saki Kawasaki. I mentally recited the name I'd finally remembered.

Oh yeah, I remember she lived close by. She was on the other side of the highway, so we'd been in different middle school districts, but the closest station to her would be one station over from me. If she was transferring to the rapid service, we'd inevitably end up boarding at the same spot.

"…"

She glanced at me as if checking what was going on with me. Our eyes met again, and she shook me off with a jerk of her head and looked outside.

…The hell?

It was now too late to say hello, but moving elsewhere would have been like admitting she was bothering me and accepting defeat, so I couldn't move.

In the end, both of us leaned against the doors for the whole thirty minutes until Tokyo Station.

When we got off the platform, I caught sight of students in the Soubu High School uniform here and there in the crowd.

It seemed they'd all arranged to come here together. *Feh, they can't even go to Tokyo on their own! Just like rural kids. Come on here, take a page outta my book. I got to Tokyo alone, you know? At this rate, maybe I'll chase my dreams in Tokyo and end up getting big, eh?*

I went up the stairs that seemed to go on forever and finally came out aboveground. But even so, I was still indoors, so I couldn't see the sun, blue sky, stars, or the moon… This is the concrete jungle. And this enormous unfeeling city was swarming with people. I was already missing Chiba. *I wanna go home.*

Swept along by the great flow of people, I aimed for the Shinkansen platform. I was swept along by the crowds so much, I started wondering if someone was going to occasionally scold me from afar for changing.

There were a lot of kids from my school at the entrance to the Shinkansen. Tokyo Station was always crowded to begin with, and it was even more of a noisy, seething morass than usual. Even in this crowded station, I'll be what I am, a solitary (Hachi)man.

"Hachiman!" A voice called my name from within the group of students. I have hardly any classmates who call me Hachiman. In fact, there's hardly anyone at all who can correctly call me Hikigaya.

And the only one who would call me by my first name with such affection would be…

"Oh, Hachiman… The township of Kyoto is brimming with such nostalgia! The hometown of my soul! Gafum-gafum."

…Oh yeah, he calls me Hachiman, too, doesn't he?

Zaimokuza approached me, clearing his throat with a bizarre noise.

"Do you need something?" I asked.

"Herm, of course I have no business! But the battery on my DS ran out already, so I was looking for a new way to kill time."

"Is that right? Man, you've brought a lot of stuff. Are you gonna hole yourself up in the mountains somewhere?" Looking over, I saw Zaimokuza had a duffel bag on his back filled to bursting. *What the hell is in there?*

He patted the bag and pushed his glasses up with his middle finger. "Aye. Just for some sword training on Mount Kurama."

"Mount Kurama, huh? That's pretty out of the way." Of course,

Mount Kurama is also a popular location, but since it's kind of far from the city of Kyoto, it's a difficult place to visit if you're going to be efficient about going to lots of places.

"Indeed, indeed! Well, 'twas not exactly my decision, but I deem training with Lord Tengu will prove interesting."

"Are you going all the way to Kibune? Well, whatever you're gonna be doing, it is easier when you don't have to decide yourself. Sounds fine to me."

"Well, I mean. I will also be getting what I desire as well. In this world, one sometimes finds a place he wishes to visit. But more importantly, I would that thou wouldst play along with my story outline and take jabs at it. I'm lonely," Zaimokuza complained, pouting his lips.

Um, I mean, it'd be a waste of time to take potshots at his cringy, juvenile story outlines, so it'd be best not to touch that. I couldn't do all that work for free.

"If you get to go where you want to go, then it's all good, right? You've got this opportunity, so go have fun."

"Indeed. Where shalt thou go, Hachiman?"

"Places and stuff. I haven't decided yet for the third day."

"The third day is the free day, is it not? Lermf, you may accompany me to the stores I might wish to visit."

"I'd be okay with that, but…" Hanging out with Zaimokuza was kinda eh, but I did have some interest in shopping itself. But there was also the matter of the Service Club request on the third day. It'd probably be best to not make any plans. "It's about time I go to the gate zone to meet up with my class."

"To the gate zone, all alone! Indeed! Well then, Hachiman. We shall meet again, in Kyoto."

"Oh, I doubt we're gonna see each other, though…"

Parting ways with Zaimokuza, I looked for where the other members of my class were likely to be. If I loitered vaguely near the fringes, I would appear to be a part of the group. I looked around for a bit and found a familiar face in a particularly noisy section of the crowd.

It was Hayama and his friends.

So then that was definitely my class.

There were auxiliary organizations dotted about here and there, with Hayama's clique at their core. So I just had to sneak into a spot on the outermost ring. Time to activate my shadow skill. This ability used to grant me the status effect of invisibility, but I must have leveled up or something recently, since it's been activating additional attacks like people saying, *You know, it's always like he's suddenly just* lurking *there.* If they're noticing my existence, my aura must be expanding.

Eventually, it was time.

The loose, wide spread of the group suddenly condensed into neat lines. Roll call was done for each class, and then we went in. Forward march! *Is this a sports festival?*

At this point, we checked that all our group members were present. That was when I finally got to encounter the people of my own group—Totsuka. Encounters in Space!

"Hachiman!"

This time, it's the real one... Solace...

"Morning, Totsuka."

"Yeah, morning, Hachiman."

Totsuka and I greeted each other and then chatted a bit as all the groups came to stand on the Shinkansen platform. The train we were to board had already arrived. Each class got into the car that had been assigned to them.

The seats on the Shinkansen are arranged in a rather strange way.

There are five seats in each row, divided into three on one side and two on the other. This arrangement makes it difficult to sit in groups of four. If you could just naturally separate into two on either side, it'd be fine, but when you have a group of three and one loner, you'll have three in seats together with one on the other side of the aisle. Either that, or a human sacrifice will be chosen from the group of three and get stuck caring for them like a dutiful child caring for their aging parents. In the case of the former, the loner will be at ease, left to their own devices, but if they're paired up with someone, this will make nobody happy. Both will be silent the whole time, and the sacrifice will eventually cave and start talking to the two on the other side of the aisle.

And it's this, the Shinkansen, which gives rise to such tragedy. Where should I position myself for this field trip, then?

There was me and Totsuka, and Hayama and Tobe.

For this quartet, the correct choice should be to separate into pairs.

But this was a class function. These things have a variety of elements tangling up in complex ways. You watch who sits where first, and the following seating arrangements are based on that. Everyone was fine until they boarded the train and started glancing at one another, wondering where they should sit. In these situations, whoever makes the first move loses the fight.

"Man, I get so excited on the Shinkansen and planes and stuff." Tobe was looking around as he walked down the aisle of the car buzzing with quiet predeparture conversation.

"I've never ridden a plane."

"This is my first time on the Shinkansen."

Ooka and Yamato came loudly stomping after Tobe. They'd evidently ended up following him in because they'd been together in the station. The other two boys in Ooka and Yamato's group followed behind them.

And another foursome was coming down the aisle: Miura, Yuigahama, Ebina, and Kawasaki. The three buddies plus one.

"I want the window seat." Golden Curls got right to point and stated the seat she wanted.

The brown-haired bun accepted that and adjusted to suit her. "Okay then, I'll be on the aisle. Where'll you guys sit?"

When the discussion was turned to them, the short black bob considered a moment, then turned toward the ponytail. "Hmm... Between the window or aisle side...which do you think gets more ass?"

"Basically, anything is fine with... Huh?" Kawasaki froze at the incomprehensible question, and drool was on its way out of Ebina's mouth.

"Close your mouth, Ebina. Come on." Miura shoved Ebina's jaw up, and Yuigahama watched the exchange with a hint of a wry smile. Even on a field trip, the four girls were having the same conversations they always did.

You made some friends. Isn't that nice, Kawasaki? Big Brother has some feelings about that.

The seating situation was not being resolved, and Hayama could no longer just stand and watch. Without addressing anyone in particular, in his calm and resonant tone, he suggested, "I figure we can just sit wherever. We can switch seats on the way anyway." Then he took a nearby window seat in a three-seat section right around the middle area.

"Yeah, you're right." Tobe followed him, moving to the one beside Hayama.

"Then I get the window," Miura declared. She spun around the seats so there were two sets of three facing each other, then took the seat opposite Hayama. As expected of Miura. She sat down where she wanted, without asking anyone's permission. "Come on, Yui, Ebina." And then, crossing her long legs and leaning back in a luxurious manner, she patted the seat beside her.

How the hell is she doing that? She acts like it's the most natural thing in the world.

"So Yumiko's there, and Tobecchi's there, and, um...," Yuigahama muttered quietly so people wouldn't hear as she considered everything.

But before her thoughts could come together, Ebina pushed Yuigahama's back. "Come on, come on, you sit there, Yui. I'll be here."

"Hey, Hina—" Yuigahama was about to complain, but Ebina cut her off, took Kawasaki's hand, and invited her to sit in front of her.

"You sit across from me, Kawasaki," she said.

"Oh, I could go somewhere else..." Kawasaki shook her head at the lineup, but when Ebina pulled her by the hand, she acquiesced. She was surprisingly easy to push.

"It's fine, it's fine! ♪" Ebina beamed as she decided the seating arrangements almost by force. As a result, a sextet was born: Miura, Yuigahama, and Ebina in a line, with Hayama, Tobe, and Kawasaki facing them.

Kawasaki didn't hide her displeasure at being forced to sit next to Tobe, and she set her elbow on the armrest and her head on her hand like she was about to take a nap. *Um, er, Tobe there is a little scared, so it'd be great if you could be a little nicer to him. You're taking all the rom-com out of this.*

Following Hayama's group's seating choices, Ooka and Yamato took the four seats on the other side of the aisle together with the other two of their group. Then the rest of the class went to decide their seats.

I was watching to see how things were going down when I felt a timid tug at my sleeve. Totsuka glanced all around, then up at me. "What should we do, Hachiman?"

I averted my eyes in embarrassment under the full force of such a tender look. I took the opportunity to survey the situation in the train car. "Yeah..."

In situations such as these, it's convention for an isolated loner to go straight for a seat on the fringe and for the others to quarantine them there. Therefore, if someone else got there first, the loner would just have to see how everything shook out and go wherever was open.

Since Hayama had gone right for the center this time, the spaces at the front and back were comparatively empty. "...Well, there's space up in front, so there, I guess," I said.

"Yeah, let's do that."

When I started forward, Totsuka just followed without asking anything. He was so pure, I could see him getting dragged into some criminal activity at the drop of a hat. *I have to protect him...* With that secret imperative in my heart, I headed toward a set of three seats at the front.

The very front was occupied, unsurprisingly, so I chose a row a little farther back from that. I put my things on the overhead rack. I didn't have much in the way of baggage, so there was a lot of space left over.

Well, it wasn't much more work to lift up two bags instead of one. "Here." When I reached out to Totsuka to lift his bag up, too, he looked puzzled but curious. Timidly, his hand crept forward and took mine.

It's so soft and small and smooth...

"No, not that, your bag..."

That's not what I meant; this isn't a handshake. Aw man, it's so smooth and soft.

"...Oh. S-sorry!" Realizing his mistake, Totsuka jerked his hand away from me. Looking down at the floor with his face bright red, he quietly said "Thank you..." and handed over his bag.

I took it and put it up on the overhead rack. I was about ready to scoop him up, too, while I was at it. *I wanna take him home~.* ♪

Totsuka was still embarrassed about his mistake as I ushered him to the window seat, and then I sat down, too.

Right then, the departure melody rang.

What a nice day for a trip!

× × ×

Suddenly, I opened my eyes.

It seemed I'd fallen straight to sleep in my seat, maybe because I'd left the house earlier than usual. "Hnn!" I stretched and heard a giggle beside me, in the aisle seat.

"You sleep too much."

"Ack! You startled me..." I jumped in my seat at the unexpected voice.

"What's with that reaction...? Sooo rude..." Yuigahama glared at me with a pouting, grumpy expression.

"Uh, I mean, you're gonna startle anyone if you talk to them right when they wake up..." *It's embarrassing when people see you sleeping, so please don't, seriously.* I instinctively wiped my mouth to make sure I wasn't drooling.

The gesture must have been funny to her, as she cackled. "It's fine, it's fine! Your mouth was closed, and you slept really quietly."

Fine, then. Actually, it's not. It's embarrassing.

Wait, why is she sitting here? It was decided long ago that Totsuka would be by my side... Looking for Totsuka, I found him snoozing beside me on the window side. But my yelp must have woken him up. He moaned quietly and rubbed his eyes a little.

Ngh! Damn it! I should have softly slid a ring onto the ring finger on his left hand while he was asleep, and then once he woke up and rubbed his eyes, he'd notice it, and I'd propose. What a waste of my strategy titled "Once she awakens...the diamond is forever." *Hachiman Hikigaya has made the mistake of his life! I've lost my chance at marriage!*

Totsuka yawned modestly behind his hand, then blinked as he took in the situation. "...Sorry, I fell asleep."

"Oh, no, it's totally fine. I don't mind if you sleep a bit longer. Once we arrive, I'll wake you up. Oh, do you wanna use my shoulder?" *If you like, my elbow or arm is fine, too.*

"I—I don't need that! You can nap, Hachiman. I'll make sure to get you up."

Ha-ha-ha, he's cute enough to get a lot of things up.

It was starting to feel like, *Are me and Totsuka gonna sleep or not? Or we could just sleep together?* Yuigahama breathed an exasperated sigh. "Come on, the both of you are sleeping too much. This field trip has just started; if you're already tired, what're you gonna do for the rest of the trip?"

"Yeah, we have to enjoy this more." Totsuka roused himself with a nod. True, it was still just the first day. It was too early to be getting tired and falling asleep.

So I thought, but Yuigahama seemed a little tired already herself. "Anyway, what's going on with you? Did something happen over there?" I asked.

Her shoulders slumped. "About that... Yumiko and Hayato are basically no different from normal... Kawasaki's been in a bad mood, and Tobecchi's been scared of her this whole time, so it feels like the conversation just isn't happening."

"I see... What about Ebina?"

"Same as always... In fact, she seems so excited about the trip, she's worse than usual."

Okay, when you put it that way, I basically get what's going on.

It was a disaster for Tobe. Kawasaki probably didn't care much for his loud personality, and Tobe was too wimpy to handle Kawasaki and her delinquent-esque tendencies. What's more, Ebina's inner citadel was a Death Star–level fortress. Without the power of the Force, Tobe was never gonna break in there.

So in all likelihood, nothing much was going to happen on the Shinkansen, since initial positioning had gone wrong. Even if the environment was unusual, if the players were in ideal positions, in the end, nothing would change. What we needed to coordinate was not the environment but the relationships in it.

"It would be nice if they could have some time alone together," said Yuigahama.

"But with just the two of them, I doubt anything would happen."

"Yeah..."

Totsuka, hearing our conversation, clapped his hands. "Oh! Are you talking about Tobe?"

"Huh? You know, too, Sai-chan?" Yuigahama asked him with surprise.

"Yeah. He told us about his crush during summer vacation, in Chiba Village."

"Oh, he did? Well, he came to talk to us about it the other day, so we're hoping the two of them hit it off. If anything comes up, could you help, too, Sai-chan?"

"If I can. I hope it works out," Totsuka said with a smile.

But this problem was rather a thorny one.

I wasn't the type to go out of my way to wish for others' happiness, but I wasn't enough of a jerk to hope for their unhappiness, either. I may have wished a little suffering on certain jerks, but I didn't feel that much for Tobe.

But looking over at Yuigahama beside me, *hmm*ing as she racked her brain, it occurred to me that maybe I had to come up with something, too. I folded my arms, pondering over the matter, when Totsuka let out a tiny "Ah!"

"Did you think of something?" I asked.

He pointed out the window. "Hachiman, look! It's Mount Fuji!"

"Huh, we've already come pretty far. Where is it?"

"You can't really see it from your seat, can you?" Pretty much glued to the window, Totsuka beckoned me. Guess that meant I should come closer. Taking him up on his word, I leaned in toward the window.

His face was really close. He twisted around awkwardly in the tiny space in an attempt to get as close to the window as possible, his face turned away from Mount Fuji so that his eyes were just giving it a side-long glance. He sighed because of the cramped position, clouding the glass for an instant.

Oh-ho, so this is Mount Fuji... And my Mount Fuji is getting close, too...

As I feared the eruption of my own personal Mount Fuji, I felt a tug on my shoulder. "Oh! I wanna see, too!" Yuigahama laid her arm over top of me, from my shoulders across my back. A chill ran down my spine. The sudden touch was startling. The smell of her lightly applied perfume hung in the air after her.

Illegal contact?! That's a foul...

But I lacked the presence of mind to shake her off or evade her, so I had no choice but to freeze in that position.

"..."

The scenery must have entranced her; she went silent for a good while. All I heard was her quiet breathing.

"Ohhh, Mount Fuji is so prettyyy. Hup." After a nice long view, Yuigahama seemed satisfied, as she finally moved away from my back and sat down in her own seat. "Thanks, Hikki."

"...Uh-huh," I replied calmly, but frankly, my heart was still pounding as if I'd been running a race.

Why does she do things like this? Listen. This innocent behavior kinda...makes a lot of boys get the wrong idea, and these mistakes can be fatal, you know? If you understand, please refrain from the following: body touching, sitting in his seat during break or after school, and borrowing something you forgot from him.

I could feel my face turning red, so I turned to Yuigahama to lecture her and maybe distract her attention. "Listen..."

"Oh, I'm gonna head back now." Before the words were even fully out of her mouth, she'd hopped out of her seat and scampered off.

She ran away... This was frustrating, irritating, annoying, a little disappointing, and at the same time, also a bit of a relief. I couldn't quite sort out all the feelings, so I breathed them out in a soft sigh.

Which was when I heard a little bird speak from my arms. "U-um... are you done, Hachiman...?"

Looking over, I saw Totsuka was still in his earlier position, like I was basically holding him down. His eyes were moist; it must have been uncomfortable.

"S-sorry!" I swiftly collapsed into my own seat and slammed my back on the armrest. "Urk..."

"A-are you okay, Hachiman?!"

"Yeah, I'm fine, I'm fine."

I waved one hand lightly to tell Totsuka all was well as I rubbed my back with my other one. A strange warmth still remained there, not so much painful as just a little uncomfortably tingly.

×　×　×

By Shinkansen, it was a little over two hours from Tokyo.

When we got off at Kyoto Station, I felt the chill as we headed to the bus stop. Fall nights were cold in Kyoto. At this time of year, it would get even colder.

Since Kyoto is a basin, geographically, the summers are hot, and the winters are cold. Put it another way, and you might also say the sharp differences in temperature bring out the seasonal beauty of the area.

In the spring, faint-pink cherry blossoms bloom on the mountain ridge, while the verdant riverbed by the Kamo River is cool in the summer. In the autumn, red falling leaves color the mountain, and in winter, snow flurries dance in the clear sky and blanket the mountains.

This was near the end of fall, around the time when you would soon be catching glimpses of snow.

Apparently, the plan for the day was to head straight to Kiyomizu-dera Temple.

Each class got into a bus.

Even here, the seating arrangement was similar to how it had been on the Shinkansen. Hayama and Tobe sat together, with Miura and Yuigahama in their row. Behind them were the Ooka and Yamato pair, and Kawasaki and Ebina together. The takeaway here was that me and Totsuka were sitting together.

But even on this bus, it seemed like Tobe and Ebina weren't getting anywhere. Not only was there less freedom in seating on the bus than there had been on the Shinkansen, we were also very close to Kiyomizu-dera Temple. With some effort, we could have walked, so on a bus, it hardly took any time at all.

We drove down the road out of the urban area, turned, and eventually reached a hill. Our bus stopped in a big parking lot crowded with other tour buses. From here, we would climb up Sannen Hill to Kiyomizu-dera Temple.

Though the autumn leaves weren't at peak season, there were still plenty of tourists. The whole Kiyomizu-dera Temple area is one of the most popular spots in Kyoto, so it was packed.

We took a group photo with the Nio gates in the background. Unfortunately, this was a scripted, unskippable event. Everyone huddled together with their best friends while the lone wolves had to question the reason for their existence.

There are three main strategies for positioning.

The first is the outranging style.

This one is easy, so you could call it a style suited to beginners. But its simplicity gives it great power. You stand about 1.5 persons away from your classmates and take advantage of the distance to inflict damage with 100 percent accuracy. Mostly to your parents when they see the graduation album. And also to yourself when you look back on it in the future. I recommend getting rid of your graduation albums and commemorative photos as soon as possible—but if you go for a half-assed method of disposal like just tossing it in the garbage at your house, then your mom will find it and save it without telling her son, and tragedy will strike in more ways than one. This style is risky.

The second method is guerrilla style.

For this technique, you mingle among your merry classmates, contort your mouth into something unnaturally wide, and with your cheeks cracking under the pressure of your dead smile, you pretend you're a part of this. This is a pretty excellent form of camouflage that prevents loners from being identified in the photo, but there will be an emotional toll before and after taking the photo, as well as the possibility of aftereffects; after the battle is over, you might get comments like *The group photo is the only time he ever approached us (lol).*

The third technique is inside fighting.

You deliberately place yourself closer to your classmates for extreme close-quarters combat. The result is that you'll be in someone's shadow, or someone else will come in front of you and cut you out of the picture. You won't be obscured from the photo entirely—you'll be about half there—so it'll be a passable memory, and it won't make your mom worry to see it. You won't be properly in the photo, but some forms of beauty aren't reflected in photographs. However, if the photographer is a real go-getter, they'll helpfully call, *Oh, there's someone in front of you, so move a bit farther apart*, so you need to be wary of that.

On this occasion, I chose the inside fight and looked for a nice spot. *Hmm, right now, somewhere behind a burly guy like Yamato should be good*. Pushing my way through my classmates, I entered Yamato's shadow and positioned myself so as to be slightly obscured by the person in front of me.

The shutter snapped a few times. Once I'd survived the group photo without incident, now we would all be touring together as a class.

I went up the stone steps and through the gate and found an impressive five-story pagoda. A sigh slipped out of me at the sight of the Kyoto cityscape.

The visitors' entrance of Kiyomizu-dera Temple was already swarming with tourists and students who had gone in before us. It would take a little while before we could get in… Multiple classes were still waiting at the group entrance.

As I was quietly standing in line with my mind in outer space, someone called out to me.

"Hikki." Yuigahama had left the line to come up to my side.

"What's going on? Stand in line like you're supposed to, or you'll lose your spot. That's life."

"You're being dramatic… And, like, this line isn't gonna be moving for a while. More importantly, I found something that looks interesting, so let's head over there for a bit."

"Later." I don't have an aptitude for multitasking. I'm the type who wants to finish the thing in front of me first. Or maybe I just prefer to get unpleasant things over with.

Yuigahama *hmph*'d at me with a little glare, expressing her displeasure. "…Did you forget our job?"

"I'd prefer to forget about work when I'm on a trip, at least…"

But of course, my earnest wish would not reach her. Yuigahama grabbed me by the blazer. "I've already invited Tobecchi and Hina, so hurry up!"

She tugged my sleeve and me to a smallish temple not so far from the visitors' entrance.

It was right there when we went in through the main gates, but it doesn't have the visual punch of the main temple, so we must have ignored it. It was simply unremarkable. Or maybe it was that Kyoto has so many temples and shrines, you have to make a big bang if you want to leave an impression.

The one peculiarity about this one was the extremely cheerful middle-aged man trying to usher tourists in.

Womb tour, it was called. Ostensibly, going through this temple building in the darkness conferred some kind of blessing.

As Yuigahama had said, Ebina and Tobe were already there, nodding along to the guy's explanation. By the way, Miura and Hayama were there, too.

"What are they doing here, too?" I asked quietly so they couldn't hear.

Yuigahama leaned in to put her mouth close to my ear. "If I just called the two of them over, it'd be kinda weird."

"Well, I guess..." It was true if we put them alone together, they'd end up hyperconscious of it. Tobe would get nervous, too, and worst of all, it would put Ebina on guard.

"Come on, come on, let's go," Yuigahama urged me, so I took off my shoes and paid a hundred yen.

They're charging for this?

I peered down the stairs to see it was indeed dark. If a dungeon in an RPG world existed in reality, it might be something like this.

"'Kay then, you go first, Yumiko, Hayato," Yuigahama suggested. "And we'll go last."

"We don't have much time, so it's probably best to just go in pretty much one after another," Hayama replied very sensibly. Well, we'd sneaked out of line, so that was fair reasoning... Well, fair enough. If logic actually mattered, he'd have said something like *Let's go through here later so we can take our time*, though… It was an ill-conceived response for him, but it seemed nobody particularly cared.

"Yeah, I suppose so," Ebina agreed.

Oh no, it's like I'm the only one thinking so much about what Hayama says! How embarrassing!

"But it'll be over quick anyway, so no worries. Right, Ebina? And, Hayato?" said Tobe. Ebina folded her arms pensively as Tobe combed back his overlong hair with a grin.

"Yeah, but it's best if we could get back early," Hayama replied with a strained smile as Miura took his arm.

"'Kay, we'll go first. Let's get going, Hayato. This looks pretty cool," Miura said, stepping down the stairs with Hayama.

"Oh man, the darkness makes it way more exciting!"

"Hmm… Oh! It's so dark… Maybe Hayama and Hikitani should be going in together…"

Leaving those rather unsettling remarks behind them, Tobe and Ebina headed down into the womb tour, too.

Phew… I'm glad Hayama and I are far apart…

"Okay, Hikki, let's go, too."

"Yeah."

We went down the stairs and turned a corner into even deeper darkness. A few more steps forward, and all the light was gone.

I couldn't pull my hand away from the handrail, which was shaped like prayer beads. If I let go now, I'd probably lose not only my sense of distance but my sense of direction, too.

Whether my eyes were open or shut, it was still just as dark. Such is the abyss. Tottering along, testing the ground with each step, I probably would have looked like a penguin if anyone had seen me.

Now that my visual stimuli were gone, my other senses sharpened in an attempt to make up for it.

I could hear Miura and the others talking a few steps ahead. Miura was muttering incoherently over and over, which somehow sounded like a prayer, and it was scarier than it ought to have been. "...Oh crap, it's dark, it's dark, it's dark, oh crap, it's dark, oh crap."

"Pretty intense, huh?" I could hear Hayama mutter, maybe just being polite, or maybe as an honest impression.

"Whoa, it's so dark! Man, this is wild! It's nuts! This is dark as you can get, dude!" Tobe continued to blather on in excitement as if to encourage himself.

In response, he got a noncommittal "Ditto." I wondered if this was a Pokémon talking at first, but that was probably Ebina.

My hearing wasn't the only thing that got sharper.

My sense of touch was similarly being honed. In the darkness, I proceeded by feel.

The air was tranquil. Since I'd taken off my shoes, I shivered from the cold afflicting my feet. But the temperature wasn't the only thing that sent a momentary shudder running through me. It was genuine fear. Things you can't see, can't understand, can't grasp, can't figure out—they all lead to fear and anxiety.

With all these unfamiliar sensations, I shuffled along, groping at each one of the large beads that made up the railing. Suddenly, my hand landed on something warm. A little surprised, I stopped. Then something lightly bumped into me.

"Ack! Oh, sorry. I can't see at all." The owner of the voice was Yuigahama. Unable to see, she patted my back and arms to make sure of where I was.

"Oh, sorry. It's so dark, I kinda got confused, too..." Well, we were in complete darkness. It was unavoidable. The blind darkness makes you uneasy, so you grab at someone's clothes or hands as a sort of emergency measure. I wasn't going to question it. *It's okay, I've held hands with Komachi very recently, and I'm n-not thinking about it, not at all, I'm totally fine.*

"You've been quiet this whole time, Hikki, so I thought you might have gotten lost."

"I do that on a regular basis." *It's racked me up a lot of EXP. And I've got super-high-speed and mental defense for going home early, too.*

When I gave her that blasé response, I could hear hesitant laughter in the darkness, some sort of snicker or wry chuckle.

I took that as my signal to start moving forward again. The pull against my blazer remained, even as I continued on my way.

The path turned again and again, and then something leaped out of the blackness filling my vision.

It was a light, vague and dimly white. It looked like a stone, illuminated with electric lights.

Arriving before the stone, I could finally see Yuigahama's face.

"Here, we're supposed to spin the rock as we make a wish," she said.

"Huh." *I don't have any particular wishes. Stable income, a safe household, and sound health, I guess. Wait, that's actually a lot.*

But I felt that wishing for something so practical from gods or Buddhas wasn't quite right. A lot of the time, you can get those things through your own effort, and if so, I'd be better off wishing for something I couldn't get.

Especially because when someone or something gives you a gift, that means it can also be taken away.

"Have you decided what you're gonna wish for?" Yuigahama drowned out my pointless speculation in the darkness.

"Yeah," I replied. But I hadn't really made up my mind... *Yeah, I guess I'll just wish for Komachi to pass her entrance exams.*

"Okay then, let's spin it together." Yuigahama spun the rock around and around like a lazy Susan at a Chinese restaurant. With her eyebrows drawn tight and her eyes closed, she looked very serious.

Once she was done spinning it, she clapped her hands twice, too. *You idiot, that's what you do at a shrine.*

"All right, let's go!" For some reason, she looked really inspired as she pushed me in the back, and we plunged into darkness again.

They must have put that rock for the climax near the end; after a little walking, we could dimly see the entrance. The light leaking down from upstairs was a sight for sore eyes. When the others in front saw the light of day, they breathed sighs of relief, too.

We all climbed the stairs and stretched wide once we made it out.

"What'dja think? Feels like being reborn, doesn't it?" the guide asked with his Kansai dialect—he asked Tobe, that is.

"Oh, yeah! Man, I feel all fresh! Is that what you mean?"

Whoa, he hasn't changed one bit since before he went in there.

I looked at the time, but it hadn't been long. Five minutes or something.

Rebirth doesn't come that easy. You can go on a trip to India or climb Mount Fuji, but you're not going to be reborn. And even if you are, it's not like you can rewrite everything that's brought you to that point. No matter how you try to change what's in your mind, if you can't revise how the people around you see you or undo your past failures, that doesn't fix anything.

People are history; the time they've spent, the experiences they've lived form who they are. If you were reborn, you would have to burn all that history and erase it. But that's functionally impossible. So then you can't wish for rebirth. You have no choice but to live with the wounds on your shins and the sin on your back.

There are no do-overs in life.

Exactly how many failures had Tobe experienced? If he'd been through as many as I had but could still act that positive anyway, that was something to respect.

But he probably hadn't.

No, I hoped so... I didn't want such a glib, shallow guy to have some trauma as the mysterious core of his personality. I didn't want him to be laughing like an idiot because he had overcome his issues. It would make him almost cool...

"Ah, wait, oh no! Maybe everyone else has gone in already!" Yuiga-hama said in a panic as she looked over toward the group entrance of Kiyomizu-dera Temple.

"C'mon, we've got time, right?" Tobe said, but we didn't seem to have as much as he figured. Even from a distance, I could see kids in black uniforms starting to move, bit by bit.

"Come on, hurry!" Yuigahama urged us, and we rushed over to merge with the line.

×　×　×

Somehow, we got back before our class entered the main temple. We went in from the group entrance, where attractions like the Daikokuten statue and iron geta were installed inside. So many people were gathered there, even touching one of them would be a challenge.

Go farther in, and there was the Kiyomizu-dera Temple platform. Unsurprisingly, it was the most popular spot in the temple. It wasn't just students from our school taking pictures there—regular tourists were in the crowd.

"Oh, wow…" Yuigahama breathed a sigh as she touched the railing. The view overlooked the autumn-red mountains and the city of Kyoto. A thousand years ago, what would we have seen beneath us? Kyoto had changed in form, but I bet the invigorating experience of seeing it from these heights has stayed the same.

Kyoto is the city where change and permanence coexist.

I felt like I kind of understood why this city had been chosen for the field trip.

As I lost myself in the scenery, Yuigahama said beside me, "Oh! Hey, let's take a picture, Hikki, come on!" She quickly popped a compact digital camera out of her pocket. The tiny pink device was very Yuigahama.

"A photo? Gotcha. Lemme have that, then."

"Huh?" A questioning look on her face, Yuigahama handed her camera over to me.

I backed up a few steps, raised the camera, and captured Yuigahama in the finder. "Say *peanuts.*" Then I pressed the button, and she rushed to make a low-effort reverse peace sign before the short electronic *beep, beep.*

"See, you got a good one, thanks to my skills," I said, returning the camera, and Yuigahama immediately checked the photo. *It's convenient you can see 'em right away on a digital camera, isn't it? But you know, if this one isn't good, she'll make me take another one.*

"I did? Oh, it is kinda flattering… Wait, no! And, like, what the heck was that that you said when you took it?!"

"Don't you know? When us Chibanese take pictures, we always say that…"

"You don't need to lie about that…"

It wasn't really a lie. In fact, I kinda wished it'd catch on. Let's all say *peanuts* for photos!

"That's not what I meant! …Let's take one together! Since we're both here and all."

Such a straightforward suggestion was hard to refuse. I figured there was no particular reason to say no to her. I could've come up with some facetious excuse about the camera stealing my soul or something, but, well, it was like she said. Since we were there and all. I hadn't brought my own camera, either, so if I was gonna be in any picture, I had to be in someone else's.

"Well, I wouldn't really mind a picture," I said. "Okay then, I guess I'll ask someone to take it for us."

"You don't need to do that. All we gotta do is this," she said, coming to stand beside me. Then she turned the lens of the camera toward the two of us and readied to press the shutter button herself. "You have to lean in close, or we might not both fit…" She took a step closer to me and gently hooked her arm around mine. "All right! Cheese!"

I heard the shutter button, then a particularly cheery electronic noise.

My eyes hovered around somewhere in the opposite direction as Yuigahama, and that probably made them look even more rotten than usual. Practically spirit-photography level.

Yuigahama whisked her arm away, and then she took a few light steps back before spinning to face me again. "Thanks."

"I-it's not worth thanking me for."

Yeah, taking a photo is normal.

Looking around, I saw quite a few people here and there lining up to point cameras at themselves and take pictures. It was probably fairly common for modern high school students. There was no need to get dramatic about one commemorative photo. People took pictures together all the time, including ones with both guys and girls. In fact, it seemed that was more common.

I was just thinking too much.

"Hey, Yumiko, Hina! Let's take a picture, too!" Arms around Miura and Ebina, Yuigahama took a picture of the three of them. It was a nice shot. I could almost see the *yay* ♪ caption.

"Hayato, you guys join in, too!" Yuigahama called out to Hayama and everyone around him, not far away, and they all shuffled in as a group. Tobe, Ooka, and Yamato all responded to her signal, too.

"Ohhh, yeah, yeah!" said Tobe.

"Oh, sure… But this is a lot of people." Smiling awkwardly, Hayama looked back at the cluster of classmates around him.

"Oh, so then we could separate into groups…"

Yuigahama's suggestion must have been lost in the crowd, or Hayama hadn't heard it, since he walked up to me and tried to give me his camera. "Do you mind?"

"…No," I replied, accepting it, and then found there was a line of people behind him.

"Like, take my phone, too."

"Here's mine, too, Hikitani!"

"And mine!"

"Oh, and mine!"

Hold on a minute here! I only said I'd take Hayama's camera…and now there's Miura and Tobe and Ebina and Ooka? Come on! And there's even more after them!

I was entrusted with a few additional cameras as well, until I accepted it from the very last person with a sigh. "Sorry, Hachiman," said Totsuka. "Can I ask you to do mine, too?"

"Yeah, just leave it to me!" *This is a very singular, irreplaceable photo. I shall put my soul into it and take the greatest photo ever!* But that made it sound like my vengeful spirit was gonna be in it. *Eugh, what a sad photo.*

"...Oh, then, Hikki, sorry. Can you take mine, too...?" A little chagrined, Yuigahama came to hand me her camera, too.

This suggestion had probably been an attempt to get Tobe and Ebina in a photo together... Well, with the whole class present, of course they were. Not to mention that if someone suggests taking a photo with everyone, that's what's gonna happen.

When I took her camera, I said, "Gotcha. Well, try again tomorrow."

"Yeah..." she replied briefly, then returned to the platform railing where everyone else was waiting, and I got ready to take the photo.

Dang, this was a lot of cameras. Almost in the double digits. *Wow, it's kinda like I'm popular!*

Actually, why didn't they just take one picture and attach it to an e-mail or share it on Facebook or something? Isn't this a time to take advantage of those social media things that I don't really get?

"Then I'm just gonna snap whatever... Okay, peanuts." *Okay, okay, peanuts, peanuts...* I took photo after photo.

The series of shots made me realize how expressive Yuigahama is. Her determination to enjoy the moment with all her might showed up on her face and in her gestures in every photo. It was a good thing the camera had an automatic focus function—otherwise, I felt like a lot of things would be going out of focus.

Miura seemed used to being photographed—though she posed differently in each shot, her expressions were basically consistent.

Hayama was a total natural, just like you'd expect from a guy who's used to attention, and though he didn't seem like he was making an effort to pose, the camera was kind to him.

Tobe was also being natural, to put it nicely, but, well, he was definitely Tobe. He was making a lot of the poses you'd see in a fashion magazine. Gaia must have been whispering at him to shine more.

Meanwhile, Ebina was smiling the whole time. I'd gotten used to that expression lately, but there was something vaguely frightening about how it was exactly the same in every photo.

We followed the tour route from the main temple, seeing the sights, and the flow of students continued toward Jishu Shrine.

Jishu Shrine is situated on the grounds of Kiyomizu-dera Temple. It's quite famous because of its gods of marriage, and it's a popular spot for visitors to come praying for romantic success. The people who come to visit Kiyomizu-dera Temple will, without a doubt, also come to pray here.

This was all the more true for the students on our field trip. The area around the shrine was full of their chattering and shrieking.

First, we would get the shrine visit done with, and then they would all go excitedly buy their charms and fortunes.

I didn't intend to buy anything in particular, so I activated my secret technique: just silently trailing behind everyone else. Well, I wouldn't have minded buying a fortune, but I suspect they're based around the idea of entertaining others, meaning you're supposed to show your fortunes off. So I've never been in the habit of doing it.

While I vaguely inserted myself into the group and watched how the class was doing, it seemed, unsurprisingly, that the number-one attraction here was the love-fortune rock.

Looking over, I saw lots of girls taking up the challenge. Their friends would secure a route for them, like security guards, so nobody would interrupt them, and then they'd start with something like, *Okay, I'm going now.*

If you can go from a rock positioned a ways away to arrive at the love-fortune stone with your eyes closed, your love is supposed to come true, kinda like that show where you get a million yen if you can perform some difficult stunt.

Also, if someone helps you with verbal instructions like you do when smashing watermelons blindfolded, then apparently, that means you'll need that person's help to fulfill your love.

Looking closely, I saw a woman of marriageable age in a suit and white jacket arrive at the stone to the sound of applause. *Our teacher-advisor is so amazing...*

As more high school girls waited their turns, boys took furtive glances at them. If the girl they had a crush on was taking the challenge, I was sure they'd work themselves up wondering if the one she liked was him. Uh, actually, I was on the brink of thinking that myself. You're allowed to have hope—it doesn't hurt anyone as long as I never put it into action and blow it all up.

Not everyone there had come for such romantic information. Some boys were just watching from afar because they were a bit curious to see. Things like this make you realize how cute boys can be.

But I felt that our dear Tobe, joining the line like it was normal, was just slightly lacking in discretion.

"I'm gonna do it on the first try for sure!" he crowed to the onlookers, and then Ooka and Yamato, who had joined him at the shrine, gave him a wild round of applause to wind him up. Tobe answered with a victory pose, then closed his eyes and, shuffling along like a zombie, headed for the goal.

"Oh man, I've got no idea. Huh? Do I just go straight here, actually? How am I doing?" Tobe asked for advice, and Yamato and Ooka amused themselves by giving nonsense answers.

"Straight, straight!"

"Behind you, Tobe!"

"Whaaa—? Behind me?!" Tobe whirled around.

"There's no point in turning around if your eyes are closed...," Hayama muttered with a sigh of exasperation. Laughter rang out around the shrine. How delightful.

As long as they were having fun, Ebina didn't have to worry about them at all. They really were good friends.

While I blankly watched the three idiots, Yuigahama patted Ebina on the shoulder, probably having similar thoughts. "Isn't that friendly enough, Hina?"

"Yeah, it is… But you can't relax until the end," she said, her face tilted toward the ground. From where I stood, I couldn't see her eyes past the lenses of her glasses. But the tone of her voice had dropped a little.

You didn't see Ebina this tense very often, and Yuigahama gave her a questioning look. "Huh? What do you mea—?"

Ebina cut her off by jerking her head up again, clenching a fist and panting through her nose. "You know! I really need them to go as far as they can on this trip!"

Go where, pray tell?

Oh, and Tobe nearly fell on his ass in the end, but Hayama caught him.

After the love-fortune stone, the kids of our class went on to opening up regular fortunes.

"Awww yes!" Miura made her joy plain with a very handsome victory pose.

Peeking at what was in her hands, Yuigahama also called out in surprise. "Whoa, Yumiko!"

"Ooh, you got the 'great fortune' one…" Even Ebina came up to her to give her a little applause.

"Man, seriously? But, like, it's still just a fortune? It's not like it really matters, y'know?" Miura was talking like this was no big deal, but the way she folded the fortune up neatly and carefully put it in her wallet gave away her pleasure. She was very much a girl in love, and it was cute.

"But actually, y'know…getting the best fortune really kinda sucks, right? 'Cause then it's all downhill from there!" Tobe teased.

"What was that?" Miura's glare was no joke.

Yup, she's scary after all.

Of course, this also frightened Tobe, so he retreated to safer waters. "Uh…great fortune… Don't see that often…"

Oh, that's definitely a thing, all right, splashing cold water over someone else's joy and making people scowl. Back in elementary school, when I went to Nikko on a field trip, I said something similar and made everyone hate me, as usual.

But Tobe's supposition that your luck tops out when you draw the best fortune isn't really wrong. Similarly, if you say it's all downhill afterward, then the opposite is also true.

"Awww. I got bad luck...," Ebina said sadly.

"But you know, since it's all uphill from here, that's actually a good thing!" Tobe casually consoled Ebina for her bad luck. Teasing Miura must have led him to this conclusion.

Huh, he's really trying at this even without our help, isn't he?

...All right, guess I'll give him a hand here. "If you're gonna tie up a bad fortune, I think higher up is better. Like, you know, the gods are supposed to be able to see it better or something." It was the most clearly superstitious folk belief thing I could have said, but, well, I had heard something along those lines before.

But my comment was so out of the blue, both Tobe and Ebina were looking all around for the source of the voice. *No, it's not a message from the gods; it's me. It's a-me, Wario.* Well, not really.

The two of them finally noticed my presence, so I repeated myself. "I hear a high spot's good. Why don't you tie it up there for her?" I said with a look at Tobe.

He seemed to understand, reaching out to Ebina. "O-oh, I get it. Hey, let me do it?"

"Th-thanks. Gotta love boys!" Ebina handed her fortune over to Tobe. But she meant it like *Gotta love boys (because they're convenient)*, which was saddening.

Tobe reached up to the highest spot to tie on the fortune. Watching out of the corner of my eye, I left Jishu Shrine feeling proud of a job well done.

Now we just had to follow the visitors' route.

We'd wandered along from the inner subtemple to the platform at the main temple to see the view, and from there, the path led on downward to the Otowa Waterfall.

They said its miraculous water was the origin of the name Kiyomizu-dera (pure water) Temple.

Lots of people were lined up in front of its three streams.

The line was long, weaving back and forth in rows divided by partitions. *Hey, hey, they're lining up like it's Destiny Land. There's no fast pass here?*

I was standing there aghast at the crowd when a violent chop landed on my head. "No going ahead on your own!"

"Uh, today isn't even the group day, so it's no big deal, come on…" Rubbing my head, I squinted at Yuigahama, Miura, and the others coming up behind her.

"Oh, there's some kinda stream here. Three of 'em."

Thank you, Captain Obvious.

"This is the Otowa Waterfall," Hayama said carelessly.

Guidebook in hand, Yuigahama *hmm*'d as she began to read. "Ummm, it says one gives blessings for studies, one for love, and one for long life."

…I see. So that's why Miss Hiratsuka's in line there with an empty two-liter shochu *bottle. That's too much to take home…*

Wait, was that true? There was nothing like that written in the explanation at the Otowa Waterfall itself. In fact, the sign even declared rather flatly: ALL THREE BRANCHES ARE THE SAME WATER! You know?

And everyone was lining up without even questioning it. So was I, though.

After about fifteen minutes of waiting, finally, it was our turn. By the way, the teacher got a scolding for taking too much of the romantic-success water.

Each of us grabbed a ladle to scoop some water.

Yuigahama, in front of me, focused on the middle waterfall and reached out with the long ladle to take some water. Bringing it to her lips, she tucked her hair behind her ear and sipped it a couple of times, her white throat moving as she gulped it down.

"Oh, wow. It's good…," she said with a sigh as she finished drinking.

This water had been famous for ages. The taste had a long history. And it was spring water, too, chilled by the season, so it had to be pleasant.

I reached out to the shelf of clean ladles to take one in hand.

"Here, Hikki." Yuigahama stopped me, handing me the ladle she'd used instead.

"Uh, that's... I mean, it's kinda sorta..."

Yuigahama sometimes had these rather girlish calculated moments, but she could also be sincerely clueless sometimes, so I couldn't tell for sure.

But this time, it seemed she was handing me the ladle with good intentions.

When she realized the significance of what she was doing, her cheeks flushed. "Uh..."

"Yeah..." *Well, that's what it is.*

I picked up one of the sterilized ladles, scooped up some water from the nearby stream, and chugged it down in one go. The cold drink was delicious.

"Y-you don't need to worry about that ..."

...But I will. I mean, if I drank from yours, I wouldn't know how the water tastes, now, would I?

Surreptitiously, **Yukino Yukinoshita** goes out to town at night.

Before I knew it, I was lying in my futon.

"This ceiling isn't familiar…" I sorted out my memories and remembered I was on the school field trip.

The first place we'd gone on day one was Kiyomizu-dera Temple, and after that, there was Nanzen Temple, and then for some reason, they made us walk to Ginkaku-ji Temple. The fall leaves had been pretty, though, and walking along the Philosopher's Walk by the river was good exercise. I think it was a nice place for Tobe and Ebina to go on a stroll.

Then after we'd gone through the schedule for the day, we'd gone to the hotel, had dinner, and then…

…why was I lying in bed here now?

"Oh, Hachiman. You're awake?" Totsuka had been sitting beside me, holding his knees. He released one leg and peered at my face.

"Uh, yeah. Um, what's going on…?" *Have I been King Crimson'd and jumped to the end where Totsuka and I have started our lives as newlyweds?*

So I wondered, but it seemed that was not the case, as I could hear loud clattering and voices from across the room.

"Man, you really got me!"

"You're too good, Hayato!"

I glanced over toward the source of the voices to see the boys from my class rambling about *pon* and *kan* and *ponkan*.

Okay, I basically get what's going on here.

It seemed my usual lifestyle rhythm, which involved a nap as soon as I got home, had backfired on me. Since we'd spent all day out doing stuff, and I'd also eaten a rather large dinner at the hotel, I'd apparently passed out the moment I'd returned to our room.

"It's past the time for the baths already, but the teacher said you could use the indoor bath," Totsuka told me.

"Wh-what?!" *So my precious bath time with Totsuka is already over?!* This was such a shock to me, I leaped out of my futon. *It seems I must kill God…*

As I ground my teeth, Totsuka indicated the door of the room.

Wh-what's this? Does he mean it like, You're such a pervert, Hachiman. Perverts like you should leave the room and have a bath in the garden pond? *I'm not that sort of pervert or a prince, though…*

I found myself worrying over this, but Totsuka continued in his gentle tone. "The unit bath is over there."

"Oh, thanks."

I'd have liked to make a unit with Totsuka and get into that bath, but I would look forward to that the next day. I mean, the field trip was three nights. I'd have two more bath-time opportunities. And what's more, for the third night, we'd be staying in Arashiyama, so there'd be a hot spring. An open-air hot tub. Yes.

I was euphoric as I washed off in the shower.

When I came out of the bath, I found Tobe sprawled on the floor, and his eyes met with mine. It seemed he'd lost the game, and his motivation, too. But then he leaped up again and said to me, "Oh, Hikitani. You're awake? Wanna play mah-jongg? These guys are all so good, I can't take it."

Hey, does that comment mean I look like I suck, so you can win? Huh?

But, well, his invitation and willingness to talk to me at all showed some of the good things about him. But I just couldn't dig his vibe. We wouldn't hit it off. "Sorry. I don't know how to score it." I rejected him casually, and Tobe didn't persist.

He gave a careless reply like "For real?" and then returned to the mah-jongg circle.

I actually can't score mah-jongg—'cause when you play it on console, the CPU calculates the scores for you.

Totsuka had joined in with the mah-jongg group, too, and it looked like they'd taught him the rules. He noticed me and waved.

Right when I was wondering what to do next and thinking about just going to sleep, the door was thrown open. "Hachimaaaaan! Drop everything and play Uno with me!"

Zaimokuza had come over, inviting me to play cards in the casual sort of way that Isono invites Nakajima to play baseball.

"…Hey, what happened with the other guys in your class?" I asked, since he'd burst in like this was the normal thing to do.

Zaimokuza pouted and clung to me. I peeled him off and made him sit.

"Listen, Hachiemon. They're so mean! Those swine told me, 'Sorry, Zaimokuza, the game is only for four people' and then made me wait my turn until someone loses."

Waiting your turn is just normal! In fact, if they're letting you join in, I think that's a good thing. Make nice with them.

"Huh. What game are they playing?" Totsuka asked.

Zaimokuza puffed out his chest.

"Mmm-paka-mm-paka! The Dream Dokapon Kingdom!"

Don't say it like it's Crayon Kingdom.

"…But why play such a friendship-destroying game on a school field trip?" I asked. Dokapon, or Momotetsu, even, will put people's personalities into relief—and I don't just mean the underhanded strategies of truly awful individuals. That's not as bad as it gets. Battle is cruel by nature after all.

The problems happen when you play the game with people who get legitimately angry about the game and spoil the mood. It really does inevitably create fissures in your friendship. Also, if I had to mention any other issues, it would be the ones who lose interest in playing and read manga or something as they tell you to just move their piece ahead.

Such an incident has occurred in my life before, in elementary school.

"So let's play Uno," said Zaimokuza.

"Oh, I'd like that," said Totsuka. "They taught me how to play mah-jongg, too, but I don't really get it."

Zaimokuza pulled the Uno deck out of his pocket and shuffled the cards like mah-jongg tiles by spreading them all over the floor. Then he started dealing them out.

"Herm, I'll take the first move," he said, and he suddenly pulled out a number of cards with *R* written on them. "Ruh-ruh-ruh-ruh-ruh-reverse!"

Shut up with your r-r-r-r-reverse; do you think it's time to d-d-d-d-duel or something?

Zaimokuza playing the reverse card meant the turn order switched multiple times, and after Zaimokuza, it was my turn, and then Totsuka's. After that, we played our cards in order, sometimes getting skipped, sometimes angrily having to draw and then retaliating with a draw four, choosing colors the others didn't seem to have. A typical series of Uno events.

Before I knew it, the white-hot competition had left only two more cards in my hand. Zaimokuza and Totsuka both held five cards each, putting me in the lead.

And it was my turn. I played a card, and Zaimokuza gave a little *hrrrmmm* and said to me, "By the way, Hachiman, where are you going tomorrow?"

"Huh? Why are you asking random questions in the middle of the game?" *Geez, he always asks such obnoxious questions,* I thought, fury welling within me, and I was about to reply when Zaimokuza huffily looked away toward Totsuka instead.

"So be it. And you, fair Totsuka?"

"Well, we're going to the Toei Kyoto Studio Park and Ryouan-ji Temple, I suppose. And then—" Totsuka put his cards down on his knees and then looked up dreamily like he was trying to remember. It was so cute, I decided to join in the conversation.

"There's Ninna-ji and Kinkaku-ji Temples in that area, too."

"Oh, that's right," Totsuka said, and he tossed out a card.

Instantly, Zaimokuza leaped to his feet and jabbed his finger at me. "Ha! Hachiman! You didn't say Unooooo!"

"Ngk! Ah…" By the time I realized, it was already too late. Totsuka had already played his card.

"Yaaay!"

"Yaaay!"

Zaimokuza raised his hands up high with a shout of victory, and Totsuka copied him and gave him a high five.

Huh? What the hell? They plotted that together? Hey, I wanna high-five Totsuka…

Dirty as I expected, Zaimokuza, dirty. Distracting me from my opportunity to say Uno is so unfair…

But seeing Totsuka all excited about it is so adorable, I'm satisfied.

"Hachiman! You've got to have a punishment!" said Totsuka.

"Aye, Hachiman! A punishment! I'm going to think of what, so wait for it!"

They were really going all in. Must be the field trip.

The others seemed to be having just as much fun, and I could hear the rising excitement of the mah-jongg group on the other side of the room over the prospect of punishing the loser of their game, too.

"So the next one to lose," said Yamato with a glance at Ooka, "goes to a girls' room to get some snacks!"

"Ah, for real?! No waaay!"

There it is… Saying you're going to go to the girls' room is a common suggestion among those types.

But Hayama prevented that attempt. "Come on. Atsugi is on the stairs to the next floor."

"Really...?" Yamato shut up then. The gym teacher Atsugi's intimidating air and mysterious Hiroshima accent gave him a reputation for being scary. And as the gym teacher, he had a tendency to be aggressive with the sports clubs so they'd see him as a tough character to handle. Well, not like I could handle him, either, though.

"Then confess to a girl! Let's get started!" Ooka immediately came up with an alternative plan, and they got right to it. Tobe and Yamato complained, but they went along with it. With a wry smile, Hayama discarded a tile.

They drew tiles and discarded them in turns, and eventually, Tobe looked at one of the tiles he'd drawn and said, "Oh, *tsumo*." When he revealed his hand, they all sighed.

"Tsk, why do you get to win the round, you wimp? Just confess."

"Screw you. Just go confess, wimp."

Ooka and Yamato sniped at him.

"Hey, you guys don't have to be like that!" Tobe shot back.

With a smile, Hayama swept the tiles into a pile. "Well, you are acting like a wimp. So your punishment will be buying juice."

"But I didn't lose this one! Eh, I'm thirsty, so I'll go anyway!"

So he's going...? What an amenable guy... Thanks to Hayama, Tobe was given an easy punishment, but still, they were kinda being dicks to him...

Watching Tobe leave the room, Totsuka muttered, "Oh, we're a little thirsty, too."

"Herm, then, Hachiman, your punishment shall be being our errand boy, too."

"All right. What do you want? You fine with ramen, Zaimokuza?"

"Mm-hmm, an attractive proposition, that is..."

"Don't consider it seriously..."

It seemed it would take some time for Zaimokuza to come up with an answer, so I turned to Totsuka instead. He smiled brightly at me. "I'll leave it up to you, Hachiman."

"Sure."

I stood up and left the room.

X   X   X

I tapped my way lightly down the stairs.

The floor above was supposed to have the girls' rooms, and rumor said Atsugi was standing guard on the stairs so that boys wouldn't go up there, but I wasn't about to bother with confirming for myself.

The juice vending machine was in the first-floor lobby.

We were allowed this much freedom before bedtime. But everyone else was busy hanging out with their friends and hadn't bothered coming all the way out here. The only people in the lobby now were people like me and Tobe, who'd been sent to buy drinks as punishments.

Tobe was off in front of the vending machine. He bought a drink, it came down with a *thunk*, and then he bought another until he had enough for everyone. When I approached, he noticed me. "Oh, Hikitani. What's up?"

"Hey."

He asked what was up as a greeting, even when he already knew the answer. Was that just something he used all the time, like Yuigahama's *yahallo*? We exchanged greetings, and I swapped places with him to stand in front of the vending machine.

Then I felt someone's eyes on me from behind, so I turned around.

Strangely, Tobe was still standing there.

"What?" I asked, suspicious that he hadn't gone back even though he had done what he'd come for.

He suddenly laughed. "Oh, it's just, you've really been working hard at this, huh, Hikitani? So I kinda feel like I should thank you? I mean, for that nice assist you did."

Uh, you don't record it as an assist unless you score a goal, though. "I haven't really done anything. And I mean, it's mostly Yuigahama. If you're gonna thank anyone, thank her."

"Ohhh, of course, yeah, yeah. But I gotta say thanks to you, at least. Like, your help's kinda got me determined to tell her now. So I'm counting on you to be my wingman tomorrow!" he said, then hurried off.

Well, he was a good guy, in a way. But for better or for worse, his loyalties lay with the mood of the moment, making him basically a slave to his surroundings.

But that nature may have been the very reason he had made no progress with Ebina. Since he was reacting to the mood on a moment-to-moment basis, he couldn't take appropriate action.

I could see difficulties in store for him...

Confessing, huh? I'm sure it'll be hard, but I hope it goes well.

To ease the wave of exhaustion coming over me, I decided to imbibe some sweet MAX Coffee.

I stared at the lineup in the vending machine in order, from the top. ...?

One more time, I stared at the drinks in order, this time from the bottom.

I carefully inspected each and every can with the utmost attention, like when I'm searching for Gagaga books at the bookstore. You've gotta look close, or you'll miss those blue spines.

But no matter how I searched, I couldn't find my (MAX) dose of sugar.

Huh...? What's going on? No matter how hard I searched, they were only selling some cheap knockoffs!

So this is Kyoto... As expected of the thousand-year home of the imperial family...

I compromised and bought a café au lait. You know, they're in longish cans and somewhat similar. I popped open the tab with a *fsk* and sank into the couch located at the edge of the lobby.

Though the guys had asked me to buy them drinks for my punishment, I didn't feel like going back to our room-turned-mah-jongg-parlor right away.

I was taking my little break with this mild sweetness when a familiar figure appeared in a corner of the lobby. Yukino Yukinoshita was striding in with purpose.

She must have just left the bath, as her hair was tied up and her clothes were unusually casual, for her. She was heading straight for the hotel's gift shop. She stared at one shelf with a particular intensity... Well, if she was eyeing something that seriously, there was only one thing it could be.

She put a hand to her mouth, considering for a while, before gently reaching out to the item as if she'd made up her mind. But that moment, she noticed what was going on around her. Of course, her eyes met with mine. I'd been watching her the whole time.

Her arm quietly lowered, and then she went back the way she'd come, pretending like she didn't even know me.

... *The usual.* I said good night to her in my head, sipping away at my remaining café au lait.

But then she walked briskly back to me. She came to stand in front of my seat and folded her arms, towering over me. "What a coincidence to see you out so late."

"You should have said that to me earlier..." In fact, I was surprised she'd deliberately come back just to say this. And what's with the arrogant posturing here?

"So what's going on?" she asked. "Did you run here because you couldn't stand to be in your room?"

"I'm just letting the youngsters handle things on their own. You?"

Yukinoshita blew a vexed sigh. "...My classmates were trying to direct their conversation at me. Why do they love talking about that nonsense so much?"

I—I wonder what they were talking about...? It wasn't like I had zero interest, but I could tell she'd get mad at me if I asked, so I couldn't follow up. It was probably best to say something safe. "But if they're trying to talk to you, that means they're interested in you, right? Isn't that a good thing?"

"You're talking as if you're completely uninvolved, but during the cultural festival, you…" She was almost glaring down at me now.

"Huh, me? …Hey, wait. I didn't do anything." I didn't know what this was about, but I decided to assert my innocence for now.

Yukinoshita pressed her temple, closed her eyes, and finally said with resignation, "…It's nothing. So what are you doing here?"

"I was tired of playing, so I'm taking a break. What about you? You're not gonna get yourself a souvenir?"

"I'm not actually going to buy anything. I was just a little curious." She jerked her eyes away.

Is that so? She'd been staring at that thing so hard, I thought for sure she would buy it, though—probably some Kyoto-exclusive Grue-bear item.

"What about you? No souvenirs?" she asked me.

"If I bought them now, they'd just be troublesome to carry around. I'll buy some on my way back."

"I see. Have you already decided what to buy?"

"More or less. I mean, I'll just buy the stuff Komachi asked for. Oh, and tell me some place that has, like, a god of academics," I requested, since we were already talking. *Please, Miss Yukipedia.*

Yukinoshita blinked and tilted her head. "To pray for Komachi passing her exams?"

"Basically," I replied.

Yukinoshita smiled. It seems many people loved my little sister, which made her big brother happy.

"Yes…" Thinking, she sat down next to me. Well, no sense in standing if we were gonna talk. I moved over a bit to accommodate her. "I believe Kitano Tenmangu Shrine might be the most famous."

"Tenmangu, huh? I'll remember that." I'd go there during our free time on the third day. I'd be buying Komachi a charm, but getting a ritual blessing as well would cost more money. And I figured it'd be a big pain to carry home a *hayama* arrow... If someone else writes a wish and hangs it up for you, do you still get a blessing out of it?

"...It's nice that you're concerned about Komachi, but how is that request going?"

Oh, whoops, I'd zoned out there. "Not good, not bad, I guess," I replied.

Yukinoshita looked down apologetically. "I'm sorry. I can't really help from another class."

"Don't worry about it. I'm in their class, but I'm not doing anything."

"You *should* be worried about it..."

As we were conversing, Miss Hiratsuka passed by. She was wearing her coat over her suit, and even though it was already late at night, she had sunglasses on for some indiscernible reason. When she noticed us, she seemed clearly dismayed. "Wh-why are you kids here?"

"Uh, well, I just came down to buy some drinks," I said. "Why are *you* up at this hour, Miss Hiratsuka?"

"H-hmm... D-don't tell anyone else, okay? You gotta keep it top secret." The oddly girlish emphasis made my heart pitter-patter. Her shyness made the word *Shizucute* pop into my head, but the next thing she said mercilessly erased it.

"U-um...I-I'm going...to go eat ramen..."

She's hopeless. Give me back those pitter-patters.

Me and Yukinoshita both looked at her with exasperation. The teacher folded her arms and then straightened up like she'd had a sudden idea. She even removed her sunglasses, too. Must have been her disguise. "Hmm. Well, if it's you two, I suppose this is perfect."

"Pardon?" Yukinoshita tilted her head, failing to infer what the teacher meant.

Miss Hiratsuka smiled at her, then sneered at me. "I'm sure *you* wouldn't tell anyone, Yukinoshita, but unfortunately, Hikigaya isn't trustworthy."

"Ouch…" *I'm absolutely gonna tell. Though I don't particularly have anyone to tell it to.*

Seeing my defiance, Miss Hiratsuka cleared her throat and added, "So I'll pay for your silence. How about with ramen?"

…Ramen, she says? In other words, she meant we should come with her?

This would be my first time eating Kyoto ramen. Perhaps due to my youth, I was already hungry again. In fact, I felt like the word *ramen* alone had made me hungry. "Well, i-if you insist," I replied.

Miss Hiratsuka gave a couple of nods.

Oh, I was looking forward to Kyoto ramen. As my mind started to drift away in anticipation, Yukinoshita, sitting beside me, quietly got to her feet. "All right, I'll go back." She gave Miss Hiratsuka a crisp bow and turned away from us.

Miss Hiratsuka called after her. "Yukinoshita, you come, too."

"But…" Turning to look over her shoulder, Yukinoshita glanced down as if a little embarrassed.

Miss Hiratsuka grinned. "Come on, just think of it as an extracurricular activity. It's still not that late, either."

"But…look how I'm dressed…" She grabbed her slightly overlong sleeves with each of her hands and spread them like she was about to curtsy.

Miss Hiratsuka took off her coat and tossed it at the reluctant Yukinoshita. "Then wear this."

Aw, what the heck, she's so cool. I could just about fall for her. The times are less Shizucute and more Shizucool after all!

"I have no right to refuse, do I?" she said.

"Doesn't look like it."

Yukinoshita breathed a short sigh, but she obediently put on the borrowed coat, apparently giving in.

"Come on, let's go." Miss Hiratsuka took us along, heels clicking as she jauntily headed out into the Kyoto night.

X X X

A few steps out of the hotel, and the night breeze was unpleasantly cold. Well, more like I'd left wearing my indoor clothes. "Kyoto's kinda chilly, huh?"

Miss Hiratsuka noticed my attire and smiled teasingly.

We continued out into the street, and Miss Hiratsuka raised a hand. A compact taxi cruising nearby stopped right by us. "Go on, Yukinoshita—get in." Miss Hiratsuka waved her in like a doorman, and Yukinoshita adjusted the coat around her, bowed to Miss Hiratsuka, and got into the taxi.

Next, the teacher let me get in before her, too. "You too, Hikigaya."

"Oh no, Miss Hiratsuka, please go ahead," I politely refused.

"Oh?" Miss Hiratsuka was half-surprised, half-impressed. "My, ladies first, is it? You've grown. But your concern is unnecessary."

"Huh…? B-but you're always a lady, no matter how old you are! Have some more confidence!"

Miss Hiratsuka smiled sweetly and grabbed me by the forehead. "…I'm putting you there because of all the seats in the back, the middle one has the highest death rate."

"Ow, ow, ow!"

With her iron claw, she flung me into the taxi. *She has more attack variety now, not just strikes. It seems we've both grown.*

"…What an idiot," Yukinoshita muttered.

"Shut up," I shot back. "I'm being kind, in my own way."

"You have no idea what kindness is…"

Miss Hiratsuka took the seat beside me. I'd assumed that, in a small taxi, three people sitting in the back would be tight, but Yukinoshita and Miss Hiratsuka were both slender, so there was actually room to spare. Phew…if we'd smushed together, I would have been a little uncomfortable.

"To Ichijou-ji Temple," Miss Hiratsuka told the driver, and the taxi set out.

Ichijou-ji Temple is a location fans of Musashi Miyamoto might know of. Sagarimatsu, in Ichijou-ji Temple, is known as the place where

Musashi had a duel with the disciples of the Yoshioka school of martial arts. Although, this is apparently not a historical fact and rather an invention of later generations.

And Ichijou-ji Temple is now one of the top most competitive ramen zones in Kyoto with rows of famous shops.

As we discussed this stuff in the taxi, before long, we were there. Taxis are fast. Faster than Salamander.

Then, when we got out, I saw a shocking sight.

"Th-this is the very first Tenkaippin…"

Yes, Tenkaippin. Not Dera-beppin. I'd only ever heard rumors of it. They say that you can stand chopsticks up in the broth and that it sticks to the noodles so well, it just disappears.

As I trembled in awe, behind me, Yukinoshita asked, "Is this a famous restaurant?"

"Oh, well, it's a national chain," I said.

"Then we didn't have to come all the way here…"

Now that she mentioned it, this was indeed true. But there was another reason I was so filled with wonder. "But…for some reason, there isn't one in Chiba. It's the only prefecture in the whole Kanto region that doesn't have one…"

Over my long personal history (of about seventeen years), Chiba has oft been praised as the promised paradise (by me), but even so, I can't yet declare it perfect, for one of the pieces missing from it is Tenkaippin.

"Well, they used to have one in Chiba, though." Miss Hiratsuka, having just finished her pre-meal smoke, came over with a scrape of her heels on the sidewalk.

"Oh-ho! What was that?" I said. "The sound of the walking encyclopedia of Chiba ramen? No, that's just your biological clock ticking."

"You were closer the first time, Hikigaya. ♪"

"That hurts, that hurts!"

The grinding of my cranium contrasted with her cheerful tone.

"Well," she continued, "they have these in every nook and cranny of Japan, but company-run branches and flagship stores just have such a different feel compared with franchise locations. I mean, there's always going to be some variation in flavor from store to store in a chain. So I wanted to give it a try." Miss Hiratsuka finally released my head, gazing at the storefront of Tenichi with sincere passion. "Come on, let's go in."

Fortunately, there were plenty of free seats inside. Miss Hiratsuka, Yukinoshita, and I sat at the counter, in that order.

"Thick," Miss Hiratsuka ordered without looking at the menu.

Well, I wanted to try the rumored thick broth at Tenichi, too. "Thick for me, too."

"…"

I hadn't heard Yukinoshita order, so I glanced over to check on her. She was speechless, timidly looking at the people around her. She tugged on my sleeve. "…Hey, does that mean the broth?"

Her expression was of something near terror. Oh, no, that's quite a reasonable feeling to have. But if this was gonna scare her off, she'd never be able to eat at Naritake. At Naritake, it's less like broth and more like pure back fat. Delicious.

Miss Hiratsuka chuckled in amusement and opened the menu. "There's also light broth. You might prefer that."

"Oh, no. Just looking at it makes me feel full…" Quite unlike her usual self, Yukinoshita shook her head feebly.

"Oh? Then we'll get an extra serving bowl for you, and you can just try a bit of ours," Miss Hiratsuka proposed. Yukinoshita still seemed intimidated, but she did eventually agree.

We ordered, and then after a little wait, they brought us the ramen.

I picked up my chopsticks and put my hands together in front of my chest. "Thanks."

Oof! My chopsticks are so heavy! I can't handle it! The thick, dripping broth coated every noodle. In Chiba, you only ever see broth this heavy at Tora no Ana. *Oh my god, this is amazing!*

"Here, Yukinoshita." Miss Hiratsuka gently laid down the serving bowl with some for her. Yukinoshita hesitated, but then she took up the chopsticks and china spoon with resolve. Tucking her long hair behind her ear, she lifted the spoon into her mouth. I looked away from the unnecessarily seductive movement of her throat swallowing the thick broth.

She wiped the broth from the corner of her mouth with a napkin, then put on a very serious expression. "…It has a particularly aggressive flavor."

Whoa, that's accurate.

As I savored my ramen, I found myself belatedly wondering if this was allowed. I ended up saying it out loud. "Is it okay for a teacher to be doing something like this, though?" I asked.

But Miss Hiratsuka wasn't worried. "Of course not. That's why I've paid you to keep your mouths shut."

"Isn't that even more unbefitting of a teacher?" Yukinoshita said with some exasperation.

But Miss Hiratsuka was unrepentant. In fact, she seemed even more laid-back as she continued to eat. "Teachers are human, and so are adults. We make mistakes. Whether we're aware of them or not."

"Won't you get chewed out if anyone catches on?" I asked. If that happened, I'd probably get dragged into it, too.

"Nope. I'll get off with complaints, sarcasm, and a private talking-to for formality's sake."

"Does that not count as being chewed out?" Yukinoshita asked.

I agreed with her.

Miss Hiratsuka finished drinking her broth, set down her bowl, and politely wiped her mouth with her napkin before turning back to us. "No. An order not to cause problems is completely different from making someone resolve it."

"I don't get the difference."

"…Yes. Perhaps since I've never been 'chewed out' before." Putting her hand in a loose fist to her jaw, Yukinoshita seemed pensive, as if sifting through her memories.

Miss Hiratsuka nodded in response. "Oh? Then I'll give you a proper scolding. Well, it's always been my intention to be scolding you, at least. But it seems I've been too soft."

"No, I've definitely had enough." I waved my hands wildly in firm refusal. Any more bodily injuries, and I'd be damaged goods; then she'd end up having to take responsibility, and I'd be the one taking her last name. Ah! Was that indeed her goal…?

Yukinoshita ignored me and my various worries and said nonchalantly, "No one's ever taken the time to scold me or anything like that, so I wouldn't mind."

"Yukinoshita, a lecture isn't a bad thing. It means someone is paying attention to you," Miss Hiratsuka said.

Yukinoshita's shoulders drooped a little. She tilted her face down, hanging her head. I couldn't tell where her gaze was.

Miss Hiratsuka kindly patted her shoulder. "I'm paying attention to you, so make all the mistakes you like."

We taxied back, and once we were out of the car, Miss Hiratsuka started walking away from the hotel. "I'm going to the convenience store to buy some alcohol for myself. See you. Take care on your way back."

Should she be doing that?

I replied to her wave with a casually raised hand, and Yukinoshita and I started making our way back toward the hotel. Neither of us deliberately took the first step. We were both silent, but it felt natural.

"…"

"…"

Yukinoshita walked a few steps in front of me. But then her feet suddenly stopped, and she glanced around.

…Well, I could get the gist of what her problem was right then. Call it experience, I guess.

"Take a right."

"O-oh." She adjusted Miss Hiratsuka's coat around her shoulders and ducked her face into the collar to avoid the wind.

I breathed a little snigger of a sigh and started walking ahead of her. I could show her the way, at least. She seemed to get what I was doing, as I heard her footsteps a few paces behind me.

But the sounds gradually diminished.

Confused, I turned around to see that she was farther away than before. "If you hang too far back, you're gonna get lost again."

"No...um..."

My bemusement wasn't getting me a clear answer. As she buried her face in the standing collar of the coat, her voice wilted.

I didn't at all understand what she was saying, but it'd be a pain if she wandered off and got lost, so I decided to wait for her to come closer. Yukinoshita and I glared at each other from a distance.

What are we doing, though...?

We stood like that for a while, and then she breathed a sigh of resignation. "I wouldn't mind if you just went on back ahead of me...," she muttered, reluctantly coming up to my side.

I wondered if taming a stray cat was like this. "Uh, there's not really any point, though. It's not even far."

"Maybe...not to you, but this makes me uncomfortable," she said evasively.

Without thinking, I asked, "What does?" Although, honestly, it would have been polite to pretend I didn't hear the question when it seemed she had so much trouble saying it.

"Um...if we were to be seen together this late...it would be a little..." It wasn't that cold, but she was adjusting the jacket to hide her face.

"...O-oh." Once she'd explicitly pointed it out, I had to think about the situation more calmly, too.

We'd met at night before, and we'd met alone. To me, there was *not* a need to be so overconcerned about it, and it did *not* bother me, and it was *not* anything strange. It was a big string of nots.

And along those lines, I'd not ever seen her like this, either.

She was looking every which way, including my feet so she wouldn't get lost.

I'd never seen her lower her eyes in embarrassment like this, or raise her hand halfway to try to stop me when I went too far ahead and then immediately lower it again.

Her awkwardness started infecting me, too, and unconsciously, my right leg and right arm started swinging forward at the same time. Even though it wasn't that far, it felt like a really long way to the hotel.

Yukinoshita and I weren't walking side by side but a fixed distance from each other just out of arm's reach.

By the time we made it back to the lobby, I was exhausted.

Ahead, there would be students around. If Yukinoshita was concerned about the eyes of others, it would be best to part ways here.

I stopped and casually raised a hand to let her go first. "See you."

"…Yes, good night… Um…thank you for walking me back," she replied, then started to leave. Though we were already inside, she was still wearing the coat. She was walking so fast, its sleeves were fluttering.

Wondering if she was going to return the coat, though it didn't really matter, I returned to my room, too.

When I walked in, the mah-jongg tournament was still going.

"Oh, Hachiman, welcome back," said Totsuka. He and Zaimokuza were playing old maid.

"Where've you been? You've been out for an age," said Zaimokuza.

"Have I?"

Well, it had been about two hours since I'd left.

"So where are the drinks and my ramen?"

"Ah." Now that Zaimokuza mentioned it, I'd been in the middle of a punishment errand.

"It cannot be—you forgot?!" Zaimokuza looked at me like I was an idiot, which was a step too far.

So I deliberately provoked him. "…Heh, of course not. I've got it…in here." I pointed straight at my stomach, and Zaimokuza's face twisted in shock.

"Wh-what?! You fiend, you went out to eat! What a formidable man…" Zaimokuza wiped sweat off his forehead as disdain gave way to respect.

Ha. That was easy.

But that wasn't going to work on the other one.

"Then go out again." Totsuka grinned broadly at me as he ordered me back out on the errand.

Wahhh, Totsuka's scaryyy…

Texting

Kyoto ←→ Chiba

How is ye olde Kyoto?

Nothing special. Also, nobody talks like that here.

Boring! I was talking with my friends today, and they say Kamogawa is great. There's a ton of couples there. Komachi recommends it~.

Of course it's popular. They have killer whales.

C'mon to Kamogawa Sea World! ...Yeah, that's not what I'm talking about. You've got too much Chiba on the brain, Bro. You do so much Chiba-ing, it's affected your mind.

Anyway, what's this about Kamogawa? Is it famous for something?

Like, the river... I think the water is pretty or something?

So they swarm around pretty watering holes? Are they fireflies?

One day, Hachiman and Komachi

Unexpectedly, **Yumiko Miura** is actually paying attention.

It was the second day of the field trip. Today, I would be touring with my group, traveling from Uzumasa to the Rakusai area.

Our first goal point of the day was the Toei Kyoto Studio Park. It was a period theme park used in real dramas, too, with elaborately made sets of a townscape re-creating places like Yoshiwara Street and the Ikedaya Inn. Plus, it had lots of fun attractions: historical costumes to borrow, a haunted house, a ninja house, and other stuff. It was a famous tourist spot.

We took the city bus from the hotel to the Studio Park.

The day-long bus pass is a powerful ally to tourists and students on field trips. It's the free pass of dreams: for a mere five hundred yen, you can ride the Kyoto municipal bus as much as you want. The Kyoto bus network is particularly developed, so you can take it to practically all the major tourist spots.

But there is an unexpected pitfall here.

This being the season when fall leaves were still in color, the buses were packed like cans of sardines. It had to be at about 150 percent capacity. The city bus was so convenient and such a good deal that tons of tourists were using it. The population density was basically rush-hour levels, and it just about broke me. *I'm not gonna get a job, I'm not gonna get a job… If it means feeling like this, then I need no employment!*

Maybe boys would be fine in such a brutal crowd, but I started getting concerned about fragile girls and Totsuka.

But the girls had Miura and Kawasaki glaring at everyone, and their intimidation kept Ebina and Yuigahama super-safe.

Yeah, um, those two are scary, huh…?

And as for Totsuka, he made sure to move into a safe zone.

"H-Hachiman, do you mind? Sorry." He looked at me apologetically from my arms.

"Hey, it's no big deal. People are just constantly elbowing me in the stomach and stepping on my feet, that's all."

"My bad! Sorry, Hikitani! But what can ya do about it, eh? This is way too crowded, man."

Damn you, Tobe…, I thought, but he was only barely maintaining his position, too. He was also being pushed from the side and stepped on from behind, and that was why he'd elbowed me a moment ago. It wasn't enough to make me mad.

"Don't forget, we're getting off at the next stop," Hayama told us. Even now, he was being considerate. I was impressed.

Finally, the bus pulled up to Toei Kyoto Studio Park and spit us out in front of the other kids on field trips and tourists as everyone crawled from the vehicle. We'd only just gotten there and hadn't had any fun yet, and we were already feeling ragged.

I would have liked to go straight to the nearby Komeda's Coffee and take a break with one of their Shiro-Noirs—ice cream on a hot Danish—but Tobe raced straight over to get tickets.

"Here, Ebina," he said.

"Thanks."

Oh, so he'd run over to buy them so he could hand her ticket to her directly—if he was too slow, Hayama or someone else would have promptly gone to buy them.

"And here ya go, Hikitani."

"…Uh-huh."

Well, it looked like he was feeling motivated, so I'd put a little effort into this, too.

We headed straight into the Studio Park. As soon as I passed through the gates, I suddenly saw some Precure stuff, but I mean, I was a grown boy, after all, so I'd go another time, when I was alone. For the time being, I'd look around the rest of the park.

We passed through an area with a smattering of Edo city buildings. Occasionally, we'd pass by some people wearing samurai outfits. They must have been staff or something.

There were *oiran* courtesans on the streets, impromptu lessons in stage sword-fighting, and even a mysterious little dinosaur that popped out of the pond... Just being among them helped me start to enjoy myself.

The pond where the dinosaur came out was especially enjoyable. You could just tell something was going to happen, but then it just poked its head out, huffed its token amount of smoke with a *fshhhh*, and then blooped back underwater again. Really surreal.

After we watched the dinosaur disappear into the pond, a strange silence hung around us. The bizarre sight had left us all frozen.

"...Let's move on," Hayama said with a smile.

Tobe unfroze and rebooted, too. "Y-yeah! Go, go, go!"

"Hey, so why don't we go there next?" Yuigahama was pointing at the most terrifying haunted house in history. She'd had her eye on it from the beginning, in all likelihood.

Well, it was a standard choice. Actually, she might have figured it would do something for Tobe and Ebina. The so-called suspension-bridge effect. Dinosaur aside—there was some hope for the haunted house.

And this place was not to be underestimated as just another haunted house. Toei's version meets expectations. Of course, they put some legit effort into the ghost sets and stuff, but the monsters that jump out at you are also Toei actors.

I thought maybe somebody in the group wouldn't want to go, but nobody excused themselves, and we found ourselves in the lineup.

"Hayatooo, I'm scaaared." Miura flirtatiously snuggled up to Hayama.

I think you're cuter when you're looking after all these kids like a mom, though, Miura. You should consider appealing to that.

"Yeah, I can't really handle this stuff, either." Hayama gave a shy *ah-ha-ha* to cover up his embarrassment. He was usually perfect, so that little sign of weakness even got me right in the heart.

Before long, it was our turn. Of course, a party of eight was too many at once, so we decided to split into groups of four.

The first member of Hayama's group disappeared inside, then the second, and eventually, when all of them were gone, our group headed into the haunted house, too.

The first part was the introduction. Since some of the ghosts were played by actors, they played a video warning us not to hit, kick, or otherwise be violent to them. But the video just made it more surreal... It's kinda like a spoiler. I mean, it's smacking you in the face with a reminder that this is totally fake.

Or so I'd thought, until now. One step in, and everything felt different.

The theme here seemed to be the Edo period. It was dark, with only absolutely minimal lighting, but the light sources were positioned to guide the eye to all the classically eerie objects. They limit your field of vision and then place items around in the vague, dark areas so that they jump out and shock you when you see them.

Calmly analyzing it like this made it...scary. Scary is scary, man.

It was hard to see the group ahead—probably Hayama's—and tell how far they were because of the darkness and the constant stream of Buddhist chanting and resentful muttering we heard around us.

It was only thanks to their typical antics that I could still tell they were Hayama and co.

"Ohmanohmanohmanohmanohmaaaagh!" Tobe, with his reputation

for going along with any vibe, was completely swallowed up by the terror of the haunted house. He was constantly terrified and never left Hayama's side the whole time. Ebina watched them with a sound like *guh-heh.*

"Yeek! I just heard something weird…" Kawasaki, walking behind me, was so frightened that she yanked at my blazer.

Um, you're gonna rip it off, so please don't? That's just Ebina, nothing sca… Actually, you're right; she is.

As I examined the design of the interior here and there, the setting appeared to be a household massacre in an Edo-period mansion, or something like that. It was a standard haunted house, but that was exactly why the interior sucked you in.

Yuigahama timidly laid her hand on my shoulder as she tottered beside me with weak knees. "I—I can't really handle stuff like this…," she said, constantly vigilant and anxious that something might leap out.

So I deployed my pet theory. "Ghosts at a haunted house aren't scary. What's scary is people."

"There you go, being grumpy again! …But maybe that just means we can rely on you." Yuigahama didn't take me seriously and just laughed.

But you know, humans really are the scary thing here.

"…In other words, the most terrifying type of haunted house is the kind where people do the scaring."

"Nope! We can't count on you at all!"

I mean, stuff scares me, too. If I'd come in there alone, I probably would have sprinted through the whole thing screaming *Sooooi! Soi! Sooooi!* or something equally nonsensical to distract myself from the fear. I might not have even been able to find the exit.

However, I didn't have to scream now, and since the others were being so loud, I wasn't that scared.

I don't know if it was for the same reasons as me, but Totsuka didn't seem very frightened, either. In fact, he even seemed to be enjoying himself.

"You look totally fine with this, Totsuka...," I commented.

"Yeah, I like this sort of thing." I could see that beaming smile of his even in the darkness.

His radiance might just end up saving us from the global energy crisis, I thought. *This will be the era of smiles, not oil!*

We moved on a little farther, and a ghost (with a person inside it) jumped out and yelled, "BRYARGH!"

Kawasaki's back went stiff and straight, and then without a word, she sprinted her way out of there as fast as her legs would go. Totsuka, who seemed more startled by her reaction, hurried after her.

I was playing it calm, but I was pretty freaked out, too. I cringed reflexively, bumping into Yuigahama beside me. Well, more like our heads cracked together.

"Ngk..."

"Ow..."

The two of us squatted down right there, rubbing our respective injuries.

"S-sorry..."

"No, I'm sorry, I was startled...," I apologized, facing her.

Tears in her eyes, Yuigahama gently reached her hand out to me, touching my head and patting it to make sure it was okay. "It didn't hurt?"

"Oh, it hurt like hell." *But that's embarrassing, so stop.* I jerked my head away, escaping her hand to stand up. Yuigahama was still squatting. "Anyway, let's go. They'll leave us behind." I extended my hand to help her up, too. I think the big-brother skill I used for my sister, Komachi, just activated automatically.

"Huh?" Yuigahama looked at my hand incredulously.

Wait, this is okay to do because *it's my little sister.* I rethought it, and I was about to put my hand in my pocket.

"Thanks." She grabbed my hand.

Well, I suppose it was just a nice thing to do. The fabled act of kindness. The act of a gentleman. I'd just done what any human would have done. There was just no helping it for a nice guy like me.

Which was why I couldn't shake off her hand.

"Then let's head to the finish point." Yuigahama smiled brightly and gently let go. Before I had the time to feel disappointed, she tugged on my shoulder. "Come on."

It was dark and chilly. We made our way forward through the haunted house, encountering blood splatter here and there, getting chased around by severed heads and fallen soldiers and such.

"This looks like the exit," I said. Light from outside seeped in through the final door. As we stepped through it, a fresh breeze blew on our faces.

"I-it's over… That was pretty scary…" Yuigahama must have been on edge. She was suddenly drained, staggering around in search of a bench. Hayama, Totsuka, and the others had already finished and were currently occupying the bench she sought.

I followed after her. Oh, I was seriously exhausted. My heart was thumping uncomfortably hard. *Isn't this, like, cardiac arrhythmia? Quick, get me some medicine.*

When I came up beside the bench to take a break, Totsuka turned to me. "That was so much fun, huh, Hachiman?"

His smile made me dizzy. *Now I'm getting light-headed?* His pretty smile was curing me with the glittering force of all the stars. It made my heart pound, bringing the feelings inside me to a new stage.

"I think we're done with this one. Let's get going to the next attraction." Hayama examined the group. It seemed there were no objections.

Miura hopped up from the bench. "Then I'm gonna call over Ebina," she announced, dashing to the souvenir shop. I'd assumed all of us were there, but Ebina and Tobe were gone, huh? I glanced at the shop and saw Ebina rapt and panting at the Shinsengumi goods, while Tobe was going on like, "Man…wooden swords are expensive…"

O-okay… Maybe the haunted house worked…?

X   X   X

Our next goal was the Rakusai area. We would be going there on the bus from Uzumasa.

But Rakusai has a lot of popular tourist spots, including Kinkaku-ji Temple, and with the fall colors still in season, the bus was packed to the rafters.

What's more, since tourists were coming out of the Studio Park, too, we would probably be waiting for quite a while. We'd already watched multiple buses pass by, and I was getting tired of waiting for nothing.

I am a man who hates full trains. A long time ago, I had to go to a university in Tokyo for a mock test, but it would have meant riding the Tozai Line during rush hour, so I gave up. I didn't take that mock test. Such is my past.

So consequently, I really wanted to avoid getting on this city bus right now.

Mentally cackling as I looked around the area for some other way—or some way out, somewhere—suddenly, my eyes landed on the taxi stand.

Hmm.

It's strange. Once you know there's an easier way, the next time around, you won't hesitate to pick the method of the undisciplined.

Yuigahama was lined up beside me, so I patted her shoulder. She was probably a little tired, as she was slow to react. She turned only her head toward me. "What?"

"Let's get a taxi," I said.

She drew her eyebrows together and *hmm*'d. "A taxi? Aren't they expensive? We're not doing anything expensive." And to put a period on the matter, she turned back again to wait for the bus.

She's kind of housewifely... She was being pretty strict about money—it was the same during the cultural festival, too.

But I couldn't let her beat me in the realm of the stay-at-homes.

Or rather, I couldn't allow her to beat me in the area of sophistry and pulling money from somewhere or other. I'm the fun-money alchemist.

"Just listen. You'd think it's expensive because of Tokyo, but Kyoto is cheaper, comparatively. Compact cars are mainstream here. In fact, it's so cheap, you'd be losing money if you *didn't* take a taxi. Besides, if we split it with everyone in the same car, it won't be that much."

"Ehhh..."

Hmm, she still didn't seem on board. I'd actually been attempting to make a decent argument, such as it was, but this wasn't enough to move Yuigahama's heart. I had to change tacks. "Hold on, calm down. Losing time here would be the greater cost."

"How?" Yuigahama was trying to casually ignore me, as if this conversation was just a way to kill time while she waited. *Agh...*

Times like this, first, you have to start by striking at their personal interests. "Do you like Destiny Land?"

"I do. So?"

Now, unlike before, her whole upper body turned toward me, not just her head. I know quite a bit about Chiba. So of course, I am knowledgeable about Destiny Land. Of my Chiba-related knowledge, the only thing I figured would intersect with Yuigahama's interests was Destiny Land and related topics. So I decided to attack from this angle. "It's popular as a date spot, too, right?"

"Yeah, it is." Yuigahama nodded with an *uh-huh*.

"I have sad news about that."

"Huh? What?"

Now her entire body was facing me. I must have piqued her curiosity.

Seeing her interest, I informed her of the rest. "Couples who go on dates to Destiny Land end up separating."

"Oh, I've heard that one before. Like it's a jinx?"

"Yeah. But, well, if you think about it, it's obvious." No mysterious powers or whatever at work here. It's a simple question of human psychology. "When you wait a long time for a ride, it'll always stress you out. And you run out of things to talk about, too. And so the irritation and the silence build and build, and you start thinking your date is really boring. It's like the opposite of the suspension-bridge effect."

"Ohhh, I get it~." Impressed, Yuigahama nodded vigorously. It seemed I'd convinced her. So then this meant just one more push.

"Don't you think right now is a similar situation?"

"You and me? Um, not really," she said with a blank expression.

Hey, don't look at me like that's never even crossed your mind.

"No...Tobe and Ebina."

"Oh, I—I get it..." Yuigahama blushed and looked down, as if embarrassed about her misunderstanding.

I surreptitiously poked my thumb toward the pair ahead of us.

Both Tobe and Ebina seemed bored, and Ebina was half paying attention to a conversation with Miura as she occasionally messed around with her phone. Tobe was a few steps behind her, swinging a wooden sword. *Wait, he bought that?*

"Y-yeah..." Nobody would claim this was going well. Yuigahama crossed her arms, mulling over it for a bit.

Well, I suppose I'll add this, just to make doubly sure. "Besides, a taxi is kinda like a locked room. Feels more intimate."

Or if it's *Conan*, it means someone will die.

Now that I'd brought it up, Yuigahama suddenly clued in, too. "I—I get it... I'll go try asking them." She called to the group lining up ahead, waving her arm. "Heeeey! Why don't we all take a taxi?" she said.

They all reacted with skepticism. Unsurprisingly, high school kids weren't thrilled with the idea, but there was no helping that. Because of the long-standing belief that taxis were expensive, they just didn't see them as an option for students.

I figured I might as well try convincing them. I didn't want to pack into a bus after all. "If we get a compact car and split it among four people, it won't cost that much."

"I see." Hayama was thankfully quick on the uptake. Once our trusty leader agreed, the rest would all follow in succession. Miura and Tobe had no complaints. Ebina nodded, too, and we quickly got Kawasaki to agree as well. It seemed Totsuka didn't have any objections, either, and he would come with us.

So we left the lineup and moved over to the taxi stand.

There were eight of us, so thinking about it normally, we'd be getting in two taxis in groups of four.

Up until we got to the taxi stand, Hayama and Miura were at the front of the line, with Kawasaki and Totsuka behind them, while I was the wall separating the remaining three from them. Now, when we got in, inevitably, Tobe, Ebina, Yuigahama, and I would be a group of four. Here, the role of wall was important.

Hey, this is me we're talking about—I always get shunted to left-over defense positions whenever we have to play sports. I have an established reputation for playing defense.

Hayama took the lead until we got to the taxi stand.

"Then go on in." I prompted Hayama, at the head of the line, to proceed ahead of us. Now the rest of us just had to get in like natural.

"Yeah. Then Yumiko," Hayama called.

"Okay!" Miura immediately took a seat. Hayama continued to stand in front of the door and called the next person into the cab. "Let's go, Tobe."

Tobe, behind me, reacted nimbly. "Oh, gotcha. Then you come, too, Ebina."

"Okeydoke. I'll see you later, then, Yui, Saki-Saki."

Tobe and Ebina both went over to Hayama and got in the car one after the other. Right as Ebina was stepping into the taxi, she gave Yuigahama and Kawasaki a wave.

"Oh, yeah, see you soon."

"Don't call me Saki-Saki."

Yuigahama replied with a casual half wave, while Saki-Saki snapped at her with a blush.

Then Hayama went for shotgun. "...We'll see you there, then."

Hayama was talking to me but not looking at me. I was sure there was something I should have said in reply, but the door closed before I could.

...*Hmm, I see.*

And so I had to get the rest of us into a taxi, too.

"So who's going to sit where?" Totsuka asked me, but I mean, the reasonable solution would be to put me in the front seat.

"I'll go in front, and you three in the back," I said.

The door opened automatically, and I made sure Totsuka, Kawasaki, and Yuigahama got in first. Then I opened the passenger's side door, sat myself down, and fastened the seat belt.

"To Ninna-ji Temple," I said briefly, and then the driver, who just looked like a softhearted person, smiled and repeated our destination.

The car quietly rolled out.

While we were waiting at a light, the driver asked me, "Are you on a school field trip?"

"Yeah, basically," I replied shortly, glancing over for a second. I didn't mean to act so curt, but I wasn't used to this small talk.

"Where are you from?"

"Tokyo."

Here's a factoid about the Chibanese: When we go somewhere and people ask where we're from, we end up answering *From Tokyo*. I mean, if you tell them it's Chiba, they don't really get it... Like, you know, it's similar to how lots of people from Kanagawa pretend they're from Yokohama.

My halting and fragmented conversation with the driver went on. *Ah, so this is a pitfall of taxis...*

Meanwhile, in the back seat, they were talking about the girls' room.

"Yeah. So then Saki started getting serious and threw a pillow, and Yumiko burst into tears."

"You don't have to talk about this..."

Through the rearview mirror, I could see Yuigahama apparently enjoying the conversation, while Kawasaki grumpily crossed her legs in the opposite direction.

Man, Miura cries too much…

Totsuka giggled as he followed up with gossip from the boys' room. "A pillow fight sounds fun, though. We were playing mah-jongg and Uno and stuff. Oh, and Hachiman lost, but then he forgot about his punishment."

Though I was only slightly separated from them, their conversation felt very far away.

As for me, I ended up feeling kind of like I had to be considerate to the driver beside me, so I didn't join in the discussion. I just stared emptily at the town as it flowed by.

✕   ✕   ✕

Ninna-ji Temple is the temple famous for the careless, giggling priest who sticks out his tongue and appears in part fifty-two of *Tsurezure-gusa*, which often shows up in textbooks.

The place had to be more popular in spring than in fall. There were apparently cherry blossoms blooming all over the place. But even in late fall, there were tourists, of course, and the temple and garden were both well worth seeing.

But regrettably, we were high school students in the prime of our youth. So the extent of our discussion was comments like "So amazing," "I know," and "It really is so amazing."

Where did the energy from the Studio Park go…?

Still, it wasn't as if I had any deep knowledge about temples, either. All I could do was impertinently mutter, "Oh-ho, so this is that famous spot from *Tsurezuregusa*…" Well, it's not like Ninna-ji Temple itself is the main subject of part fifty-two, though.

We looked around the temple and garden for a while until we were all silently wondering *Can we go now?*

Yuigahama, as the one particularly sensitive to our impatience, prompted us. "Righty then, let's move on!"

Mysteriously, we were all more excited to leave, and we all followed after Yuigahama and left Ninna-ji Temple.

Now then, our next goal point was Ryouan-ji Temple. Not only did this one have a cool name—the Temple of the Peaceful Dragon—it had a famous rock garden. Even more cool. By the way, Tenryuu-ji Temple has an equally cool name, the Temple of the Heavenly Dragon, but first place is a duel between Konkai Koumyou-ji Temple (Temple to the Golden Light of Virtue) or Kyouou Gokoku-ji Temple (Defender of King and Country Temple). Adashino Nenbutsu-ji Temple is kinda like the secret unlock character here.

It was about ten minutes walking from Ninna-ji Temple to Ryouan-ji Temple. We headed off at a slow and steady pace, red leaves fluttering down around us.

I was strolling at the very back, a habit of mine when I was walking in a group. Yuigahama should have been in the lead, but she gradually slowed her pace until before I knew it, she was by my side.

"It's not going good, huh?" she murmured, looking a little glum. She must have been talking about Tobe and Ebina.

"Of course it isn't. I can't even manage myself right. I can't be taking care of other people, too."

"…Yeah…that's true."

"And besides…"

"Besides?"

And besides, the trouble wasn't Yuigahama's fault. This wasn't just something I wanted to say to make her feel better. It was fact.

We had Tobe's natural personality to contend with, plus the fact that Ebina didn't even consider him an option. But more than that, more than anything, one of the group was doing things that didn't make sense. I was sure this was one factor getting in the way.

I didn't know what was motivating this strange behavior, and I didn't think there was much point in mentioning it when I couldn't be certain of it. Suspicion and misgivings are not to be voiced out loud; they're things you should bottle up inside yourself. Especially when they're really bad. If you go and say them and they turn out to be true, you're out of luck.

Suspicions that stay suspicions don't hurt anyone.

Yuigahama was waiting for me to continue, so I told her something unrelated. "We don't have to be so aggressive about it. If it's not gonna happen, it's not gonna happen."

"But I want you to really try." Yuigahama's shoulders fell a little again, and her feet seemed to drag as they scuffed over some fallen leaves.

"Don't take this too far. It'd suck if Ebina gets annoyed by it."

"Oh…"

"These things really do work if the person in question is even a little bit interested, though."

"Hmm…," Yuigahama replied listlessly.

No, it really does. It's awful.

As we walked and talked, we noticed Hayama and the others waiting ahead of us. We'd arrived at Ryouan-ji Temple.

We went through the visitors' reception and onto the temple grounds to look out over a big pond. Apparently, this was called Kyoyo-chi Pond, and it covered about half of the whole area. Aristocrats of the Heian period would amuse themselves boating here.

A fence of woven bamboo was built along the road to the shrine, going up the stone steps.

Going into this place called Houjou—well, basically, it's a temple hall—we were finally face-to-face with the rock garden.

Kare-sansui refers to a style of garden that doesn't use water, expressing the form of a garden through stones and such. *I guess this white sand represents the surface of the water. Hmm, I see. I bet these concentric circles around the rocks are supposed to be ripples, probably.*

Everyone was a little tired from walking around and sat down to gaze at the rock garden vacantly. I decided to do the same and, with a heavy sigh, made to seat myself at the edge of the bench.

The person next to me scooched away slightly. I pardoned myself with a casual bow and a hand gesture in thanks, and then the person spoke to me. "Oh, fancy meeting you here."

I turned to look with a "Huh?" and found the one sitting there was Yukino Yukinoshita.

"Oh, you're here, too?"

"I am."

Looking over, I saw what appeared to be her group. Some proper, modest, quiet-looking girls were all sitting in a line. The suspicious looks they shot at me were a little uncomfortable… *Well, an outsider might find it strange for me and Yukinoshita to be together.*

But from where I stood, Yukinoshita was way stranger just by being herself.

Whether or not she had real friends in her class, she could be part of a group, although she couldn't mess around with them on an equal basis the way Yuigahama did. I more got the impression these girls had gathered to worship her from afar.

Well, you'll get different impressions of a person depending on your perspective.

For example, this rock garden. Supposedly, you can't see all fifteen stones placed in it at once from any single angle. Depending on your point of view, they change. The people who made this garden were probably thinking something more grand and philosophical, but being the shallow person I am, all I could come up with was this cliché analysis.

The world was full of so many things I didn't understand: the meaning in this rock garden, people's true faces, and how to engage with others.

As I lost myself in thought staring blankly at the rock garden, Yukinoshita stood up beside me and then sat down again.

I looked at her as if to ask, *Why the heck did you just stand up…?* Yukinoshita noticed and replied, "This place is also known as the garden where the tiger carries her cub across the river, so I was wondering which part represented the tiger."

Oh-ho. She's curious about it because tigers are cats, isn't she?

A tiger carrying its cub across the river, huh...? I stood up to look at it, too, wondering which part was the tiger.

Yep. I have no idea.

But Yukinoshita seemed so at peace as she drank in the landscape that I figured she must have found some insight.

I dunno; maybe this is a moment to say "Deep" or something. But even that thought is particularly shallow.

This gazing went on for a while.

"Oh, Yukinon."

I hadn't even realized Yuigahama was next to me. When she noticed Yukinoshita, too, she moved to sit in between me and her.

Yukinoshita smirked and stood up. "Shall we go elsewhere?"

"Yeah, let's talk over there," said Yuigahama.

With a flutter of her hair, Yukinoshita spun around. "I'm sorry. I'll be leaving you for a bit. I don't mind if you move on without me," she said to her classmates from Class J, and they looked at her with adoring, sparkling eyes as they nodded their assent.

It's like they're her lovestruck underclassmen at a private school for rich girls... Well, if push came to shove, I wouldn't say they were *that* close.

As I was pondering Yukinoshita's relationship with her classmates, a voice came down to me. "What're you doing? Hurry up."

Oh. So I'm going, too. When I stood up as well, the girls from Class J glared daggers at me, and it was a little scary. *I'm not, like, gonna get stabbed by Yukinoshita's fangirls anytime soon, am I? Am I gonna have to start stuffing manga magazines under my shirt tomorrow?*

They decided to leave Houjou and walk a circle around the garden. I followed after them.

"How is the request going?" Yukinoshita asked.

"Hmm... Not too great." Yuigahama summed up the situation thus far.

Yukinoshita looked down, a little apologetic. "I see. I'm sorry I've made you do everything."

"Oh, no, don't worry about it." Yuigahama waved her hands below her chest in tiny motions.

The gesture seemed to relieve Yukinoshita, and she smiled. "I can't really say this will make up for it, but I have been considering the matter."

"Considering what?" I asked.

Yukinoshita looked at me. "There are some famous Kyoto locations women tend to enjoy. I figured they might be useful for the free day tomorrow."

"Ohhh, awesome, Yukinon! Okay, let's go there tomorrow, then!"

"With Tobe and everyone else?" I got the feeling that wouldn't be much different from how today had been.

"No," said Yuigahama. "We'll follow after them, and if anything happens, we'll help them out."

"I can't say that sounds very classy." Sneaking after people and spying on them didn't seem very admirable.

"Well, whether we follow after them or not, if we just recommend a tour to Tobecchi and the others, they'll probably go along with it. So if anything happens, we can go meet up with them."

So we'd plan out their date and propose the idea to them, huh? Well, if we stayed nearby, then they could call for us if there were any issues, and we could potentially help out.

"I can't say it's a very sound idea, either, but we have nothing else," said Yukinoshita.

At any rate, we'd settled on a plan for the next day. I had no idea how we should do this, nor how it would benefit Tobe.

Right about then, we finished a full circle of the garden and returned to the main gate.

"We're going to Kinkaku-ji Temple now," I said.

"Then I'll head back," said Yukinoshita.

"Okay, see you again tomorrow," Yuigahama replied.

"Yes, see you tomorrow."

Parting ways with Yukinoshita, we met up with Hayama's group. We still had places to go.

We walked the easy slope from Ryouan-ji Temple to Kinkaku-ji Temple, and the twisting road took us past Ritsumeikan University.

Seeing Kinkaku-ji Temple ended up using all our touring time. It was past five now. From Kinkaku-ji Temple, we waited for yet another bus and returned to the hotel. Hayama called our homeroom teacher to say we'd be late, and in the end, by the time we arrived at the hotel, the boys' bathing time had already passed.

And so I ended up using the inside bath on the second day, too.

No, it's still okay—there's still the third day! I won't give up!

×　×　×

Dinnertime in the banquet hall was truly packed.

Why is it that when high school boys go on a field trip and they serve themselves rice at dinner, they give themselves *Nihon Mukashibanashi*–level portions?

Thanks to that, I didn't get any rice at all.

I think there was a big mah-jongg tournament going on in the room right then, since according to dinnertime conversation, every room had had a mah-jongg game the previous night. So now they were going to decide who was the champion.

If I were to go back to the room now, I would probably encounter the aftershocks of the tournament, which would keep me from the bath. And if I couldn't get into the bath, then the chances of some unexpected incident between me and Totsuka would be zero.

Then it was best not to go back for a while.

I was feeling peckish, so to satisfy my stomach, I wandered out of the hotel. If a teacher were to find out, they'd probably be angry, but this was where my (self-generated) active camouflage was useful. I made it to the convenience store around the corner without anyone questioning me.

First, as was my usual habit, I cruised around the magazine corner. *Hmm… Sunday GX, Sunday GX…*

As I was searching for the magazine, an imperious voice called out to me. "Oh, it's Hikio."

Before I could find *Sunday GX*, which I love but had just forgotten to buy, someone else found me instead. I replied to the unpleasant nickname with a particularly vile, rotten glare.

But the one who'd said it, Yumiko Miura, had her eyes on a magazine and not me.

So then why'd you talk to me…?

It seemed that in her mind, I was basically a natural phenomenon. She'd mentioned me just now in the same way you'd be like, *Oh, it's raining* when you start to see drops.

But, well, the distance she maintained made things easier for me, so I was fine with it. If she wasn't being considerate to me, I didn't have to be considerate to her, either. Without turning toward her, I picked up *GX* and immediately started flipping through it.

"Listen, like, what are you guys trying to do?" she said suddenly, and I jumped a little.

I'm not a fan of the scary tone…, I thought as I faced her. But she was still picking out fashion magazines.

She must have guessed that I'd turned toward her, though, as she continued the conversation on her own. "Could you stop trying to interfere with Ebina's business?" Maybe nobody taught her that you should look at someone when you talk to them. Her eyes never left the magazine.

She flipped another page. "Are you listening?"

I wanted to ask *her* that, but I suppose I hadn't said anything in the first place. I'd say it now, then. "I'm listening. And it's not like we're really interfering with her business."

"You are. It's obvious." She suddenly closed the magazine. It seemed she finally meant to actually talk *to* me. "And it's annoying," she said, reaching out to the magazine beside the other one. She carefully removed the elastic band around it and opened it, too.

Aren't you not supposed to do that…? I thought, but I was basically guilty of the same offense, so I couldn't say anything, either—not to her, at least.

"So it's annoying you, is it?" I said. "Well, there's someone else who wants us to. One person's gain is another's loss. That's normal. Give it up. Besides, it's not like it's hurting you directly."

"What?" For the first time in this crude exchange that hardly qualified as conversation, Miura looked at me. The queen's eyes were filled with animosity. "I'm gonna be the one who's hurt."

"…" That was unexpected, and it confused me a little. This was Miura, so I'd assumed she would arrogantly enlighten me as to just how much annoyance she was suffering right then. Following which, I'd figured I would argue down each of her points with care, piss her off, and then make myself scarce.

I had guessed wrong. I didn't expect her to speak about it in future tense.

I must have looked quite silly, going silent like that, as Miura gave me a hard look. "Listen, you're with Yui, so you understand Ebina, too, right?"

"I…I-I-I'm not *with* Yui at all…" Hearing this unfamiliar revelation made me a panicky, stuttering mess. *Hey, what the heck, this is too random! I-I'm n-not with her, not at all!*

Seeing me dripping blobs of gross sweat, Miura gave a wholeheartedly derisive smile. "Why are you getting the wrong idea about that? Ew. Of course she wouldn't be *with* you. That's not what I mean, like, you know? I mean, you'd get it, since you talk with her and stuff. Ew."

…You didn't have to say it again at the end.

So she didn't mean "going out with" but just "hanging out with as a friend," huh?

But even understanding that much, I still didn't get what Miura was trying to say. "What do you mean? I don't think they're at all alike."

"Well, since their personalities are different…" Miura's gaze softened just slightly. "Yui's, like… She can tell how people are feeling, and she goes along with everyone else, right? Though lately she's started being more open with what she wants to say."

Miura was right—when I'd first gotten to know Yuigahama, she'd been constantly sensitive to the reactions of others and the social atmosphere, establishing a place for herself by assimilating and adapting.

"Well, yeah…"

"Ebina's the same. She's the same but kind of in the opposite way." Miura smiled with just a hint of sadness and returned the magazine to the shelf. "She goes along with things by ignoring the mood."

The same as Yuigahama, but opposite. The way she put it—going along with things by ignoring the mood—fit so perfectly. "Oh, huh, now that you put it that way, I get it."

"That's how she is. That's why this stuff is so dangerous. It's just been working out somehow, 'cause Ebina's good at handling it."

So basically, Ebina maintained an appropriate distance from others by acting out that character and making others go along with it. She wasn't naturally a weirdo—she was only encouraging others to treat her like a weirdo.

Miura continued, her tone nostalgic. "If Ebina just keeps her mouth shut, lots of guys are into her, so a lot of them ask me to introduce them to her. But if I do, she always rejects them one way or another. I thought she was just shy, so I was real persistent about it. So then what do you think she said?"

"I dunno," I said with a shrug. Of course, I couldn't answer a pop quiz with no hints at all.

Miura quietly looked down. It was a gesture unusual for the Queen of Fire, and somehow sad.

"'Oh, then I'm done.' She was smiling. Like I was a total stranger."

Miura's quote played in my mind particularly vividly. Ebina's tone, smile, and eyes were cold as she stood just a step away, allowing no intrusion.

"Ebina doesn't really talk about herself, and I don't really ask. But…I think she hates that sort of thing."

I didn't think that was quite it. I figured if Ebina were about to lose something, she would choose to break it herself instead. She would give up on it and throw it away rather than making the many sacrifices needed to protect it.

She would probably throw away the relationships she had now.

"Y'know, I'm having plenty of fun right now. But if Ebina stops hanging out with us, things might not ever be the same. We might not be able to do stupid stuff together anymore," Miura said, her voice shaking a little. "So could you not do anything you don't have to?"

This was probably the first time Miura had looked at me and actually seen me. The feeling was clear in her gaze.

This was why I would respond with as much sincerity as I could muster.

"You don't need to worry about it."

"How can you say that?" Miura asked me, as if it were the obvious question.

Well, it was. Miura had zero reason to be trusting me. If you want someone to trust you or have faith in you, first, you have to gain a mutual understanding, then start building it up steadily, one piece at a time, until they'll trust you to handle things.

Such trust had not been built between myself and Miura.

But still, I said with the utmost confidence, "It'll be fine. Hayama said he'd manage it somehow."

"Whaaat? Well, if Hayama says so, then whatever," she said, smiling.

Even so, **Hayato Hayama** can't make a choice.

It was the morning of the third day of the field trip.

We were allowed to wander around independently today. We could all spend the time as we pleased, with or without our classes or groups. We could be with club friends, or girlfriends and boyfriends. We weren't confined to Kyoto city, either—we could go out to Osaka or Nara. Since it was a free day, anything was okay. Of course, so was being alone.

Perhaps the way this drained me of anxiety was what had helped me sleep so hard.

I did remember Totsuka shaking me awake at some point, but my faint memories seemed to tell me I'd said *Go on without me. I'll catch up soon* like a super-badass.

As a result, the Hayama, Tobe, and Totsuka trio went to have breakfast without me, and I spent a short time getting some extra sleep.

But I couldn't sleep forever—partly because I would miss breakfast, but also because we were staying at a different hotel for the evening of the third day. So I had to pack up my bag and put it in the lobby so they could carry it off.

I said my farewells to my beloved little futon that so craved my indolence and got up to dress myself. I washed my face and threw on some random clothes and packed my bag while I was at it.

…Right, now I just had to eat, and then once I came back to the room, I could leave immediately. Figuring I'd eat breakfast first, I left the room with a yawn.

"Morning, Hikki."

"Uh-huh." The corners of my mind were still occupied by sleepiness, so I didn't really question the fact that Yuigahama was in front of the door.

"Come on! Let's go!"

She's sure awake for so early in the morning. "Yeah, breakfast... It was in the big hall, right? On the second floor?"

"No, no, we canceled breakfast."

"Oh, it's canceled... What?" The unfamiliar word made me finally wake up. What did she mean, breakfast was canceled? This wasn't a fighting game. Canceling doesn't come that easy. "What do you mean, *canceled*? Breakfast is supposed to give you your energy for the day. It's not good to skip it."

"You get so intense about the weirdest stuff..." Yuigahama sounded exasperated, but then she took charge and tried to push me back into the room. "Just pack up your things, and we're going."

"Uh, I have no idea what's going on here, though..." But fortunately, I didn't have much luggage, and I'd long since finished packing up. It wasn't much trouble anyway, so for the moment, I did as I was told and went back into the room to get my pack.

"Okay, bring that out to the lobby, and let's get going."

"I don't mind taking my stuff out to the lobby, but...breakfast...," I said, but I think Yuigahama was really excited about the free day. She was humming to herself, hardly listening to me at all as she briskly went ahead.

Um...breakfast...

× × ×

Hotels are so convenient these days. At tourist spots and stuff, they have a service where they send your bags to your next destination. This field trip was no exception, and they had arranged for us to use that service to have our things sent to the next hotel before we got there. The place we'd be staying at for the third night was in one of the top, most scenic locations in Kyoto: Arashiyama. By making use of this wonderful system, we were able to enjoy our free day to the fullest with nothing to burden us.

By the way, I hadn't had breakfast that morning, so even my stomach was unburdened.

After we left the hotel, Yuigahama made me walk a while. It's often said that the city of Kyoto is laid out like the lines on a Go board, but the streets were indeed straight, and the intersections were perpendicular, too. Maybe that was why Yuigahama didn't get too confused about the way there.

Following her, I eventually spotted the white building of a coffee shop on the street. Beside it was a Kyoto-ish traditional-style shop. But according to the sign, it seemed both of them were the same place.

"Oh, I think this is it," Yuigahama said.

"What's *it*?"

"The place we're having breakfast."

"Huh? Hey, isn't breakfast on the second-floor hall?"

"I told you—I talked to the teacher and canceled it," Yuigahama said, going into the apparent cafe.

Huh? You can cancel it? I know it's a free day, but isn't our school too free?

The traditional-style building had a courtyard, too, and we were escorted to the terrace seating. On the terrace, elegantly drinking coffee, was Yukinoshita.

"Oh, you're late," she said.

"What? What is this? What's going on?" Still unable to grasp the situation, the only thought I could come up with was that she looked perfectly natural drinking coffee on a terrace.

"It's *mouningu*." Cool and composed, Yukinoshita challenged me with an English vocabulary test.

But of course, I know what *morning* means, at least. "Uh, I know it's morning."

"Not that. I mean a café breakfast, like a morning set, or morning service."

"Oh, the thing Nagoya's famous for." There's a lot of stuff in Nagoya besides that, like *tenmusu* and the Mountain café and stuff. And people from Nagoya end their sentences with *mya*, so perhaps Yukinoshita thinks they're felines.

"…Well, let's go with that."

"But they have it in Kyoto, too, huh?"

"Yep, yep. And this café is super-famous, too." Yuigahama summoned the server and quickly finished ordering.

It was true—this elegant storefront appeared to be popular with women. *Oh, so this is the recommended ladies' tour Yukinoshita looked up, isn't it?*

"I just saw Ebina on the traditional side, so I think they may be here as well," said Yukinoshita.

"Oh, so Tobecchi's going straight into the tour!"

I get it. Hearing all this, finally, I understood what the goal was. This must have been a part of Yukinoshita's list of famous spots that tend to be popular with women. Yuigahama had passed that information to Tobe, and Tobe had summoned his courage to invite Ebina, and thus they had all come here. *Huh, he's been working at this.*

Meanwhile, the breakfast plate we'd ordered arrived.

It included toast, ham, scrambled eggs, salad, coffee, and a glass of orange juice, too. It was pretty standard fare, but the nice presentation whetted the appetite.

"Let's just eat first," said Yukinoshita.

"Yeah, let's."

"Right!"

We all put our hands together before digging in. There's something strange about putting your hands together in front of a Western-style breakfast.

As we ate, Yukinoshita explained our upcoming schedule. "First, let's go to Fushimi Inari Shrine."

"For the path of torii, huh?"

"I've seen that on TV," Yuigahama said, and Yukinoshita nodded. It was a famous spot, and the line of crimson torii gates was sure to be beautiful. Well, I could get why women liked it.

"And then after that, Toufuku-ji Temple, since we can stop by there on the way back from Fushimi Inari," Yukinoshita continued.

"I don't know that one." There was no hit in my Japanese history database. I didn't think it was a World Heritage site or anything.

Yukinoshita set her cup down with a *clink* and put her fingertip to her mouth in consideration. "Well, perhaps so. You might not go there often on school field trips, but…"

Yup, when you're on a field trip, everyone generally goes to all the same spots. They really tend to select the most typically "Kyoto" spots, like with our trip to Kiyomizu-dera Temple on the first day. That's inevitably what happens when you restrict it to famous historical landmarks and World Heritage sites. The other way you could narrow things down for a field trip, I suppose, would be to base it on Japanese history. I think it'd be interesting to try a tour of locations related to the Bakumatsu years and the Shinsengumi. However, Honnou-ji Temple is deeply disappointing, so you've got to watch out for that one.

"What's famous at Toufuku-ji Temple?" Yuigahama asked.

"If you go and see, you'll know right away." Yukinoshita giggled. She seemed to be insinuating something. "And after that, Kitano Tenmangu Shrine."

…She remembered that random chat we had?

"Sorry," I said.

"It's for Komachi, right?" Yukinoshita said.

"What, what? Does Komachi have something to do with this?" Yuigahama asked as she munched on her toast.

"I'm praying for Komachi to pass her exams."

"I knew it… Sister complex…"
Call it brotherly love. Brotherly love!

× × ×

The weather was clear as we surveyed Kyoto from the intersection at Fushimi Inari. We'd been blessed with sunny skies for these three days.

"Ohhh, wow!" The view made Yuigahama breathe a sigh of wonder.

Meanwhile, on a bench off to the side, Yukinoshita exhaled deeply, totally exhausted.

Well, I could get that. Fushimi Inari Shrine is made so that you pass through a whole slew of torii gates as you go up and up and up. Though it's all stone steps, given the steepness and amount of exercise you're getting, frankly, it's kind of a hike.

Our current spot was still just the beginning. There were even more torii waiting higher up. But it's probably uncommon for casual tourists to go any higher. Most would come this far, feel a moderate degree of accomplishment, then go back down.

We had more plans after this, so we probably wouldn't have time to go up to the top.

Most of all, there was a certain someone here who seemed to lack the endurance for it.

"We'll have a little break," I said.

"All right…," Yukinoshita agreed.

I sat down on a bench and had some bottled tea. I was feeling kinda hot, so the cool breeze felt nice.

While we were taking that short rest, more sightseers showed up. Yukinoshita saw them, slowly opened her mouth, and said, "Let's start heading down."

"Are you okay?" I asked.

"I caught my breath. That's enough," she said, starting her descent. But going down was its own kind of hard. Once it was close to noon,

the number of tourists swelled, and we had traffic jams with people who were coming up at the same time.

Finally, we reached the bottom again.

"That was quite crowded…," Yukinoshita said, sounding weary. It seemed she'd been more affected by the crowds than the hike.

"I'm sure it'll be about the same from here on out," I said.

"…" She didn't say anything, but I could tell from the cold expression on her face that she was already sick of this.

Lately, I've been feeling like I could pass a level-three Yukinoshita certification test.

I'd expected this. I mean, I'd taken it for granted. We were headed to Toufuku-ji Temple, and the place was packed with tourists.

Apparently, Toufuku-ji Temple was one of the top spots in Kyoto for fall leaf-viewing. Of course, it's famous, but it's unfortunately a little ways away from central Kyoto, geographically, so it's kind of hard to get there on a school field trip. The location prides itself in its high popularity not only because of the fall leaves but also because of the Tsuuten-kyou Bridge built into the temple.

As I stood on the bridge over the stream flowing beneath me, the varying shades of the leaves filled my whole field of vision. Coupled with the calm temple atmosphere, it made for a truly elegant sight.

The fall leaves were no longer at their peak, so it had probably been much prettier before. But the area around the Tsuuten-kyou Bridge was still packed.

"Oh, it's Tobecchi."

In the crowd, we found Tobe and Ebina.

The two of them were taking pictures with the fall leaves in the background. Serving as photographer was Hayato Hayama, the guy who never forgets to be cheery, even among the mobs. I thought the sparkle I saw was his teeth, but it was just his camera flash.

"So Hayama and his group was with them, huh?" I said.

"It may have been that we just didn't see them when we ate breakfast, and they were all together," said Yukinoshita.

"Yeah, well," said Yuigahama, "when it's two people all alone, it can feel awkward, so it might be easier with them there."

"...But then it's no different from usual." They may have been in a new locale, but they were still just hanging out as a group. If we introduced an uncertain element like me, or if Yuigahama did a little matchmaking, we might have been able to stir things up a bit, but...

"But we can't split them up," Yuigahama said, stopping my train of thought. She was right.

"Basically. We don't want Ebina thinking about it too much." Otherwise known as being self-conscious. It's the most annoying feeling. It was important to not make her feel wary. Betray their expectations and fulfill their hopes: That's rule number one of entertainment.

"When a boy is coming to confess his feelings to you," said Yukinoshita, "you can anticipate it from how much everyone around is tittering about it. You hear what people are saying—whether they be teasing or ridiculing him. Generally, you have precursors before he calls you out to talk."

"Are you speaking from experience...?" I said. *Oh yeah, I tend to forget it because she's such a jerk, but the boys do like Yukino Yukinoshita. She is pretty after all.*

"It's an unbearable feeling for the one on the receiving end."

"Huh."

"You feel like a spectacle, an object of public humiliation. It's a tremendous nuisance," Yukinoshita said with sincere loathing.

Ebina had probably experienced it before, too. She was pretty in the pure and natural way—didn't even dye her hair—so any boy was guaranteed to fall for her once. So it wouldn't be surprising for her to be sensitive to the social atmosphere with boys.

"But then it doesn't seem like it'll go anywhere...," said Yuigahama.

Hmm, yeah, Hayama's crew was there, so it wasn't going to just happen when the moment came, either...

That was when Hayama and company noticed us and waved.

Yukinoshita and I made the safe choice of ignoring it, but Yuigahama waved back, like *Heeey!* They must have taken that as a signal of some sort, and all four of them came over to us.

"Hey." Hayama's short greeting was probably directed at me and Yukinoshita both, but Yukinoshita gave me a quick look.

Uhhh, I'm not your translator here... "What other places are you guys going to?" I asked just to be polite.

Instead of Hayama, Tobe replied. "We're thinking we'll go to Arashiyama first."

"Oh, really? We're going there soon, too." Yuigahama smoothly played along.

She's the one who suggested that plan... What girl skills.

Despite the amiable mood between the friendly trio of Hayama, Tobe, and Yuigahama, winter had come a little early in the back.

"..."

"..." Miura's and Yukinoshita's gazes intersected wordlessly. Perhaps it was my imagination, but I felt like the leaves started falling faster.

This is scary. I wanna go home now... I looked away reflexively, and my eyes met someone else's.

"Hikitani." Her voice was casual and singsong. I finally realized the discordantly cheerful tone was Ebina. No, maybe I could tell it was her *because* of the dissonance.

Her eyes were dark in a way they never would have been normally. After addressing me, she started walking off.

It seemed she was heading away from Tsuuten-kyou and toward the garden. She slipped through the gaps in the crowd without looking back. I almost thought she would disappear just like that.

It was like she was wordlessly telling me to come with her.

So then, I just had to follow.

The garden was brilliantly colored with red leaves, and lots of people were stopping to enjoy the view and take pictures.

I possess the ability to avoid people practically automatically, so a crowd of this size was nothing to me. But I wondered if I could catch up to Ebina even with my ability.

In other words, she also possessed the same habit.

On the edge of the tour route, where she could watch the sight-seers coming and going, Ebina waited for me with a wide smile. I finally caught up with her and came to stand beside her, looking at the crowd.

"You haven't forgotten what I came to talk to you guys about, right?" She took one gentle step closer to me. It was quiet, like she didn't want it to be noticed.

I couldn't react, and silence fell between us. Apparently not fond of the pause, Ebina broke the dam and started talking. "So?!?! How are the guys getting along?! Are they *intimate*?"

Yeah, there's no mistaking this. It's one hundred percent Ebina. The Hina Ebina that I know—that we know. "...I think they're getting along. They're playing mah-jongg and stuff at night," I said, understanding that this was probably not what she was asking.

Ebina puffed up her cheeks in a pout. "But I can't see that! That's not juicy! I like it more when the boys are all together when I'm around."

I could tell what she really meant by that.

It was the reason she'd come to consult with the Service Club.

But even understanding this wouldn't tell me how to deal with it—not yet anyway.

"Well, we're going to Arashiyama, too, so then...," I said, though this wouldn't even buy me time. Everything would be settled in just a few hours.

"I'm counting on you," she told me, and her voice was horribly heavy in my ears.

X   X   X

We headed for Arashiyama via a different route from Hayama's group, which left Toufuku-ji Temple before us. We stopped by Kitano Tenmangu—my choice—on the way.

I prayed at Kitano Tenmangu, bought a charm, and while I was at it, wrote up a wish on an *ema*. If they accused me of having a sister complex for writing one, I really wouldn't be able to argue, so I had the others wait a little ways away.

"Sorry to make you wait," I said after I was done.

"No prob."

"Then let's get going to Arashiyama."

Arashiyama is known as a Kyoto scenic spot. It's basically like a grab bag of good things about our country, showing off the charms of every season: spring cherry blossoms, summer's green leaves, fall's red, and a coating of snow in winter—and there are hot springs, too.

We took the Keifuku Rail to Arashiyama. The train car was reminiscent of the trolley age, which really put you in a traveling mood. We changed trains at Katabira-no-Tsuji and spent some more time on the train.

When we got off at the station, I saw the mosaic mural of the fall leaves and the color-gradated line of mountains. *Oh, I get it. This is why adults want to go here.* A sigh escaped me.

"…" It took Yukinoshita's breath away, too.

First, we went to the Togekkyo area, and after taking a peek at the Music Box Museum, our feet carried us toward Sagano. Rickshaws whisked by in both directions, and eventually, the road led us to a street lined with various shops. The pretty streets were relatively hip, with their rows of eateries selling fast food and junk food. As we passed, their fragrant smell was inviting.

To Yuigahama.

She chomped down on a croquette, guzzled fried chicken, and stuffed her face with beef buns. *W-well, you know, we never ate lunch, so there's no helping it, right? You could call this a lunch replacement.*

Yukinoshita was watching this scene with an expression of horror and must have felt she had to say something. She sighed hesitantly, then commented, "You'll spoil your dinner…" like a mom.

Yuigahama's expression turned to sudden realization, and then she timidly proffered her junk foods to me. "Aw… Then I'll give it to you, Hikki."

"I don't want those." Why'd she take just a single bite out of everything? If she'd split one in half, at least, I would have eaten it.

Yuigahama stared hard at the bun and croquette she carried in either hand, then looked at Yukinoshita, nonplussed. "Huh? Then what do I do with these, Yukinon?"

"Agh… I'll have just a bit." It was so unusual to see Yukinoshita taking a big bite, I found myself staring. There was something emotional about this, like Yuigahama had tamed a wild fox squirrel.

As I observed this scene, Yukinoshita glared at me. "You help, too."

"Agh, well, I guess I can eat some."

"Oh. 'Kay then, here." Yuigahama tore half off her beef bun and handed it to me.

Well, if that's how we're doing it, okay, I guess. I obediently accepted it and tossed it in my mouth.

After I had munched a little, Yuigahama burst into giggles. She was having fun with this.

When she split her croquette in half and handed that to me, too, I felt like a dog getting treats. It wasn't bad. Food tastes great when you're not the one working for it.

As we ate, we strolled down the streets of Arashiyama. We decided to keep going straight instead of turning onto the road to Tenryuu-ji Temple.

Then we heard the whoosh of the wind blowing through from the left. Looking up, I saw a rampant, dense forest of verdant green bamboo, wind rustling the leaves. The tunnel of bamboo seemed to go on forever, so many of them growing long, huddling against one another's shoulders, I couldn't even guess how many stalks there were.

The sunlight that made it through the cracks between them was softer, and cool air wafted around the whole path with a breezy whisper.

This was the bamboo forest the way it was featured in Arashiyama tourist guides, and on TV.

The path itself was the height of simplicity, but the lines of bamboo went so far, you couldn't see the end of it. It felt like it was sucking you in, almost like a maze.

"This place is amazing..." Yuigahama stopped and looked up. Bathed in the light falling between the gaps of the bamboo grass, she quietly closed her eyes.

"Yes, and look down." Yukinoshita softly walked up to the brush-wood fence. Entering the shadow of the stalks, the leaves of the bamboo rustled noisily. She pointed at her feet.

"Lanterns, huh?" I said.

"Yes, they must light it up at night."

The contrast between the warm light of the lanterns and the pale, bluish bamboo forest would surely draw out the beauty of the Arashi-yama night. The familiar sight I'd seen here and there in travel magazines rose in my mind.

It seemed Yuigahama was thinking the same thing, as she spun around excitedly. "This is it! This is a good spot! I think!"

"For what?" I asked. She was being too vague. Not only did she not provide context, she'd even added "I think" at the end, too.

Yuigahama stopped in place and looked down in embarrassment. "If someone's gonna...c-confess to you..."

Why the passive wording...?

Yukinoshita giggled in apparent amusement at Yuigahama's behavior. "The atmosphere is quite nice, isn't it? I think it might be a good location, too."

"R-right?!"

"So if Tobe's gonna try his luck, here's the place, huh?" I said.

The sun would set soon. These lanterns would be lit, just as Yukinoshita said, and the bamboo forest would shine with bright light.

A cold, late autumn wind blew through the trees.

×   ×   ×

I finished the last dinner I'd be having on this school field trip and returned to my room.

Normally, now would be the time for our class to go to the baths. But the bamboo forest would only be lit up for a limited time. If we were going out, we had to put off bathing until later and sneak out now.

Tobe was pacing around restlessly in our room at the hotel. "Aw maaan, I'm getting nervous! Man!"

Yamato whacked Tobe on the back, and the impact made Tobe hack a cough.

"It'll be okay," Yamato said in his heavy bass voice.

"Tobe with a girlfriend! You'll probably stop hanging out with me," Ooka said, glancing at Tobe.

Tobe automatically retorted, "No way. And, dude, I can't even think about that now. Oh man." And the anxiety returned right away.

Yamato whacked his back. "It'll be okay."

At this rate, they'd start an endless loop. But anyway, they looked like they were having a good time.

"This is kind of making me nervous, too." Totsuka is a good boy. I was feeling kind of on edge myself, although I'm always on the edges of any social situation, really.

Hayama, who had been silent until then, slowly stood up. "...Hey, Tobe."

"What? What's up, Hayato? I'm pretty wound up right now, y'know."

"Oh, it's nothing..."

Their shallow, inarticulate conversation went on.

"Whaaat?"

"I was going to wish you luck, but seeing your face, I changed my mind."

"Wow, ouch! Oh, but now I'm kinda less nervous."

Hayama left the room, careful not to allow Tobe to see his glum expression.

...So his attitude about this still hasn't changed, huh?

Hayama's attitude during this field trip—even before—had been strange. And since this was Hayama, who could pull off anything without a hitch and never rocked the boat, he made it hard to notice something was off. But Hayama had kept the boat too steady. That's why someone like me would notice.

I left the room that was bubbling with excitement and followed Hayama outside.

As he headed to the river, I called out to him. It's a special service for me to make the first comment in a conversation like this. It's really rare, you know. "You're being pretty damn uncooperative, aren't you?"

"Am I?" Hayama replied without turning around. It was like he'd expected I would come, and the way he was so calm about it suddenly turned my mood sour.

"You are. In fact, I feel like you've been getting in our way." At the very least, the Hayato Hayama I knew always arrived at the answer absolutely closest to correct. And since he would espouse such fair reasoning, he was always bound by it. I think that's the kind of person he is.

That was why it had felt wrong when he hadn't chosen the totally obviously correct answer of supporting his friend.

"I didn't mean to, though." Smiling ironically, he turned to face me. What a liar.

"Then what *were* you meaning to do?"

"...I like the way things are now. I like hanging out with Tobe, Hina, and everyone else," he stated, looking straight at me. "That's why..." He was about to go on.

But before he finished, I understood, and I knew what I would say in response. "...If that's enough to destroy those relationships, then that's all they ever were, right?"

"Maybe you're right. But...what's gone won't come back." It was like he was speaking from experience. But I wasn't interested in interrogating him about his implications. I had no interest in Hayama's past.

He had no intention of going into it, either. He just hid it behind a smile. "Maybe we can get through this like nothing happened. I'm decent enough at managing that."

"That still won't undo it," I shot back quickly. Without realizing it, I was speaking with certainty.

There are some things in life you can never regret enough.

Some remarks, you can't take back.

You could be talking as usual one day, but then suddenly, there's a distance between you, and after that, you stop talking. The messages you've been exchanging so frequently then stop. And that's if things go relatively well. Both of you will smile stiffly at each other, reassuring yourselves that no, you're not bothered, you're behaving like a friend should. But still, you won't be able to erase the awareness in a corner of your mind that holds you back and makes you act more distant, and though neither of you is really to blame, that's the end of it.

Hayama closed his eyes and opened his mouth. "You're exactly right. I think Hina most likely thinks the same way."

"Of course. In fact, you're weirder for wanting to enjoy those shallow relationships." I lightly kicked a pebble at my feet to stave off my anger. It rolled toward Hayama, and he scooped up the rock and stared at it. He might have been trying not to look at me.

"Maybe... But I don't think they're shallow. The environment here is everything to me right now."

"No. It *is* shallow. So what'll happen to Tobe? He's pretty serious, isn't he? You're not gonna consider how this'll affect him?" I said, cornering him.

Hayama clenched the rock. "I've told him over and over to give it up, because I don't think she'll open up to him, the way he is now... But still, I can't read the future. So I didn't want him rushing to a conclusion." Hayama flung the rock in his hand at the river. It skipped along the surface a few times, then sank. "Sometimes, it's more important not to lose something than it is to gain something else." Hayama stared hard at the surface of the water, like he wanted to see where the rock had gone. He clearly wasn't gonna find it, no matter how he searched, though.

At the end of the day, Hayama and I were both talking based on the assumption of harm. And Hayama was saying there's an end to every relationship, so if you feel one is truly important, you should try to hold on to it, because you know you'll lose it eventually.

But that's just rationalizing.

"That's a selfish excuse. That's just what you want."

"So then…!" Hayama's voice was sharp. He glared at me, anger plain in his eyes, and I glared right back at him without wavering.

He must have felt ashamed at getting emotional, as he took a deep breath to suppress his feelings and slowly formed his next sentence. "…Then what about you? What would *you* do?"

"Who cares about me…?" There's no use in thinking about what *I* would do. Hayama and I are different. And of course, Tobe is, too.

My stories really don't matter, and they're totally pointless. So I don't want to talk about it.

"In other words," I said, "you don't want anything to change."

"…Yeah, that's right," Hayama spit. His voice was more distressed and upset than I could have imagined it ever being.

But even so.

The desire to keep things the same…

…that was the one thing I could get.

I wished I didn't.

It's not necessarily truly the right thing to communicate your feelings and open up about everything. Some relationships you can't take to the next level. Sometimes you're not allowed to cross that line. Some relationships won't let their boundaries get crossed. Dramas and manga always cross the line and give you a happy ending, but reality isn't like that. It's crueler, less kind.

What's most important can't be replaced. And if you lose something irreplaceable, it's gone forever.

Being the person I was, I couldn't tell him off for being gutless or make fun of him for being a coward. It's fine if the right choice is to hold back. It's fine to stay complacent forever.

I couldn't open my mouth and reject the answers he'd found.

I could find no mistake there.

As I was unable to deny or refute this, I heard a short, resigned sigh. "You're right... This is just me being selfish," Hayama said with a lonely smile.

I didn't like that smile.

"Don't you underestimate me, Hayama. I don't believe what people say that easily." I'm the guy with the garbage personality, the one who always immediately reads into everything people say. "So I'm not going to believe this is just you being selfish, either."

"...Hikigaya." His face was filled with surprise. Not that there was any need for it.

This is probably what a certain someone else wants, too.

I'm sure there's someone like me.

A girl who uses lies to pretend and protect something.

Hayato Hayama will not stand by and let people get hurt. I'm sure the reason he can't do anything is because he knows someone will be hurt. If that line were to be crossed, the pain would come, and something would break.

Who can deny the righteousness of someone who suffers to keep that from happening? Who keeps from intruding?

Our time in high school is limited—this goes without saying. We live in this laughably small world for a hopelessly short time.

Who would blame you for wanting to hold on to that?

I didn't have to lose it to understand.

Hayato Hayama cannot choose. He has so many things, and every single one of them is important to him.

Hachiman Hikigaya cannot choose. He never had a choice in the first place, and he can only do one thing.

Ironically, the inability to choose is all we have in common, while everything else about us is different.

I didn't understand what Hayama was trying to protect.

And that was fine. That was why there was something I could do.

As I left the river beach, Hayama called after me. "You're the one person I didn't want to rely on…"

That goes for the both of us, you idiot.

I'll sing the praises of love and friendship, but that's just for the victors. Nobody lends their ear to the laments of the defeated, those who have lost it all.

So then I'll listen. I'll sing it out loud.

This is the fox's ode to sour grapes.

This is a requiem for all those who, no matter how attracted they are to someone, can only try to hide their weakness.

His and her confessions will reach no one.

One by one, the lanterns lit up on the path of the bamboo woods. The dim white lights illuminated the fresh green stalks, a few paces between each glow. The sun set, and when the moon rose, a pale aura enveloped the area.

If you could visualize kindness, I'm sure it would look something like this.

This mix of coincidence and calculation had been staged, dramatized, and beautifully packaged into the very picture of benevolence itself.

This was the stage that had been set for Tobe.

Everyone was telling little lies in order to construct this situation.

Yuigahama had been the one to call Ebina out here. She'd probably made up some kind of excuse and brought her here.

Ooka and Yamato must have had their own thoughts on the matter. This wasn't purely about supporting Tobe—they were getting a great show out of this, though they hid it behind their meek expressions.

Even Miura, who wasn't there, knew what was about to happen, though she didn't ask about it, didn't stop it, and was clearly pretending not to notice it.

Hayama wanted to be supportive but couldn't be. But regardless, he was there.

They were all lying.

The only one of them who wasn't lying, Yukinoshita, was blank-faced in a rather colder manner than usual.

In the deepest part of the bamboo forest path, we awaited Ebina's arrival.

Hayama, Ooka, and Yamato were committing to staying out of Tobe's way. Tobe was taking deep breaths, staring down the path. When I went to go talk to him, he was stiff from the anxiety of staying ready for her to come at any moment.

"Tobe," I said.

"H-Hikitani... Agh, man... I really can't take any more of this..." He smiled at me awkwardly.

"Hey, what'll you do if she says no?"

"Come on, isn't that pretty harsh to say right before I'm about to tell her? Huh, that actually made me less nervous... I get it—you're tryin' to test my determination again?"

"Look, just answer me already. Ebina's about to come," I said more harshly than I'd meant to. I couldn't handle his jokes.

Tobe must have realized this, and his expression turned somber. "...Well, I wouldn't give up." His gaze was somewhere beyond the bamboo forest. "I'm not a really serious guy, you know? So I've only ever had nonserious relationships. But I'm pretty serious this time."

That was all it took for me to understand. This was why I could say what I really thought, no lies, no deception. "...All right. Then do your best, right till the very end."

"Yeah! You're a good guy after all, Hikitani." Tobe whacked my back.

"I'm not, you moron." I shook off his hand and returned the way I'd come. We were on standby in a spot right after a curve in the path, where it would be hard for Ebina to see us when she came from the other direction.

Upon my return, Yuigahama said, "So you *can* be nice, Hikki."

"What brought this about?" Yukinoshita added. Both of them smiled as they teased me.

"You've got it wrong, seriously. At this rate, Tobe's gonna get rejected," I replied to them.

Their expressions fell a little. "You may be right," Yukinoshita agreed.

"Yeah…"

That was why I knew what to say to deal with that. "There is actually a way to settle this all without conflict."

"How?" Yuigahama asked me, tilting her head a bit.

But frankly, I didn't really want to say it.

Yukinoshita must have sensed my hesitation. She breathed a short sigh and cracked a little smile. "…Well, we'll.leave it to you."

Yukinoshita nodded in response. I was grateful they weren't asking.

As we spoke, Ebina came into view. Yuigahama's invitation had done its work.

We sent Tobe off from the corner of the path.

Passing the evenly spaced lanterns one by one, Ebina approached him.

Tobe greeted her with a nervous look.

"Um…"

"Yeah…" Ebina's reaction was tepid.

Just watching them from a distance started up a dull pain in my chest.

First of all, Tobe was going to be rejected.

And then the two of them would avoid each other's eyes in the classroom, put on fake smiles, and gradually become more guarded and distant around each other, until finally they just stopped associating at all. Or he might keep trying until they were shuffled into new classes. But the eventual ending was the same.

But even if it wasn't going to happen now, just maybe, things could be different further down the line. Did Tobe understand that possibility? Did he understand he was risking their current relationship? He had to be at least a little prepared for that.

But what about everyone else?

Tobe wasn't the only one who saw that relationship as important. Other people in their lives were stakeholders, too.

That was why *she'd* made that request.

That was what was causing this distress for *him*.

The wishes of third parties had come together. They didn't want to lose this. Maybe the arrows were pointed in different directions, but they were similar in that they wanted the same goal.

"I, um…"

"…" Ebina didn't reply. She politely laid her hands in front of her, listening quietly. She wore a clear and robotic smile.

Yeah, it's just the look I imagined she'd have.

If I was to pull off this request somehow, there was just one escape route I could use. I could keep Tobe from being rejected while also maintaining the relationships of their group and ensuring they could all still be friends.

There really was only one way.

The important thing was timing—and the impact of this special move.

You hit them with something outside the realm of their awareness, something that knocks everything topsy-turvy. *Think—what would gain the most interest? What could give someone the initiative? What could change the atmosphere here in an instant?*

Good grief. It drives me nuts that all I can think of is this cheap trick. Not to mention that it's a trick Zaimokuza got me with just recently. Ugh, feeling indebted to him feels gross.

"L-listen…," Tobe stuttered, screwing up his determination.

By then, I was already moving.

Ebina's shoulders twitched at his words.

Just over ten more steps.

Tobe paused a second and looked at Ebina.

Would I make it?

Ebina's eyes moved to a lantern at her feet.

If I'm going to say it, now's the time.

"I've liked you for a long time. Please go out with me."

Ebina's eyes went round when she heard it.

Of course. I was startled, too.

As was Tobe.

His mouth was hanging open, since I'd stolen the words he'd meant to say.

Ebina was confused to hear a confession from me, but she quickly came up with the correct response. "I'm sorry. I don't want to date anyone right now. No matter who confesses to me, there's no way I'll date them. If this is over, I'm going, okay?" She gave a head bob of a bow, then ran off at a trot.

Tobe was frozen, mouth still hanging open. Having lost his moment, he couldn't say what he was supposed to say—or anything at all. His head slowly jerked around toward me.

"There you have it," I said with a shrug.

He combed his hair back and looked at me with reproach. "Hikitani... that's not fair... I mean, it's good I found that out before I got rejected, but..." *Not fair, not fair,* he said over and over, like he was an animal and those two words were his cry.

Then Hayama, who must have been watching from close by to see how things would go, walked up to poke Tobe lightly in the head. "That just means it's not the right time yet. Right now, it's fine to simply enjoy things as they are, isn't it?"

"Well, I guess. But, like, she said *right now*, right?" Tobe gave a little sigh. And then he dragged the soles of his shoes over to me and bopped my chest with his fist. "Hikitani, sorry, but I'm not gonna let you beat me." With a charming grin on his face, he pointed at me, then walked off toward where Ooka and Yamato were standing, apparently satisfied, where they baptized him with arms slung over shoulders and whacks on the back.

Hayama went after Tobe, too. As we passed by each other, quietly, so that only I could hear, he said, "Sorry."

"Don't you dare apologize."

"I knew this was the only way you know how to handle things, but...I'm sorry." His expression was one of pity—not contempt or scorn. Just sympathy for the abject.

My fist wanted to fly out in shame and anger, but I kept it in check. Even after Hayama was gone from my sight, that look was still branded clearly in my eyes.

They all left in a hurry, and suddenly, everything felt colder.

The only ones left were me, Yukinoshita, and Yuigahama. I was a little far off from the both of them. Relieved it was finally over, I walked toward them so we could leave.

But Yukinoshita just stood there stiffly, glaring at me. Her cold, accusing look slowed my feet.

Come on, don't be such a bully. What Hayama said just now actually hit me pretty hard.

But of course, she couldn't tell how I was feeling. The bladelike glint in her eyes never dulled. Yuigahama was just looking down uncomfortably beside her.

"...I hate the way you do things," Yukinoshita finally said when I was within a few steps of her. She pressed a hand against her chest and glared at me. Emotions that had nowhere to go were welling in her eyes. "It's so frustrating that I can't quite explain this properly, but...I really hate the way you do things."

"Yukinon..." Yuigahama gave Yukinoshita the most pained look. I heard her swallow, and then she lowered her eyes again.

When I didn't reply, Yukinoshita opened her mouth like she had something to say, but nothing came out. She bit her lips as if to keep them shut. Red leaves danced in the wind, and Yukinoshita's eyes moved away from me to follow them.

"…I'm going back now," she said icily, then walked past me. She must have wanted to leave as soon as possible, as she was walking faster than usual. I could start after her now, but I wouldn't catch up.

Yuigahama smiled weakly. "I—I guess I'll go, too." She sounded like she did when she was forcing herself to act cheerful. At least that was easy to understand.

"…Yeah," I answered, starting to walk away. Yuigahama followed after me, one step behind. She chattered on in an attempt to bury the inevitable silence. "Man, that strategy was awful, huh? I mean, it sure was a surprise, and it did take away her chance to reject him."

"Mm-hmm."

"But yeah. It really startled me. For a second, I thought you were serious."

"Of course I wasn't."

"Of course not. Ah-ha-ha…"

Our vague conversation continued, and when we drew near the path's exit, Yuigahama's footsteps stopped. "But…" When she started another sentence, I stopped, too. Suddenly, she tugged my sleeve, and I turned around without thinking. "But…don't…do anything like that again…okay?"

I wanted her to stop smiling like that. I couldn't stand to see something so pained and pitiful. Without a word, I averted my eyes.

That smile took more of a toll on me than the pity or the anger directed at me.

"It was the most efficient way to do it. That's all." It was the only thing that would come out of my mouth. I could have explained it in more logical terms. I knew I could use the fanciest rhetorical flourishes to rationalize what I'd done. But the words just coiled up in the pit of my stomach and rotted there.

"It's not about being *efficient*…" Her head was hanging, but I could still hear her voice clearly.

"Some people here don't want things resolved. Of course, they'd prefer things stay the way they are, so it isn't going to work out for

everyone. So then you have no choice but to find a way to compromise, somehow." As I spoke, I became aware of it myself: *Agh, this is just mincing words.* It was just an excuse to falsely lay the responsibility for what I'd done on the shoulders of some formless someone. It was what I hated most in the world: deceit.

Yuigahama had to realize that.

There was a sniffling sound.

"Tobecchi didn't get rejected, Hayato and all the guys are on good terms as far as I can tell, and Hina doesn't have to worry about it, either... Now, tomorrow, things can be like they always were. Maybe we'll just move on, and nothing will change." Her trembling voice kept me from arguing. Her shaking fingertips would not let me move.

Unable to face her head-on, all I could do was stay silent and still.

"But... But..." For an instant, her fingers released their gentle hold on the hem of my blazer, but then she grabbed it again, with more force this time. "...You should...consider people's feelings more," she said, and I could faintly hear her breathing. "...You understand so many things, so why can't you get that?"

I do understand. I know that if things change, you can't go back.

No matter what it becomes, you can't take it back. I could say that for certain.

But my blazer felt really heavy now that Yuigahama was holding it. She wasn't that strong, but the weight was tremendous. Heavy enough to crush me, it felt.

"I hate that," she muttered feebly, and then like a little girl's, her grip slid off.

She took one, two steps away from me.

I couldn't follow her.

I...just looked at the sky.

The pale, shining bamboo forest tunnel was cold and clear enough to freeze me solid.

I couldn't see the moon anymore.

X   X   X

You can see out over the city from the roof of Kyoto Station.

There's a mix of modern buildings with temples and shrines, blended with the bustle of people.

A city can maintain what it's had for a thousand years, but it still changes from day to day.

It's extolled as the imperial city of a millennium, and yet, it changes. They glorify it *because* it doesn't change. People love it because its fundamental nature, its core, has been preserved faithfully for all this time.

In other words, doesn't that mean that no matter how something might be distorted, its true essence will never change?

So then human personalities won't change, either. They can't change. This is nothing other than evidence that they can't.

But I want to believe that, often, the right thing is to stay the same.

It was the final day of the school field trip. We just had a little bit of time to wait for the Shinkansen. I wasn't window-shopping for souvenirs but waiting here for someone.

I could see her going to the trouble of climbing the long outside stairs. She had whispered in my ear as she'd passed by me on the bus to Kyoto Station.

"Hello, hello~. Did I keep you waiting?"

I replied with a shake of my head.

She had shoulder-length black hair and thin-framed red glasses with clear eyes behind them. She was petite in both face and body. She would make for a great picture sitting behind a library counter.

The person who had made this recent request of me, Hina Ebina, was standing there. "I figured I'd say my thanks," she said.

"You don't need to. The issue you came to us about hasn't been resolved," I replied briefly, then turned my gaze back to the city of Kyoto.

But I heard her voice from behind me. "Superficially. But he understood, didn't he?"

"..."

Silence was my only reply.

I saw Ebina as an irregular presence.

She acted bubbly, but she was actually quite canny, and that was exactly what made me want to read into the things she said.

A quiet-looking girl who has no qualms about approaching me sets off my alarm bells. My middle school–era experiences have taught me to habitually try to find the hidden meaning behind the words and actions of girls like this.

Which was why it seemed off to me that she flaunted her slash fangirl side, and when she came to consult with the Service Club, it made me want to speculate as to her true motives.

Her request that we make sure the guys were closer, in other words, meant she wanted the boys distanced from herself, and she wanted to prevent Tobe from confessing his feelings to her.

She'd probably asked not only the Service Club to do this but also Hayama. Which was why Hayama had been so conflicted and half-assed about helping us.

"Thanks for this. You've been a big help." Her cheerful tone made me turn around, and I saw her smiling with seeming relief.

But if she can smile like that, she has to be capable of more, too, I thought, and something I didn't need to say rolled out of my mouth anyway. "...Tobe's a useless piece of trash, but I think he's a good guy."

"It's not going to happen! You get that, right, Hikitani? If I dated anyone now, it wouldn't go well."

"That's not—"

"Sure it is," Ebina interrupted. "Because I'm rotten." Her smile was frozen, and her excuse sounded just like someone else's.

"...Guess that's that, then."

"Yes it is. Nobody can understand, and I don't want them to. That's why I can't have a decent relationship."

Was this ultimately about her hobbies, or about her? Well, it wasn't something for me to ask.

We exchanged little smiles, and then she poked her glasses up. The glare on her lenses hid her expression from me. "But," she added, lifting her face. Her cheeks were a little red, and she wore her usual bright smile. "Maybe things could work out, if I dated you."

"Don't even joke. If you throw around comments like that, I might inadvertently fall for you."

If someone else had been here and heard such a terrible attempt at humor, they would've burst out laughing. Ebina laughed, too, shoulders shaking as if it were the funniest thing. "I kinda like the way you can be honest with people you don't give a damn about."

"What a coincidence. I kinda like that about myself, too."

"I kinda like the way I can just spout off things I don't mean, too."

We both puffed out our chests with gloomy smiles.

"You know, I'm happy with the way I am now and how things are going in my life. It's been a long time since things have been like this, so I don't really want to lose it. I enjoy where I am and who I'm with." Ebina's gaze was pointed far away, toward the bottom of the big stairs. I couldn't see anything there, but she must have been looking at someone.

Ebina descended the stairs one at a time, eyes carefully at her feet as she added, right before she left—

"That's why I hate myself."

In silence, I watched Ebina's small back grow distant.

I looked for the words to say to her, but I couldn't think of anything.

I couldn't praise or blame anyone for small lies they tell themselves.

You care about it, you don't want to lose it—so you hide and play pretend.

That's exactly why you're sure to lose it.

And then, once you have, you mourn it. If you'd only known you were going to lose it, then it'd be better not to have had it in the first place, you think. If letting go makes you feel so much regret, you should have given up on it.

In a changing world, some relationships probably have to change, too. And I'm sure some will end up broken so badly they can't be repaired.

That's why everyone lies.

—But I was the biggest liar of all.

Bonus track!
The girls will rock you. ♡

This bonus track is a novelization of the script from the limited special edition *My Youth Romantic Comedy Is Wrong, As I Expected*, Vol. 7, plus drama CD. The script features an episode set immediately after the main story in Volume 6. Please understand that since this is a rewrite, some parts will differ slightly from the drama CD.

Uchiage: a party to celebrate the completion of an event. People say this word constantly, but it never sounds quite right to me. Why use a word that can also mean things firing in the air or waves crashing out of the ocean? The only places that should be happening so frequently are the beaches in Florida or Tanegashima.

As long as you're on this earth, anything that rises high will come back down again; it's the law of nature. Therefore, if you're going to an *uchiage* party, your feelings are bound to plunge downward, too.

Once upon a time, the Greek hero Icarus aimed high using bird wings made of hardened wax, with courage as his only companion. But as many are aware, he tragically fell and lost his life in the end.

So aiming for the heights brings only death, and trying to fly without knowing your own limits should be called not courage but foolhardiness. That doesn't make you a hero. It makes you an idiot.

A true hero reads the room, *fears* the room, and so does not participate in *uchiage*.

From this, let us derive a conclusion: The wise and the brave do not fear loneliness, and the feeling that one must join in on something is what ensures they will not go.

I'm not going. When I say I'm not going, it means I'm not... I swear I'm not gonna go, okay?!

✕   ✕   ✕

The cultural festival, which had felt much longer than it was, finally ended. However, only regular students could really call it over. As a member of the miscellaneous section of the Cultural Festival Committee, I still had a duty to write a report.

But, like, I still don't really get why it's me who has to write this thing. Well, that's work. When your superiors tell you to do it, you just have to do it, no matter what. It's not about whether you can or can't. You're just gonna...

This task seemed to me to be unreasonable, unjustifiable, and unfair, but finally, I could see the end of it. Occasionally, my own excellence scares me. Pen racing along, I reached the conclusion, finished the whole thing off, and took a break.

"...Right, guess that's it," I muttered, and Yuigahama's head jerked up.

"Oh, Hikki, are you done writing the report for the cultural festival?"

"Yeah, basically. I'll do the rest at home."

Once Yuigahama had confirmed I was done, her gaze shifted over to Yukinoshita. "What about you, Yukinon? Are you done with your career path form?" she asked.

Yukinoshita's pen stopped. It seemed she was. "Yes, I just have to submit it now," she said.

Yuigahama leaped out of her chair and flung both her arms wide. "Okay then, let's go to the after-party!"

"Not happening."

"I'd rather not."

Yukinoshita and I mysteriously synchronized, and then there was a moment of silence as Yuigahama slumped back down into her chair dejectedly. She gave the both of us an anxious, entreating look. "Y-you're really not going?"

"I just said I'm not. If I did, I'd just ruin the mood," I said.

With a bright smile, Yukinoshita said, "That's always the case with you. Perhaps I should use some of the club budget to purchase a mood cleanser."

"Hey, don't say stuff like that, even as a joke. It reminds me of that time in middle school when the girls in my class sprayed me with 8x4." I.e., the deodorant spray. I could never forget that day near the end of spring. It was after gym class, and Suga, who had the seat next to me, slowly— Actually, never mind. This one makes me kinda depressed.

Yuigahama's sensitivity must have picked up on my signals, as she said with pity in her voice, "Ack, that's sad...b-but at least it wasn't Febreze! I often spritz a little when Daddy goes by!"

"That doesn't make me feel any better, and now I feel sorry for your father... Be a little nicer to the poor guy." I was supposed to be the object of sympathy here, but now I was feeling sorry for someone else instead. Good grief, the dads of teenage girls have it rough. They say kids don't understand how their parents feel—and this was a prime example.

Yuigahama stared into space, seemingly lost in thought as she muttered, "Oh yeah... Father...*father*, huh...? Th-that feels kind of weird..."

I didn't really get what all the mumbling was about, but I would reiterate what was my one clear conclusion: "And so I'm not going. I mean, it's a waste of time for me to go anywhere there's gonna be a crowd."

"A waste of time? No it's not," Yuigahama protested.

But it seemed Yukinoshita shared my opinion. "It's true. If Hiki-gaya and I were to go, there would be nothing for us to do. Our time would be spent simply being there."

"It'll be okaaay! Come on, I'll be with you!" Yuigahama pressed with a thumb jabbed at herself.

But things would never go that well. "That's half the problem."

"Huh?" Yuigahama blinked.

"I'd go because I got invited by someone I get along with, right? But come on, if they're friendly with me, that means they're popular and have lots of friends. They'll be in high demand wherever they go. While they're talking with other people, I'm at loose ends. I'll never fit in with the crowd, so I have nothing to do but focus on eating. That's why I make sure not to go to these events in the first place," I explained.

Yukinoshita added, "Formal parties and ceremonies are social pleasantries and nothing else, which actually makes them less stressful."

"I get the sense you've experienced this personally. It's kinda scaring me..." Yuigahama winced a bit at Yukinoshita's smile.

Ooh, I feel like I just saw the dark side of a wealthy socialite.

Yukinoshita brought us back to the point. "Neither I nor Hikigaya are enthusiastic about this, Yuigahama, but if you can provide a good argument for the merits of going, I believe there is room to consider it."

"Yeah, yeah," I said. "Like not having to use conditioner, or how it's got moisturizer in it, or how foaming it up turns it into a duck."

"Why is that all about shampoo...? And wait, was that last one even shampoo?"

Oh, that last one was mousse, huh? "Anyway, whatever is fine. Just shoot," I said.

Yuigahama put a hand to her mouth, tilting her head. "Hmm... Oh! If we all go together, i-it'll be fun?"

"That's extremely subjective and unpersuasive," Yukinoshita said flatly.

"O-okay, okay, okay then...eating together will make the food better!"

"Dealing with all the people there means you can't even think about the food." This time, I was the one shooting her down.

But Yuigahama wouldn't be discouraged. "Having a great time with your friends…is…h-healthy…"

"I doubt it's healthy to get yourself wound up so late at night." Yukinoshita calmly fired a shot of rationality.

But still, Yuigahama did her best to wring some kind of benefit out of going. "U-um…it's an important opportunity to make memories?"

"Oh yeah. This is that thing where you write it as *memories* but it's actually pronounced *trauma*."

It seemed even Yuigahama was out of ideas at that point, as she held her head in her hands, halfway to tears. "Ngh…ahhhhh…h-hold on just a minute! I'm thinking!"

She's still not giving up…?

"All right. Then, Hikigaya, while we're waiting, why don't we have you point out the disadvantages?" Seeing Yuigahama's tenacity, Yukinoshita smiled sweetly and made a malicious suggestion. Well, I went along with it, so that made me a bad guy, too.

"Okay. Well, first of all…it costs money."

"Penny-pincher…," Yuigahama muttered sadly in a low tone.

Meanwhile, Yukinoshita was wearing a cheerful, beaming smile. Aha. *I know where this leads.*

"Going straight for the financial argument. I'd expect nothing less from you, Hikigaya."

"Yeah. Money management is a vital skill for a househusband after all!" I replied with pride.

Looking exasperated, Yukinoshita said, "I meant that sarcastically…"

"Hikki's already used to that. But it's true; it does cost quite a lot. Even if you're not going to a restaurant, a pot-pa or a *tako*-pa or curry-pa costs quite a bit." Yuigahama was intoning some kind of spell.

What? What'd she say? I wondered, and I was not the only one.

Yukinoshita was equally baffled. "What? Pa? …Huh? I'm sorry. I don't understand in the slightest what you just said… What language was that?"

"Oh, that was short for hot-pot party, *takoyaki* party, and curry party."

"How do you have a party with hot pot or curry? Do you put candles on top of curry rice?" I asked. *Or do you do toasts with the pot?*

Yuigahama answered cheerfully, "We all get together at someone's house, make the food, and eat it!"

Is that all...? I wondered.

But Yukinoshita's concern focused on a different point. "Would you be included in the cooking...? Please never invite me to one of those events."

"Don't worry! I'm in charge of drinks!"

"At least you're aware you're a terrible cook," I muttered. Aaand we were quite off topic. "...Anyway, paying money to go to some party or get-together so you can go and be miserable is a crazy idea. I'm serious."

"O-oh...okay... I guess..." Yuigahama started trying to think of something else to say, and Yukinoshita glanced over at me.

"You have more, don't you, Hikigaya?"

"Yep. —Like when you tell yourself, *Okay, let's do this,* and you try talking to people and end up saying too much."

"Urk." Yuigahama cringed. "Yikes...I get that. If you're thinking *I've got to talk, I've got to talk* when you're with someone you don't really know, you can end up saying stuff you shouldn't..."

"We're slowly convincing her," said Yukinoshita.

And, well, it was a foregone conclusion at this point. "So can I take it that it's unanimous that we're not going?"

"No objections."

"What?!"

Yukinoshita agreed with my statement, and majority rule meant it was determined we would not go.

But Yuigahama still wouldn't give up. She was desperately racking her brain. "Hnnnng, there's got to be something, there's got to be something...... Oh! ...Being with you...makes me happy." After struggling to come up with something, that was the idea she had finally found.

"..."

"..."

Yukinoshita and I went silent. We were taken aback, even.

Yuigahama must have taken that silence as a rejection, as she sighed in resignation. "Agh, guess it's no use after all..."

"...Heh. Well, I suppose we'll call that a merit." Yukinoshita smiled softly.

Joy clear on her face, Yuigahama turned back to Yukinoshita. "Huh? Then you'll come with me, Yukinon?"

"Yes, I'll come with you, just for a short while."

Well, if Yuigahama and Yukinoshita were together, there wouldn't be anything to complain about. I'd feel bad if they thought they had to babysit me the whole time just because I was there, so it was best for me to not go. "I'll pass. The way all the others'll see it, I'm basically not invited anyway. Don't worry about me. Go and have fun," I said.

Yuigahama's hands fidgeted on her lap, and she eyed me with some reserve. "I—I am worried, though..."

"...Agh...don't worry about it."

"O-okay..."

At this rate, I was gonna end up stressing over it, so I decided to take my leave quickly and efficiently. "I'm heading out, then. Komachi's probably already made dinner."

"Say hello to her for me," said Yukinoshita.

"Uh-huh. I will."

"Huh? Hey! You're really going?!"

"Yeah. See you." I slid open the door and stepped out into the hallway. It was already pretty late. The school building was sinking into the setting sun.

And this was how the curtain closed at last on my cultural festival. The madness of the event was distant now, and even the lingering heat of excitement had cooled from the school's halls. Only a few words remained in my ears, like the roar of the ocean, lighting a faint glow in my heart. I found myself thinking it wasn't a bad ending to a cultural festival to go home feeling this way.

…My youth romantic comedy really was all wrong, as I expected.

As I was leaving…
"Y-you think I'll let it end here?!"
"You don't know when to give up…"
…I got the feeling I heard something like that.

×   ×   ×

I got home and opened the front door, then climbed up the stairs to the living room, on the second floor. "I'm baaaack."

"Ohhh? Bro, welcome home!" Noticing me, Komachi poked her face out.

"Komachi, is dinner ready?"

"Huh? Oh yeah… I thought for sure you'd have an after-party or something, so I didn't make anything…"

"Hey, that's not like you. I always come straight back home from everything, choir recitals, graduation ceremonies, whatever. This is no different." I think it'll probably be the same for my coming-of-age ceremony, too.

"Hmm… But you worked so hard on this one, Bro." She sounded unconvinced, somehow.

But I was certain. "And that's exactly why I don't want to go to the after-party. I don't want to be any more tired."

"Hmm, hmm! I guess you could look at it that way. That's very you. Yeah. Oh well. All right, then I wonder what we should do for dinner…" Komachi folded her arms to think, when her phone gave a little *tee-da-lee.*

"Komachi, your phone is ringing."

"Yeaaah." She grabbed her phone and accepted the call. "Hello, hello, it's Komachi."

"Oh, Komachi? It's me, it's me," I heard faintly through the mouthpiece, but it wasn't clear from what Komachi said after that who it was.

"Oh, hello. Thank you, I'm always grateful for your assistance."

"Are you an office worker?" I was starting to wonder if Komachi would end up being the one to get a job and support me.

But she reacted to me coldly. "Bro, shut up. Komachi's still talking on the phone here. I'm sorry… Oh-ho, oh-ho. Ohhh. Yes, that's right. I understand. Just leave the rest to Komachi~. ☆" There was a beep as she hung up, and then she drifted into thought for a moment. "Hmm, so then first…" She started texting furiously.

"Immediately texting right after a call? You're sure busy."

"It's important to do things before you forget. Okeydoke, and send!"

"Huh… I would appreciate it if you didn't forget your big brother's dinner," I said, and Komachi spun around to face me.

"Oh, about that. Since I didn't make anything, let's go out to eat."

"Huh? We can eat at home. If you want, I can just cook." I was feeling too lazy to go out now, and I wanted to take it easy at home.

But Komachi was stubbornly refusing to give in. "No, no, you worked hard on the committee, Bro. We should go out and have fun. Think of it as a reward or something."

"If that's the deal, then your home cooking would be the better reward for me, Komachi." A remark that was worth a lot of Hachiman points slipped out of my mouth. The sincerity was what gave it such a high score. In Hachiman points.

Komachi staggered dramatically, as if she'd been shot with an arrow through the heart, but then she immediately countered. "B-Bro! Y-you big jerk! Where'd you learn such a high-level technique?! You're already garbage to begin with, so if you learn how to toy with girls' hearts, too, then you really are destined to be one of those guys who leeches off a woman's finances for sexual favors."

"What a horrible thing to say…," I muttered.

"Anyway, the decision's been made. We're going out. Let's go!"

Komachi took advantage of my moment of weakness after suffering such an enormous blow. As instructed, I ended up going out.

× × ×

I strolled around the town with Komachi in search of dinner.

"Okeydoke, maybe this area'll be good," she said.

"We ended up just coming back near the school… So, what are we gonna eat? Ramen? Curry?"

"Since it's a special day, let's have something nicer."

As we were tossing easy, meaningless banter back and forth, a figure dramatically stepped toward us. "Oh-ho, I can't ignore that remark."

"Gah! Miss Hiratsuka!"

The beautiful teacher made a particularly cool entrance, but her next remark sort of ruined it. "Ramen is a wonderful food. One might even call it the soul food of the Japanese! You know the old wisdom. *Article the first: Softness of* menma *is to be valued. Article the second: Sincerely revere the three treasures—noodles, broth, and toppings.*"

"What is this? The Ramen Seventeen Article Constitution?"

And what is this waste of a beautiful woman? Talking to her was so cringey I didn't even want to engage with her, but my little sister dove in headfirst.

"Oh, Miss Hiratsuka, you're late."

"Sorry. I was a little busy dealing with some cultural festival cleanup."

"Komachi invited you here…?" I asked.

"Komaaaachiii!" Someone was running to us from the distance, calling Komachi's name, as a second figure walked toward us slowly.

"Yui! Yukino! Yahallo!" Komachi called out.

"Yahallo!" Yuigahama greeted her cheerfully in turn, while Yukinoshita did so more sedately.

"Good evening."

"Yuigahama and Yukinoshita? You guys didn't go to the after-party?" I asked.

Perfectly nonchalant, Yuigahama replied, "Yeah, we went. We all had a toast and hung out for a while, and then we left early."

"Was it okay you did that?"

"Aw, it's fine! There were tons of people there, and when it comes to these things, you only remember the people who were near you at the very beginning and the very end."

"She frightens me with the things she says sometimes...," Yukinoshita muttered.

Yep. I was thinking it, too, just now. *Ooh, she's kind of scary.*

"Anyway, more importantly, why are you all here...?" I asked no one in particular in an attempt to figure out the reason behind this gathering, and that was when I heard someone else running up to us.

"Hachiman!"

"Totsuka... Why are you here?" *Could it be...fate?* I was struck with this certainty but turned out to be wrong.

Yuigahama replied easily, "Oh, I ran into Sai-chan, too, so I went and invited him."

"Invited him? To what...? Wait, you were at the after-party, too?" I asked Totsuka.

"Yeah, I figured I would just stay a little while and then leave, so I'm glad she invited me."

"What...did you say...? If I'd known you were there, I'd have gone, too..." Damn it, I wanted to be cheek to cheek with Totsuka on the dance floor, lit by the soft light seeping into the room amid the sounds of the festivities...

Totsuka must have sympathized with my regrets, as his head dipped a bit. "Oh, you meant to go to the after-party, too, Hachiman? Then maybe I should have stayed..."

"No, it's okay. My reason to go isn't there anymore anyway! So what the heck is this get-together...?"

The very moment I wondered this, yet another one burst in.

"Hyah! Master Swordsman General Yoshiteru sallies forth at the appointed time!"

"Give me a sec; I'm trying to ask for an explanation... Hey, why is Zaimokuza here, too? C'mon, who's doing all this inviting?"

And what's more, he was clearly the only one there whom no one had anticipated showing up. There was no way any of the others could have invited him. However, completely ignoring all that is what makes Zaimokuza, Zaimokuza.

"Just who the hell do you think I am?! Wherever you go, I'll be there, Hachiman!"

"Listen, that's creepy. You like me too much. And hey, Komachi, why'd you get all these people together?" I decisively looked away from Zaimokuza to turn the conversation toward Komachi instead.

My sister's reply was as cheery as it could get. "The real after-party starts now, Bro! Let's have some fun to blow all that fatigue away!"

"Uh, I'm the type who wants to take it easy at home when I'm tired, though..." *Fun would only make me more tired...*, I thought, but I just couldn't get Komachi to understand, and Yuigahama put pressure on me, too.

"C'mon, it'll be nice! We'll call it our own private after-party!"

"Eugh..." I made my reluctance clear.

But Yukinoshita, who I'd thought had maintained a similar attitude toward this the whole time, coolly said, "Why don't you give up? I meant to just go along with this briefly and then go home early, but I've already acquiesced..."

"Agh..." I expelled a deep, deep sigh. Whatever the case, once a decision was made, there was nothing I could do about it. So I would meekly play along.

We wandered aimlessly through the bustling crowds, searching for a place to go.

This was when Yuigahama said awkwardly, "Um, what should we do?"

"You didn't think about this…?" I groaned. *Why so reckless? Are you Botchan?*

It seemed leaving it up to Botchan would get us nowhere, so instead, Sai-chan suggested, "Maybe we should just go into a restaurant?"

Komachi responded to Totsuka's suggestion with a question of her own. "Yeah, but then what would we eat?"

Instantly, Zaimokuza reacted. "Herm. What sort of meat, Hachiman?"

"You've already decided it's gonna be meat?"

"I'll have anything! Beef, pork, chicken, barbecue, horse, white meat, wild boar, venison, mutton, or lamb!"

"You meat maniac. And wait—chicken and white meat are the same thing…"

Actually, the way he casually inserted barbecue into that lineup turned it into a kind of mini-game. Which one of these is not like the others?! The correct one is…me!

I'd assumed Zaimokuza's opinion wouldn't be held in any regard, but surprisingly, the girls were responsive. "Ohhh! Komachi agrees with meat!"

"I'm feeling the meat, too. Meeeat!"

"Yaaay! Meat!" Komachi and Yuigahama were loudly going into total meat mode.

In contrast with the two of them, Yukinoshita was calm. "I'm… perhaps in the mood for seafood… Like spiny lobster."

"What, you a fan?" *Adding it at the end makes you sound particularly passionate about it.*

Totsuka followed up with "I'd like to have something with more veggies."

Miss Hiratsuka agreed. "Same here… For the antiaging properties."

"One of you is taking this too seriously… Anyway, we've got zero consensus here." Nobody was making an effort to compromise on anything. *It doesn't look like anything's gonna get decided after all.* I was thinking like a spectator, when Yukinoshita suddenly looked at me.

"How about you, then? …Isn't there anything you'd like to eat?"

"Oh yeah. I guess I didn't say what I wanted. Nobody ever asks my opinion when I'm in a group, so I forgot to say."

"What a sad tendency… I believe today, at least, you can state your preference." For once, Yukinoshita gave me the freedom to say what I wanted. Oh, I normally do, but it was unusual for her to go to the trouble of asking me for my opinion.

Guess I'll have my say, then. "Okay. Then, some kind of carbs," I requested.

Miss Hiratsuka nodded. "Mm-hmm. Meat, seafood, vegetables, and carbs… If that's the situation, let me think over this a moment."

Leave it to an adult to handle all the requests so calmly.

The similarly calm Yukinoshita said, "But if we stay around here, I think we might bump into some of the other classes. It would be nice to find somewhere not too crowded."

"Yeah," I agreed. "I don't want to be stuck in some awkward situation where we're glancing at one another but nobody's making a move."

"Do you have to put it like that…?" Yuigahama replied wearily, but she quickly got over it and folded her arms, trying to think up a place we could go. "Maybe there's some nice restaurant that isn't so well-known around here somewhere?"

Yuigahama's description must have stuck with Miss Hiratsuka, as she seemed to hit on something. "Now that I think of it, I know someone who's fairly in the know about these things… Wait just a moment. I'm going to make a quick call." She stepped away for a bit to dial someone. "Oh, sorry this is out of the blue. It's me."

Watching her from afar, Totsuka tilted his head. "Someone in the know… I wonder who she means."

"I dunno. But someone familiar with a lot of obscure but good restaurants would have to be someone who parties a lot, so it's probably no one good," I said.

Yuigahama's expression turned sour. "That's pretty narrow-minded of you…"

"Indeed it is. Some people are no good even if they don't party a lot. I won't name names, though." Yukinoshita smiled at me.

Hey, you're making it pretty explicit here. "Come on, don't give me that nice little smile."

Finished her phone call, Miss Hiratsuka returned. "Sorry for the wait. There's a nice place just past the train station—somewhere we can have meat, fish, and veggies. I reserved a table, so let's go," she said.

So we followed after her and came to a shop with the traditional split curtains hanging in front of the entrance.

"Oh, this is it. I'll check our seats," Miss Hiratsuka said, and she pulled open the sliding door with a rattle and went inside.

While we waited for her, we examined the storefront.

Looking at the curtains, Zaimokuza muttered, "Hmm, Yoshie's Okonomiyaki and Monjayaki…"

"From the curtains, I figure someone named Yoshie runs the place." I had nothing else to do, so I did Zaimokuza the favor of conversing with him.

Yuigahama, who seemed equally at loose ends, joined in. "It'd be surprising if someone else ran it, huh?"

During our incredibly trivial conversation, we could hear voices within the restaurant.

"Sorry for taking so long."

"Uh-uh, it's totally fine."

Miss Hiratsuka was discussing something with someone inside—it seemed she was with the person who had found her this restaurant.

Noticing their presence, Totsuka took a little peek into the shop. "Oh, it looks like someone else got here ahead of us."

"Then we might as well go in, too," said Yukinoshita.

"Yeah!" Komachi followed her inside.

The rest of us passed through the curtains, and I closed the door behind us. But then, when the person in front stopped, I suddenly pitched forward to keep from slamming into her.

Yukinoshita, in the lead, had screeched to a halt.

Why'd she stop? I wondered, looking ahead, and I discovered an unexpected presence.

Sitting in a seat at the back was Yukinoshita's older sister, Haruno Yukinoshita. She waved a hand, a smile on her face. "Heeey, Yukino-chan!"

In contrast with Haruno's cheer, the younger Yukinoshita was ice-cold. "...Why are you here?"

"Shizuka-chan invited me. Tee-hee." Haruno giggled innocently, but Yukinoshita's glacial stare didn't waver at all.

"..."

"D-don't give me that nasty look. That hurts, geez. It's a special day, so can't we be good sisters just for today, at least?"

"Just for today, hmm?" Yukinoshita glared straight at Haruno.

"Yes, for one day." Haruno was smiling, but her eyes were locked on her sister's. The tension between them did not abate.

"Well, fine..." Yukinoshita blew out a breath, and then finally, things relaxed enough that we could have a normal conversation.

Do that at home, guys, okay?

It seemed Yukinoshita was on board now, as she walked to the back of the restaurant, and we followed after her.

Haruno waved casually at the rest of us coming up behind her. Yuigahama noticed her and called out. "Oh, Haruno!"

"Gahama-chan! Yahallo!"

When Haruno beat her to her own greeting, Yuigahama replied with some confusion and a little distate. "Y-yahallo, Miss Haruno."

"Are you trying to be polite...?" I muttered.

When I followed in after Yuigahama, Haruno raised a hand to greet me, too. "And yahallo to you, too, Hikigaya!"

"Hey," I replied with a casual bow, and then Komachi pushed me aside to come forward. *She's weirdly into this...*

"I think this is the first I've spoken with you properly! Thank you so much for always dealing with my brother. I'm his sister, Komachi. And this is Totsuka and Snowflake."

"Oh, my, my, thank you for always being a good friend to Yukino-chan. I'm her sister, Haruno." She bowed politely after Komachi briefly introduced Totsuka and Zaimokuza. Well, I'm not sure if that counted as an introduction for Zaimokuza.

"H-hello..." Totsuka greeted her a little nervously.

Haruno replied kindly, "Oh, hello. Be good to Yukino-chan, okay?"

And then, having waited until the time was ripe, Zaimokuza took the stage. "Burrraaah! I believe this is the first I've laid eyes upon thee! I am Yoshiteru Zaimokuza, master swordsman general! Prostrate thyself before me!"

Agh, there he goes..., I thought.

But Haruno just laughed. "Ah-ha! What a unique character! You're funny! ♪ I think I'll have a good time talking to you."

...For real? The way she handled him left me speechless.

And Zaimokuza was ecstatic. "H-herm-herm! 'T-tis an honor and a pleasure to make your acquaintance!"

Watching Zaimokuza's meaningless salute to Haruno, I said to Yukinoshita, beside me, "Your sister's social mask really is perfect... I couldn't never manage Zaimokuza like that."

"Oh, indeed. She is impressive, if I may say so of my own sister."

I couldn't figure out if she was being ironic when she said that or not.

A very wound-up Zaimokuza zoomed loudly toward us, rambling at warp speed. "H-H-H-H-H-Hachiman! Ye gods! Finally, an angel has descended upon such a hopeless man as me! Right?! That meant this is it, right?!"

"Hold on and calm down, Zaimokuza. Listen, if you translate what she said into modern Japanese, it means... *You're weird and gross. Talking to you is the most I can handle, and any more than that is a whole lotta nope.* ☆ *So gross.*" I gave him my calm analysis.

This seemed to cool his head, and he started to accept reality. "What? What a most perfect translation! 'Tis as if you had the very seal of Solomon! Is that your Solomon Style?"

"Naw, it's not a special power or anything. It's just one of those things people like you and me used to misunderstand in middle school. Figure it out already."

While I was admonishing Zaimokuza, Komachi stepped forward. "But anyway, Haruno, you're really pretty! No surprises there, since you're Yukino's sister… Oh! A new bride candidate! Not bad, Bro!"

"Not bad what?" I asked.

Komachi gave me a cheek-splitting grin. "Komachi just keeps getting more and more big-sister candidates! Aside from the ones here, there's, like, um… Taishi's sister Kawa… Kawaa… Kawa-something, too."

"You should remember her name…"

Remember, um, Kawa… Kawabata, at least.

Komachi swiftly forgot about Kawa-something and hopped over to Haruno. "Anyway, for Komachi, having more big-sister candidates is a great thing! I'd love to call you my big sister, Haruno!"

"This girl is so funny, huh, Hikigaya? A second little sister, huh? Awww~. You're sooo *cuuute*, Komachi-chan! I'll take you home with me~. ♪" When Komachi approached, Haruno petted her head and wrapped her in a tight hug.

In her arms, Komachi was on her way up to the heavens. "Oof, so soft and happy…"

"All right, could you please get your hands off my sister?" As her big brother, I had to firmly and resolutely take my sister back now.

When I went to pull them apart, Haruno smiled mischievously, looking into my eyes. "Whoops… So am I allowed to put my hands on you, Hikigaya?"

I was startled—but I wasn't about to let something like that rattle me now. I made an effort to keep calm. "Depends on how you do it. If you mean like punching or kicking, I'll have to say no—Miss Hiratsuka is the only one allowed to hit me."

"So he's resigned himself to it…," Yukinoshita said with exasperation, and Haruno gave a lamenting sigh.

"Oh, that's the sort of contrarian remark I expected. I'm impressed."

I wouldn't say *speak of the devil*, but right then, Miss Hiratsuka came walking up from the back of the restaurant.

"Oh, have you all said hello to Haruno? I've spoken to the management, and they're letting us take the table in the back, so go have a blast. And we start with a toast. Take your seats."

It seemed she'd gone to find us some group seating. *There's someone you can count on. Still wish she didn't punch me.*

When we were all in our seats, Miss Hiratsuka picked up a glass. At that signal, the rest of us raised our glasses, too. Turning around to sweep her eyes over everyone, Miss Hiratsuka led the toast. "All right. To a successful festival!"

"Cheers!"

We all drained our glasses.

The main dish here was *monjayaki*. Well, there was no main anything, really; it started with the climax.

Monjayaki.

Given it's fairly inexpensive, you can eat it for a good while, and you can also enjoy adding a variety of different toppings to suit your own taste, so high school kids tend to go for it...I think. I don't really know what high school kids like.

It's extremely simple to make. First, you fry up the toppings and then use them to make a donut shape. In the biz, we call 'em "nuts." So you pour the batter right in the middle, and then once it starts bubbling, you mix it all up and wait awhile. I can't say it looks pretty, but it tastes a lot better than it looks.

There are many things to be learned from *monjayaki*.

For example, how you shouldn't judge people based on appearances, and how you can't judge light novels based on their titles, and...nothing else in particular, nope.

As I was lost in thought, a savory scent wafted toward me. Glancing at the flat grill, I saw the *monjayaki* was about done.

Haruno noticed, too, and said, "It's looking pretty good now."

"Oh yeah. Well then, let's dig in," said Miss Hiratsuka, and on that cue, we all took up our spatulas and started eating.

Shocked, Yuigahama yelped, "What the heck?! This is good! Oh my god! It's way better than it looks!"

"Hey, don't talk about how it looks. If I look too hard at it, I won't want to eat it anymore," I said, a little irked.

Haruno's sharp ears picked this up, and she leaned over toward me. "Oh my, Hikigaya. It doesn't look like you've eaten much. Oh well. Big Sister will help you. All right, say *ah*." Beside me, she gently held out her spatula. Her body pressed up close to me.

I twisted around in the small space in an attempt to avoid it. "Uh, um, I'm fine eating at my own pace."

"Come on now, go ahead! You worked so *hard*, Hikigaya, so I think I can do this much for you. Here, Hikigaya. Say *ahhh*."

Even though I refused and refused her, this woman just kept pushing. *She feels soft and smells nice, and I can't— Ah, hey! Don't touch my thigh…hngh.*

As I started to doubt whether I could take much more of this, a voice cold like ice water poured over us. "Haruno. Nothing good will come of spoiling him, so stop it."

"Y-yeah. U-um, that kinda stuff is, uh, um…," Yuigahama added, somewhat flustered.

With the two girls both telling her off, Haruno lowered her hand, blinked, and gave a mean smile. "Oh my, so you're joining in, too, Gahama-chan? Oh-ho…this is getting kinda fun."

One other person at the table wore a similar smile. "Oh-ho indeed! I'd agree this is a pretty interesting development, in Komachi terms."

"I don't get that feeling at all, though," I said. "Things are just getting awkward."

Haruno and Komachi might be a dangerous combination. Put the two together, and they're Twenty Million Powers. But mixing black and black only gets you more black… It's just like Gin said, really…

"But does this count as a party? We're simply eating *monja*." I asked the question that had struck me as I ate my food.

Yuigahama's expression turned uncertain. "Huh? I—I dunno…"

You don't know, either…?

Yukinoshita put her hand to her jaw and tilted her head. "What should we do, specifically?"

At times like these, the thing to do is bring up other specific examples. And then based on those, you come up with an approximation to help you grasp the overall picture. With this thought in mind, I decided to ask about the most recent party-like event, the one to celebrate the cultural festival.

"What did you do for the after-party?" I asked.

Yuigahama stared into thin air with a cute little noise and thought back. "Huh? Well, like, we had it at a live music venue…and we all just kinda partied and had fun?"

"That explanation functionally tells us nothing." With absolutely no concrete details, I was still in the dark. So I was forced to ask someone else who'd gone.

When I glanced at Yukinoshita, she said, "Some people who performed during the cultural festival were onstage."

"There was also a DJ, and people were dancing," Totsuka added as well.

Oh, dancing. "Hmph, good thing I didn't go…"

Haruno nodded with big-sister-like composure as she listened to the others describe the party. "Yes, yes, that's nice and healthy. Once you're an adult, after-parties are all about drinking."

"Is that right?" I couldn't really imagine that, so I looked at Miss Hiratsuka, our resident adult.

"Yeah. You go around saying hello to everyone, pouring drinks as you go, and if someone's glass is empty, you quietly order an extra drink."

"Whoa, that sounds exhausting." Yuigahama put in a lot of effort in the realm of social consideration, so she was a little boggled. For me, that would be totally impossible. I'd probably just end up causing trouble for my coworkers, so it'd be best if I didn't get a job. I'm sure unemployment can be its own form of kindness.

Yuigahama's remark made Miss Hiratsuka smile. "Hey, it's not all bad. There are bingo tournaments and Secret Santas, too."

"Bingo!" For some reason, Zaimokuza reacted to that word. Not in any meaningful way.

"Just mentioning that part makes it seem pretty fun~," commented Haruno.

"I think I wouldn't mind joining in if there were prizes!" Komachi reacted, too.

Hey, that's, like, material greed, isn't it?

But Miss Hiratsuka ignored their excitement with a soft little sigh. "But when you're the one who has to run it, it's hell…"

"Huh?" I replied instinctively. Her phrasing had unsettled me.

But Miss Hiratsuka didn't continue immediately. She raised a hand to call the server. "Oh, a whiskey and soda, please." Then she downed it all in one go and started talking. "First of all, underlings have to handle the reception and cloakroom. You deal with guest after guest while they're all pouring in. If you're bad at it, the flow bottlenecks in front of the counter, and that puts a hell of a lot of pressure on you. And then, right as you start to think you've survived and maybe you can relax, you have to spend the party time watching people's stuff so it doesn't get stolen. Some people will leave partway. And then by the time you're freed from cloakroom duty, the party is already in full swing, jazz, and blues. Oh, another whiskey and soda, please."

"Y-you're drinking really fast…" Totsuka was scared (how cute).

Unbothered by his fear, Miss Hiratsuka gulped down her new drink and set down the glass. "And what's more…"

"There's more…?" *We've already heard some pretty awful stuff…*

Maybe it was the booze, but Miss Hiratsuka had no intention of stopping. "Of course, you have to deal with the guests' bags and coats when they leave, too. And that's when all kinds of issues crop up—like their bags go missing, or they never checked them in, and then you think it's over, and *then* you're running over to reserve a spot for the after-party, and on top of *that*, you have to catch a taxi for the bosses to take home, and just when you think everyone's *finally* gone, you're left holding on to some lost item whose owner never shows up… Oh, sorry, another whiskey and soda." Miss Hiratsuka was downing her drinks at an impressive pace.

Haruno chided her. "Shizuka-chan, you're drinking too much, okay?"

"That was all just complaints…" Yukinoshita looked rather tired and exasperated after being subjected to all that.

But her hard-heartedness stirred some sympathy in me for Miss Hiratsuka. "Hey, let her complain, at least. I'm sure she can never say this stuff normally."

"Oh, you're surprisingly understanding about this," our teacher said.

Hey, I was a slave to the system on the Cultural Festival Committee. I understand a thing or two.

I'm sure she was dying to do some grumbling at times like these. Generally, if you complain, people always tell you you're not the only one having a hard time. Why do I have to have a hard time just because everyone else is? What's the causal relationship here?

Miss Hiratsuka smoked a cigarette as she continued listlessly. "Agh…you kids have tomorrow off, but I have work, you know…"

"Aren't you sulking a little too much…?" I gave her a mildly exasperated look, but when her eyes met with mine, she suddenly became energetic.

"All right then, let's do it."

"Do what?"

"The top three remarks I can't stand hearing from bosses and superiors!" She was winding herself up and up even though the rest of us were not, and I was not going to encourage her.

"We're not doing that. We are *not* doing that." *I don't wanna do such a sad segment… It'll make me even more averse to getting a job…*

I doubted anyone wanted to do it, but she was really excited about it.

"Well then, in third place…"

"So you're going to do it whether we want you to or not…" Yukinoshita shivered, and Miss Hiratsuka poised to make her announcement.

"In third place! *If you're not taking notes, that means you got everything, right?*"

Her delivery, obviously an imitation of someone, landed a critical hit in Yuigahama's memory. "Oh… They said that to me at a part-time job…"

"Now that I think of it, they told me that at my part-time job, too. And when I did it perfectly, it just made them even grumpier…," I muttered.

As the mood at the table got darker and darker, Miss Hiratsuka blew away our gloom with her excited presentation of number two. "In second place! *I've got something to talk to you about tomorrow, so please make time for that.*"

As we listened, the scene grew even grimmer.

"The polite way of putting it actually makes it scarier…," said Totsuka.

"That would bother me so much, I wouldn't be able to work all day…," said Yuigahama.

Even Yukinoshita agreed. "And they indicate a specific time, but they don't tell you what it's about…" All three of them stared down at a corner of the flat grill.

Perhaps concerned for the futures of these young people, Miss Hiratsuka gave a classroom-style explanation. "That one is pretty rough, so watch out. You'll spend all night wondering if you should skip work the next day. Agh, seriously, what am I gonna do tomorrow…?"

"They just told you that today, huh…?" Komachi gave the thirtyish teacher a look of pity.

Unable to take it anymore, Yuigahama cried out, "Not allowed! No real stuff allowed! It'll make me too sad!"

"Ha-ha-ha! That sort of thing is no big deal. Now, what you've all been waiting for: number one!" Miss Hiratsuka laughed it off bravely, but this was too much for me.

"There's something even worse…? Enough… This hurts…"

"Nobody's waiting for it…" Just as Yukinoshita said, nobody wanted to hear this—or rather, I think hearing it might ensure that all of us would never want to enter the workforce, ever.

But there was no sign Miss Hiratsuka was stopping.

"In first place: *'I told you if there's anything you don't understand, then ask, right?'*

"*'Come on, I wanted you to think over this much on your own, at least…'*

"*'Hey, why did you just do it without consulting me?'* in an endless loop."

Instantly, those three lines spun around in my head like an ouroboros. "No matter what you do, you're screwed… Is this a bug in the world or what?"

"The ultimate triple threat, from which there is no escape! So this is the Tenchi-matou! Defense, Attack, and Magic all in one stance!" Zaimokuza gulped, wiping sweat off his brow. That three-stage attack was bound to take down half of all fresh employees.

As the revelation crushed our spirits, the one person who looked unaffected, Haruno, grinned. "Well, the world is an unreasonable place, so there's no helping it."

"I don't wanna get a job…," I moaned.

We'd been forced to witness the ugly side of society. A murky cloud hung over us.

In attempt to cheer things up, Haruno suddenly suggested an idea. "Now it's all gloomy. We should play a game!"

"Yeah!" Komachi quickly got on board.

But somehow, I didn't have a very good feeling about this… "Not these two together...," I muttered, but it seemed nobody else realized the danger they posed.

Totsuka tilted his head in a pure expression of curiosity. "What sort of game would we play?"

"Oh, that's a good question." Haruno pointed at him.

Then Miss Hiratsuka, now finally calm, joined in on the conversation. "Well, the standard is the king's game, I figure."

"That's something a middle-aged man would pick." Yuigahama offered her artless impression.

This silenced Miss Hiratsuka once again. "Hngh..."

In the corner of my eye, I could see Zaimokuza trembling. "Th-the king's game, with girls... The dream situation...... D-d-d-d-do you want me to bring you support from a sponsor? Bandai, the company that brings good times!"

"Calm down. Bandai isn't a sponsor."

In fact, we're actually recruiting sponsors. There's still time!

Someone else at the table reacted to the term *king's game*. She quietly straightened her posture, turning a piercing gaze toward us. "The king's game... If we're competing for a throne, I must win. Might I ask the rules?"

"Hey, it's not like that at all!" Yuigahama cried out in shock.

Miss Hiratsuka, now revived, folded her arms with an *mm-hmm*. "I should explain. In the king's game, we draw straws to decide on a king, and that person can give any order. We call out, *Who's the king?* ♪, and we all draw at once. You got that? It's *Who's the king?* ♪ Okay?"

"She's way too into this..."

"It's cute how she's so excited about the *Who's the king?* ♪ bit...," I said.

After learning the rules, Komachi's eyes sparkled. "You can order anything... That sounds amazing!"

Seriously, my little sister is such a scheming— Wait. "Ah! If we can order anything, then Totsuka..."

"Chance!" Zaimokuza was on the same wavelength as me. I didn't even finish my sentence, but he understood, which means Totsuka's cuteness is universally appreciated, right?

Totsuka, now a being on par with an international super-idol, seemed scared of this game. This only increased his cuteness factor by 40 percent. "It's a little bit scary, if it's *anything*."

"True… I'm sure certain people among us would give nasty orders." Yukinoshita glowered in my direction.

"Hey, you," I said. "Could you quit it with the glaring?"

Since some opposing opinions had been presented, Haruno suggested something else. "Okay, so instead of the king's game, then, let's do the Yamanote Line game."

"Oh. I'm fine with that," Yuigahama agreed.

But as a resident of Chiba, I didn't really know the Yamanote Line game. "I don't ride the Yamanote Line much, so I wouldn't know it."

"So then the Sobu Line game. It doesn't matter what you call it. You all know the rules?"

It doesn't matter what you call it…?

Haruno scanned the crowd to confirm, and Yukinoshita belligerently replied, "No problems here."

Making sure everyone else was okay with it, too, Miss Hiratsuka leaned forward. "All right then, let's get started. The call for this is *Sobu Line game, yaaay!* ♪"

"She's got it bad for this. It's kinda cute…," I muttered. I could almost get into her super-excited, nearly giddy mood, which was freaking me out.

Still as cheery as could be, Miss Hiratsuka called out, "Sobu Line game! ♪"

"Yaaay!" Everyone called out in response.

She followed up with "Who's the Sobu Line?!"

"Is this how this game goes?!" Surprised, Yuigahama did a double take.

"Oh. Me."

"Herm, and I am a user of the Sobu Line."

"And you guys are gonna keep going, too?!"

Wait, this isn't how the game goes...? Am I wrong? Yuigahama?

"This *is* different from the king's game from earlier, isn't it?" Yukinoshita muttered, folding her arms with a *hmm*.

Yes, this is different from the game we were just discussing, isn't it?

Looking over the crowd of people who, including me, didn't know the rules at all, Haruno gave a wry smile. "Looks like I have to actually explain the rules... Well then, my lovely assistant: Please tell them."

Assistant? Who? I thought, and Komachi's hand shot up.

"Heya, I'm your lovely assistant Komachi! All righty, I will now explain the rules of the Sobu Line game. Basically, you request something, and then everyone answers in rhythm!"

"That's way too basic... You could turn that into a programming language."

But Komachi didn't care and continued her sloppy explanation. "It's like the everywhere anytime game, but, like, you know. So anyway, let's get started~!"

"First, we have to decide on a subject," Haruno said.

Totsuka considered with a *hmm*. "It's hard to think up something out of the blue..."

Seeing his hesitation, Miss Hiratsuka said, "When you're playing this game at parties or group dates, it's typical to pick a theme that can provide a foundation for conversation after the game. You should remember that."

Komachi nodded, impressed. "Ohhh, is that right? The more you know!"

"Though I get the feeling Miss Hiratsuka's not capitalizing on that at all. That's sad..." *Why does she understand so much and yet still can't get married...?* I could almost shed a tear for her.

Ignoring me, Yukinoshita tilted her head. "But what sort of topic would stimulate conversation?"

"If you go with your hobby or favorite foods as a theme, you'll have more things to talk about afterward. Like, *Oh, so your hobby is fishing; I'd like to go, too.* Something like that."

Miss Hiratsuka's example answer made Yuigahama's eyes sparkle. "You're right! Wow! You're a super-natural!"

"It's sad you're so shrewd about it, and you still can't get results…"

Why can't she get married if she can do all that…?

"All right then, let's make the subject hobbies."

"Let's give it a shot!"

Haruno picked a subject from the examples Miss Hiratsuka had given, and Komachi gave the start signal.

And of course, the one to lead the game was Miss Hiratsuka herself. "Sobu Line game! ♪"

"Yaaay!" everyone replied.

Then Miss Hiratsuka announced the topic, and I could almost hear the *whee* ☆ in her voice. "Everywhere, anytime, a hobby you're really into right now~."

First came Komachi. "Karaoke!"

We clapped to the beat, and Yuigahama followed. "You beat me to it! Um, cooking!"

Huh? Really? I thought as we moved on to Yukinoshita.

"Horseback riding."

Singing, horseback riding… She's got a wide range of interests.

After that was Totsuka's turn. "Tennis!"

And my racket and ball, too… was something I did not have the time to say, as there was another clap on the beat, and then it was Zaimokuza.

"Herm, writing my draft."

I see; so that's his hobby… Well, never mind him.

Next was Miss Hiratsuka's turn. "Going for drives."

Ohhh, I can see her with a cool hobby like that.

And next was Haruno. Following the clap, she went along with the rhythm to announce her interest. "Travel."

Huh, sounds like university students have some spare time on their hands, I thought, and then there was a clap, and all eyes gathered on me.

"Huh? My hobby...? P-people-watching...?"

"..."

The *Huh? What's that supposed to mean?* silence was rather painful.

"You're out, Hikigaya," Miss Hiratsuka declared.

"Huh? Hey, wait. People-watching is a legit hobby!" I attempted to argue, but the reaction from the others wasn't favorable.

"That basically means you don't do anything, doesn't it...?" Yuigahama said.

Yukinoshita added, "In your case, that's less a hobby and more of a behavioral pattern, isn't it? It's the kind of creature you are, isn't it?"

"Don't talk about a person like they're a wild animal. I mean, if I'm out, then Yuigahama's out, too! Cooking is *not* your hobby!" I said.

Yuigahama was quite indignant. "Rude! I love watching people cook!"

"Watching people cook? That's novel...," commented Yukinoshita.

Ignoring Yuigahama's groundbreaking choice of hobbies, Haruno gave a somewhat mocking smile. "I really don't know about calling people-watching a hobby... At the very least, I've never heard it in my sphere."

"Of course not. Anyone who says people-watching is their hobby generally doesn't have friends. It's on a higher level, so to speak, permitted only to the chosen ones," I announced with pride.

Yukinoshita put her hand to her temple and said with exasperation, "That's just a bad habit."

Huh? I-is people-watching...bad?

As I was busy being rather shocked, Komachi chided me. "Bro, if you're gonna overcome lonerdom, you should get a proper hobby."

"It's fine. I have no plans to overcome my lonerdom anyway, and I don't even want to. I mean, there's something wrong with the idea that it's unpleasant to be alone."

"Here he goes again...," groaned Yuigahama, sounding suddenly tired.

"What you're saying is not at all incorrect, but you're the wrong person to say it," said Yukinoshita in a similar tone. They both seemed ready to resign themselves to their fate.

Don't give up, guys!

Haruno clapped her hands. "Oh, but speaking as an older sister, I think it's good to have a hobby, you know?"

Miss Hiratsuka gave an appreciative *hmm*. "Haruno, you always say things that sound so reasonable on the surface."

"Shizuka-chan, that's a horrible way to put it!"

"It's the truth." Yukinoshita added another blow, and Haruno puffed up her cheeks in a pout.

"And you're being mean, too, Yukino-chan! But I really am concerned about Hikigaya!"

"You? Concerned? Please make your jokes at least somewhat believable."

"I'm serious! I mean, he's going to be living a lonely life all by himself, right? So I think he should at least have a hobby to throw himself into."

"Hey, that was super-nasty," I said. "That was about three times worse than you, Yukinoshita. Is no one gonna do anything about this?" *Why do these sisters wound me so much?*

As I searched for comfort, I found the angel for my ears, oh, Totsuka. His voice had reached me. "But it's fun to hang out together with someone who shares your hobbies, huh?"

"Okay, everyone, hurry up and think up a hobby for me. Chop-chop, what if you don't make it in time?"

"Why are you suddenly acting all bossy...?" Yuigahama huffed at me.

But of course I would get bossy about it. I mean, if I could acquire a hobby to have in common with Totsuka, I'd have half the world, you know?

Everyone seemed to be trying to think up a hobby for me, folding their arms and tilting their heads and going *hmm*. They're all such good people...

The first one to arrive at an answer was Yukinoshita. "The safe answer would be reading, wouldn't it?"

But Yuigahama's reply was merciless. "Huh? That's kinda dull."

"...Is it dull? ...I... I find it fun, though." Yukinoshita sounded a little hurt, a heavy air hanging around her.

Picking up on this, Yuigahama swiftly backpedaled. "Ack! I-I'm sorry! With you, Yukinon, it works, so it's totally okay!"

"Oh-ho...Yukino-chan got upset. Wow, Gahama-chan," Haruno marveled.

"Wait, so it's unacceptably boring if *I* read...?" If you think about it, that just hurts me indirectly...

"But it's true more active hobbies have a healthier image," said Komachi.

Zaimokuza crossed his arms and put on an arrogant attitude. "Herm, so then what about *sabage*?"

"*Saba...ge*? ...*Saba*?" Yukinoshita tilted her head at the unfamiliar term.

"It means survival games, Yukinoshita. Basically, intense play fights with airsoft guns," Miss Hiratsuka explained.

Yukinoshita smiled at me with understanding. "I see... I think that might be perfect for you, Hikigaya. You would have an aptitude for sniping from blind spots and things of that nature."

"Hey, don't act so happy about mocking my invisibility."

"Yukino-chan, you can't say things like that," said Haruno.

Oh-ho, as expected of the big sister. So she does actually scold her sister for this behavior?

"Hikigaya wouldn't be able to get together enough people, so he wouldn't be able to start a game in the first place. It would be cruel to give him undue hope."

"Your sense of humor is pitch-black! Are you the coffee sisters? You're gonna keep me wide-awake here." *What is up with these two?*

As I was suffering at the hands of the Yukinoshita family's DNA,

Miss Hiratsuka offered her own suggestion. "Hmm. Then maybe fishing would work. You can do it by yourself, and I do it quite a lot. I-if you like, I might even teach you."

"Herm. As do I... But this is bait!"

"Old meme. Okay, next, next." As I casually brushed off Zaimokuza, other suggestions piled up.

Yuigahama was the next to speak. "But, like, hobbies where you need equipment are hard for a high school kid. That stuff costs money." This was a rather budget-wise opinion, but, well, she was right.

Yukinoshita also agreed, nodding. "Then we should make it something that could be considered an extension of his current lifestyle."

My normal lifestyle... *Oh, it's kinda...well...*, I was thinking, when Totsuka looked up at me.

"What do you do at home, Hachiman?"

"Huh? Well...not anything, really... There's nothing I can really point to..." Yes, nothing I could point to in front of everyone...

I quietly averted my eyes, but as if she had read my mind, Haruno smiled and brought the conversation around to Komachi. "Komachi-chan? Could you tell us?"

"I—I wanna know, too!" said Yuigahama. "I mean, um, I guess."

"Oh, this sounds intriguing." Miss Hiratsuka also expressed interest.

So Komachi went *hmm* as she mentally sketched out my typical routine. "Um, well..."

"No, don't, Komachi," I warned, but of course, she wasn't going to listen.

"When my brother gets home, he lies around watching old anime on Chiba TV, and after that, he studies in his room. Or reads books and plays video games."

"Whoa, boring." Yuigahama's impression was really damn honest.

"Leave me alone... I have a good time. It's great when *Wataru* and stuff is on."

"Herm. I do something similar on weekdays."

That's Zaimokuza for you—loath as I was to admit it, he understood.

Actually, he was the only one who did. Everyone else was acting rather aghast.

In an attempt to help, Totsuka said to Komachi, "He's got school and club, so there's nothing you can do about that, right? So then what about weekends?"

"Um, on weekends, after Super Hero Time, he watches Precure... and cries about it..."

"Whoa, at that age..." Yuigahama, like the rest of them, was horrified.

Objection. I mean, like, you guys aren't watching it? What the hell is with that? These days, even preschool kids are watching it, you know? Don't get left behind, okay? Don't you love the smiles and glitter?

"He also goes to the library and bookstores and stuff, but he's always doing the same things, you know?"

"As long as he's having fun, I can't be upset," Yukinoshita said with pity.

"Shuddup. I don't wanna hear it from you. I mean, you're not much different, are you? You don't have friends, and you like reading," I shot back.

Yukinoshita swept her hair back off her shoulders with a derisive snort. "Don't compare us. I...," Yukinoshita began, but Haruno cut in.

"Heh-heh-heh, when Yukino-chan lived at home..."

That made Yukinoshita freeze. "Haruno, don't. Just don't."

But something like that was not going to stop her. This was just like what had happened with me. Haruno smiled gleefully and continued. "Come on, it's not like this will cost you anything. On weekends, Yukino-chan would pour tea and read in the living room, or watch movies. Occasionally, she would play piano."

"Ohhh, that's very Yukinon," Yuigahama said.

Totsuka nodded as well. "I don't think it's anything to be

super-embarrassed about. It's elegant and cool." It fit Yukinoshita's image perfectly.

"Yeah, it comes off like something a fine young lady from a rich family would do. I think it fits you," I said.

"I-is that so…? T-to me, it's normal, so it's hard to see it that way…" With everyone singing her praises, Yukinoshita twisted around uncomfortably. Her voice was calm, but she was blushing a little.

"That's so wonderful!" Komachi said, and Haruno joined in, too.

"Right? But Yukino-chan is even more wonderful when she's in her room."

"Hold on right there. How do you know that? Stop, Haruno. Please stop." Yukinoshita started getting more serious about putting a halt to this until she was all but begging. But I think her pleas just made Haruno want to keep going.

The ultimate grin on her face, Haruno continued gleefully. "When she's in her room, she'll cuddle a Ginnie the Grue pillow and search for cat videos online, and she'll watch them like it's the most serious thing."

"…Agh." Yukinoshita breathed a deep, utterly woeful sigh of mixed shame and grief.

"Uh, um, er, well, I guess…" Yuigahama tried to be considerate and smooth things over somehow.

Yukinoshita slowly lifted her head. Her eyes flashed open. "…Yes… well…even if I did, hypothetically…*hypothetically*…so what?" Seeing her straighten up and swell with pride was strangely awe-inspiring.

"Whoa…she fought back… That's some ironclad emotional resilience," I murmured.

"Ohhh. But if we're talking about cats, then my brother also plays with our cat a lot at home. So maybe cats are kinda like a hobby for him, like Yukino."

"What kind of hobby is that? The number-one recommendation of top breeders?"

Yukinoshita reacted to a certain word Komachi had said. "Cats…"

"H-Hikki! Dogs! Dogs are good, too!"

"Cats…"

"Dogs!"

Yukinoshita and Yuigahama glared at each other for a second. The two of them engaged in a silent battle of stares. And then, for some reason, their eyes turned to me.

"Cats, right, Hikigaya?!"

"Dogs, right, Hikki?!"

"Uh, um, don't ask me… Also, Yukinoshita, you get way too intense about cat-related contests."

Neither of them listened to me, instead repeating their own positions.

"Dogs!"

"…Cats."

Watching them, Komachi and Haruno couldn't hide their excitement and rose to their feet.

"Flaaame waaaar!"

"Beat her down, Yukino-chan!"

"And so the time has come for: *My Classmates and Acquaintances Fight Too Much!* commentated by Komachi Hikigaya. Cat lovers versus dog lovers clash in this dog fight— W-wait, is it a cat fight? Well, whatever! Cat and dog fight, ready, go!"

And then out of nowhere, a gong clanged.

"Ah! Hikki, you like Chiiba-kun, and he's a dog! See, Hikki's a dog person!"

"Hmm… I see." *It's true—Chiiba-kun is a dog… He* is *a dog, right? If he is, I may not be able to deny that I am a dog person.*

The commentators were excited to see my heart swayed a little.

"Ohhh, and a preemptive attack from Yui lands a critical hiiiit! Miss Hiratsuka, what's your analysis of that attack?"

"Hmm, a cunning strategy to manipulate his love of Chiba."

But Yukinoshita was not about to take this lying down. "Not bad, Yuigahama. But in order to walk a dog, one must go outside. So a shut-in like Hikigaya would be a cat lover, right?"

"Ngh, it's true; I don't leave the house very much, so I can't argue…"

"And Yukino isn't letting up, either! Her brilliant counter connects! What do you think of that, Haruno of the Yukino faction?"

"It's very like her to lead her opponent into taking damage. As expected of my little sister."

"All right! Neither side is relenting, and no one knows where this battle will go!"

The commentator and analyzers here are really just bullshitting… And why is my sister so into this? "Komachi, whose side are you on?"

"That's a foolish question, Bro. Komachi is on *your* side." Komachi gave a cute *tee-hee*.

She's cute, but man, she kinda pisses me off…, I thought, shooting her a little glare, when I felt a couple of tiny tugs on my sleeve.

"Hachiman, Hachiman."

Hearing my name, I turned around to see Totsuka. "Hmm? What is it, Totsuka?" I leaned close to him, and he practically whispered in my ear, "Rabbits."

"Huh?" He was so cute, I hadn't quite heard him.

But Komachi's commentating helped me understand what he meant. "Whoops! And here, a third contestant, the rabbit faction, bursts in!"

"Rabbits, Hachiman, rabbits. They're cute, too, you know?"

I wanted to say *You're way cuter*, but it was not to be. Someone else appeared to prevent me.

"Th-that's right, Hachiman! 'Tis always the role of a rabbit to invite you to a new world!"

Zaimokuza wasn't entirely wrong.

"…Yeah, that's true. All that cuteness just now nearly opened up a new world for me…"

"Indeed! Welcome to the Underground…"

"Stop it, Zaimokuza. Don't whisper in my ear." I could still feel his incredibly cool delivery in my ear, and it was a little gross.

While I was busy shooing Zaimokuza away, Totsuka was passionately lecturing on the appeal of rabbits. "You know, Hachiman, having a pet bunny is lots of fun. They're so fluffy, they're quiet, and their snoots are so wiggly when they eat!"

"Bunnies are great, Hachiman! In the name of the moon, they'll punish you! And there'll be more fan service, too!"

"It's strange, Zaimokuza. When you say it, I like rabbits less." *Does he actually even like rabbits?*

But now, unexpectedly, there were two people on the rabbit side. This new development made Komachi the commentator belt out even louder, "It looks like there's been a tag in! And now this is almost like a battle royale!"

And then even the commentators got dragged into this factional dispute. "If this is going to be a tag-team fight…then I'm with the cats, I suppose," said Miss Hiratsuka. "I've been thinking about getting one soon."

"Shizuka-chan, that's basically dooming yourself to lifelong single-dom, you know?"

"Quickly! Someone hurry up and marry this woman!" *Or else I'll have to! Get a move on!*

Now that Miss Hiratsuka had declared she was a cat person, Haruno considered the question. "Hmm. So you're a cat person, Shizuka-chan? If I'm forced to choose, then dogs, I suppose. They're loyal and always obedient."

"Your reasoning is scaring me," I muttered. How can she say stuff like that with such a brilliant smile?

The fruitless conflict went on.

"Dogs!" Yuigahama cried.

"Cats…," Yukinoshita declared.

"Rabbits," Totsuka said cutely.

"A three-way bloodbath! In the end, who will wear the shining crown of victory?!" Komachi riled them up, and all three of them looked at me.

"Hikigaya." It was an order. I didn't have a choice.

"Hikki." Her tone sounded expectant.

"Hachiman…" His look inspired my protective instincts.

"Ngh! The ultimate three-way choice between cool, passion, and cute…"

"Come on, what's your answer, Bro?!" Komachi pushed me to respond. If I didn't answer now, this situation would inevitably turn disastrous. I could tell half-baked excuses would not be accepted.

So I have no choice but to steel myself, huh…?

"…I'm…going…w-with Totsuka…"

"Why name a person?!" Yuigahama demanded.

"Answer with the name of the animal," added Yukinoshita.

The two of them got mad at me, so I corrected myself. "U-urk… rabbits."

"Yay! Hachiman, let's go see rabbits sometime!"

And then the gong rang, signaling curtain close.

"Aaand match over!" Komachi declared. "And the winner is Totsuka! Um, does this mean your hobby is Totsuka, Bro?"

"Aye, 'tis a good hobby!" Zaimokuza declared enthusiastically, for reasons unknown.

$$\times \quad \times \quad \times$$

The battle over, once things were finally calmed down again, Haruno brought the conversation back to the beginning. "A good hobby… When you think about it, that's kind of a hard one, huh? Hmm, I know a lot of people who are into cars and motorcycles…"

"But I don't have a license," I said.

"Yeah… There's also photography or music." Haruno offered a few more hobbies.

Yuigahama jumped on one of those. "Music! That's kinda cool!"

"Listening to music is a hobby, too, but what you're talking about, Yuigahama, is playing an instrument, right? I suppose the most familiar, classic instruments would be piano and guitar," said Yukinoshita.

Komachi also recommended playing an instrument. "You should do one, too, Bro! Music is great!"

"Uh, no, I'm not gonna do that…and hey, can *you* even do anything like that?"

"I can! Komachi can sing and dance, and even sing and fight!"

"Huh? What the heck? That's novel…"

Seriously, when did my little sister turn out this way…?

"It'd be cool if you played guitar or something!" Komachi was aggressive about this suggestion. It seemed this was her top choice.

But I did have an actual reason as to why I wouldn't do it. "Naw. Now that I'm in my second year of high school, starting guitar this late would just be uncool."

"I dunno…" Totsuka tilted his head doubtfully.

"No, it is, if you really think about it. Look, it comes off like you're doing it because you want attention from girls."

"I don't think so, though…," Yuigahama countered.

I decided to unleash my pet theory to overcome her argument. "It will! According to my personal research, eight times out of ten, the reason a middle school boy starts playing guitar is because he wants to get girls."

"N-now that I think about it, we have a guitar at our house for some reason…," Komachi suddenly realized.

Yes, she would also have seen it. "Exactly. It's the manifestation of budding youth that I inherited from our father: the Hikigaya family guitar."

"But I feel like I've never seen anyone play it…" Komachi trembled.

"Of course you haven't. When a guy starts guitar because of girls, he'll only consider playing in front of other people once he's good enough."

"An exemplar of someone who never improves," Yukinoshita said, chagrined.

"Exactly. Those guys generally get discouraged when they can't nail an F chord. Source: me."

"Lame..." Yuigahama mumbled something or other.

But when something's impossible, it's just impossible. "I mean, holding down an F chord just can't be done. It's Fleming's left-hand rule on the frets. Don't you underestimate humanities types."

Totally wrecked her argument. There was no longer a single reason standing as to why I should play guitar.

I basked in the glow of victory for a few moments, but Yuigahama just moaned. "Uuurgh... At this rate, we'll never find a hobby for you, Hikki..."

"Hikigaya, you never fail to amaze," said Yukinoshita. "No one is better than you at shooting down every idea from the get-go."

"Huh? Th-this is my fault...? My personality is the reason I can't find a hobby?" *I-I'm starting to feel like a real waste of a human being...*

When I started getting down on myself, Miss Hiratsuka said to me in a kindly chiding tone, "You don't need to worry so deeply over it, Hikigaya. Hobbies aren't something you force yourself to discover. Besides, starting something because other people want you to and joining in on fads are what you hate most, right?"

"Well, that's true..."

"If you're looking for something you want to do, you should just look around. There should be plenty of interesting things in your life now."

I found myself actually touched. *Will I find something like that one day? If I reexamine myself, will I find I already had what I was looking for all along?* "Miss Hiratsuka..."

But Haruno cut in to our sentimental moment for some teasing. "Yeah, yeah, the world is brimming with excitement. For example... Shizuka-chan playing the bass. Hint, hint."

"Haruno, don't tease me. I just made a really great speech."

"But that concert was great, huh? You were so cool," Totsuka gushed.

But Komachi looked down in disappointment. "Awww, I went home, so I never got to see it."

"What, you didn't see it?" I said. "Well, I only caught the end."

"Hachiman! Me too! I didn't see it, either!"

"Yeah, yeah. Why are you trying to make yourself look cute here?" I casually ignored Zaimokuza.

"Komachi wants to hear it, too…," my sister squeaked, sounding tormented. "I wanna hear Yui and Yukino singing!"

"Yeah, yeah!" Haruno agreed. "I'd love to see that side of Yukino-chan!"

"Absolutely not," Yukinoshita refused.

Yuigahama didn't seem into it, either, expressing a negative opinion. "I had fun, but it really was embarrassing."

"Besides, I doubt there'll be any more opportunities for us to perform," Miss Hiratsuka agreed.

Haruno gave us all a mischievous grin. "Oh, if that's the issue, we're good."

"Huh?" Yuigahama and Miss Hiratsuka both said at once.

$$\times \quad \times \quad \times$$

Our footsteps echoed through the silent venue.

Yuigahama, walking in front of me, looked around. "Looks like the after-party's over. Everyone's gone home."

"Yeah, it's all cleaned up. Is this where they had it?" I asked.

Yuigahama spun around to face me. "Yep, yep," she replied.

"Oh, but the stage is still set up." Just as Totsuka said, the instruments were arranged onstage.

"That was because I went and asked them to leave them for us." Haruno, coming in after us, strolled toward the platform.

Yukinoshita, following after her, asked, "Haruno, what's this about?"

"Hmm? Oh, we used to hang out here a lot. I just called upon my connections." Haruno got up onstage and twanged some instruments for a quick test. "Yeah, there's no problem with the settings on these. See? This is for you guys." She came down and returned to Yukinoshita.

"If you've gone to all this trouble, then I guess we have to... I'll do it!" Miss Hiratsuka headed for the stage with a new fire burning in her.

Yukinoshita gazed at it from a distance and softly whined, "Why me, too...?"

Haruno smirked. "My, my. You're so nervous now that Hikigaya is watching that you can't do it?"

"What are you talking about? I can hardly think of another boy who looks so unperturbed. No one could feel nervous, looking at *that*."

"Oh? Well, it's true; he does calm your nerves."

"I feel like you mean something else by that phrasing..."

"Now, now, let's just get ready, Yukino-chan."

"You don't have to pull me; I'll go. Agh..."

Haruno dragged her younger sister up onto the stage, and little by little, they got things ready.

Watching, Totsuka couldn't seem to hide his anticipation. "Wow, I'm kind of excited. There's nothing like that feeling before a live show starts."

"Right?! It's funny how you get more and more pumped even when nothing is happening," Komachi replied, looking equally giddy.

Meanwhile, someone else was getting himself stimulated in a rather different way: Zaimokuza. "Oh-ho! They are indeed remarkable! I love, *love* live shows, too! Love live! Hey! Someone bring me a set of glow sticks and a glow stick bandolier!"

"That's getting a little too prepared..." I sighed.

"I-is there a regulation length for modified electric glow sticks?!"

"I dunno... Ask the management." *I can't deal with this guy...* I separated from the three of them and walked to the rear of the venue.

Zaimokuza's called after me. "Oh-ho! Hachiman? What's wrong? Where are you going?"

"I always watch from the very back. Like at a movie theater or whatever." I continued all the way to the back wall and leaned against it.

All I could hear was tuning strings and test bangs on drums in the distance. The venue was quiet—and then came the slow approach of footsteps.

When I noticed, I looked over to see Yuigahama.

"Hikki."

"Yuigahama? What's up? You don't have to set up?"

"Oh, no. Since I don't play an instrument. U-um, Hikki, you said you weren't really watching our show during the cultural festival, right...?"

"Hmm? Yeah," I replied.

Yuigahama paused for a couple of slow breaths, then slowly put the words together. "Oh... This time, really watch, okay?"

"Well, I can't really pretend I'm not at this point... But I am." I couldn't pretend forever that I wasn't watching. And anyway, I had the feeling that, soon, I would be able to face her properly.

It wasn't like I'd go to the trouble of saying it out aloud now. That was the most I could say at the moment.

"Yeah. A-and, you know...I'm paying attention to you, too!" Though slow and faltering, she nevertheless managed to express herself honestly, and this was probably the best she could do right now.

Then she escaped to the stage at a run.

"...Ah, hey...you don't have to say that and bolt," I muttered, even though I didn't have the words to give her a decent reply.

X   X   X

The mikes onstage just barely picked up their voices, so I could hear them.

"Sorry to make you wait! Oh, Yukinon, I still only kinda remember the lyrics. For all intensive purposes."

"It's *intents* and *purposes*."

Watching their characteristic banter, Haruno smiled. "It's okay, Gahama-chan. Yukino-chan will be singing, too."

"If that's what you think, you're sorely mistaken. Letting someone constantly lean on you won't help them, in the end." Yukinoshita's posture was grumpy, but I knew she'd help Yuigahama out again, in her own way.

I think Miss Hiratsuka could see right through her, too. She was grinning. "Come on, now. Just sing together, you two. Belt it out there loud enough to reach the very back of the hall," she said, then looked to the back wall. The two girls followed her gaze to me, too.

"Agh…"

"…Will do!" they replied—Yukinoshita reluctantly and Yuigahama cheerfully.

"Oh, it looks like they're done setting up," said Totsuka.

"Yaaay! I've been waiting for this!" said Komachi. The two of them cheered up a storm, and in the edge of my vision, I saw Zaimokuza with a glow stick, flailing about wildly with his upper body.

I leaned against the wall and looked at the stage.

I did say I'd watch after all.

And then the curtain rose onstage.

X　X　X

And so another festival had concluded, and what was done was done.

Whether it be fireworks or a rocket, once you fire something up, it generally doesn't come back. But just as fireworks become memories and rockets become stars, something is left behind. So for some reason or another, I pulled out that guitar and started fiddling with it. It wasn't like anything specific had changed in me. I just sorta happened to do it.

But as I plucked away on the guitar, the door to my room was suddenly thrown open.

"Bro, quit twanging on that thing! Shut up!" Komachi cried, and then immediately, she closed the door again.

And I was left there frozen, holding the guitar and looking kind of dumb.

"You're the one who said I should have a hobby... Agh, I give up..."

Afterword

Hello, this is Wataru Watari.

It's almost spring, isn't it? And spring is the season of meetings and partings. I would like to part with work hell already.

Good-bye, life of an hour and a half of sleep a night! Hello, cardiac arrhythmia and physical reexamination! There has been some stress, too, but I'm doing all right. I'm okay with staying up all night tonight again, too!

And so, this has been Volume 7 of *My Youth Romantic Comedy Is Wrong, As I Expected*.

The moment you think the story has nothing to do with them, it is, in fact, their story, and in truth, when you probe deeper, it was their story all along. I don't understand what I'm saying here.

And so as such, starting from here, the story moves in fits and starts.

And now, the acknowledgments:

Holy Ponkan®: I've got to think of a title greater than Holy soon! How about Supreme Kai? Your work in both the regular edition and the special edition was absolutely amazing. Thank you very much.

To Sou Sagara: Thank you for miraculously writing comments on the book band for me during that busy period when the anime was being broadcast at the same time. And while I'm thanking you, I'll make sure to advertise the anime: Starting in April, the anime *My Youth Romantic Comedy Is Wrong, As I Expected* will be on TV! Please see it!

To all the staff involved with the production of the drama CD: I'm very sorry for forcing such a terrible schedule on you. All your efforts have made this drama CD really fun. Honestly, thank you so much.

To all the cast: The way you've breathed life into the characters has made them feel even closer to my heart. During each dubbing session, I was so filled with emotion! Thank you very much.

To all the writers: You guys never invite me drinking. But that's because I shouldn't just be waiting for an invitation, right? Thank you very much for all the consideration you've shown me.

To everyone involved with the media franchise: I feel deeply obliged for all the trouble I continue to cause for you. I'm really looking forward to being able to see new adaptations into various media forms. Thank you very much. I'm grateful for your continued support.

And finally, to all my readers: We've finally reached the latter half of the battle. I'm incredibly thankful: It's because of all of you that I've been able to continue writing this. Thank you so very much. I hope you will continue to stick with me.

Now then, on that note, I will set my pen down here.

On a certain day in February, in a certain place in Chiba, under warm sunlight, while sipping *hooot* MAX Coffee,

Wataru Watari

Pre-Field Trip Study Report

P. 3   **Sugawara no Michizane** was a scholar, poet, and politician of the Heian period. He's revered today as the god of learning (Tenman-Tenjin). Due to political maneuverings of a rival, he eventually lost his position and died in exile. Various natural disasters followed his death, leading people to believe it was the doing of his vengeful spirit, and seventy years after his death, he was deified.

Chapter 1 ⋯ **Hachiman Hikigaya**'s life at school is, in fact, extremely peaceful.

P. 6   **Superhuman Hardness** is a measure of the hardness of Chojin/Superhumans in *Kinnikuman*.

P. 6   **"You said diamond is unbreakable, didn't you?"** Diamond Is Unbreakable is the name of an arc in *Jojo's Bizarre Adventure*.

P. 6   **"I wouldn't even get a bit on *Where Are They Now?*"** *Ano Hito wa Ima* (Where are they now?) is a TV show about old celebrities and what they're doing now.

P. 7   **USJ** is Universal Studios Japan, the theme park.

P. 7   **"A punchline from the home o' comedy, y'all!"** Osaka is famous for *manzai*, a form of stand-up comedy done in pairs, and the home of some major *manzai* theaters. Osaka is so deeply associated with comedy that it's common for Kanto people to put on an Osaka accent to try to be funny.

P. 7   **"I reckon Conan said somethin' 'bout that."** Hachiman is referencing a line from *Detective Conan* where Conan is teasing his detective rival, Heiji, by making fun of his Kansai accent. The line has since become something of a meme.

P. 8   **"...and you're Cell telling Vegeta to laugh."** This is from *Dragon Ball*, when Cell mocks fun of Vegeta for treating him with contempt. Now Cell is so powerful that Vegeta can't damage him at all.

P. 8   The **Bon Odori** is a celebration of the dead that falls in either July or August. It traditionally involves a folk dance.

P. 11   ***Sispuri*** is the portmanteau of *Sister Princess*, a dating game / visual novel about a boy who lives with twelve sisters. It's basically *Sister Complex: The Game*.

P. 12   **"Totsuka's seriously an angel."** This is a reference to an Internet meme, "_____ is seriously an angel." It originated with an *Angel Beats!* joke about the character Kanade Tachibana that went "Angel-chan is seriously an angel" and expanded from there to include pretty much any cute character. It's generally not something you'd say about anyone 3D.

P. 13   **JSDF** is the abbreviation of Japan Self-Defense Forces.

P. 13   **"'Well, I guess we need to find another couple of people without a full group yet and dock with them.' Of the ones left over, whoever**

left the most vivid impression would carry out the operation with us." In the anime *Vividred Operation*, "docking" involves two girls merging into one super-being.

P. 15   "*Domo*, greetings, it is I, the ninja Hikigaya." This section is referencing *Ninja Slayer*, a series of novels published piecemeal on Twitter. They claim to be a (shoddy) translation of some English novels, but this is just part of the fictional backstory. The story is deliberately American-style pulp, the kind of novels Americans would write about Japan around the 1980s, and everything is spelled out in katakana with lots of strange slang to make it look American. Kinkaku-ji Temple in Kyoto is relevant to the plot of the story.

Chapter 2 ⋯ Nobody knows why **they** came to the Service Club.

P. 23   **Ryotaro Shiba** is most well-known for the novel *Ryoma Goes His Way*, about Ryoma Sakamoto, a pivotal revolutionary of the Meiji period (Kyoto was the capital city until the Meiji Restoration, and so much of his activity was there). *The Tatami Galaxy* is a modern-day novel set at Kyoto University.

P. 24   "Though actually, the names are about all that's similar about them." Kyoto Tower is a thin, pointy tower somewhat like Toronto's CN Tower, placed atop a nine-story hotel, while the Chiba Port Tower resembles a triangular prism. They don't look anything alike.

P. 24   **Kinkaku-ji** and **Ginkaku-ji** Temples are some of the most well-known temples in Kyoto. Kinkaku-ji's nickname (Temple of the Golden Pavilion) comes from how it's literally painted gold. Likewise, Ginkaku-ji was initially planned to be painted silver, but this never happened.

P. 25   **The Philosopher's Walk** is a pedestrian path along a canal lined with cherry trees, popular with tourists during the spring in particular. Its name comes from how the Kyoto University professor and philosopher Kitaro Nishida is said to have used it for his daily meditation.

P. 26   The **Shinsengumi** was a police force in Kyoto during the Meiji period and is a popular subject in anime and historical dramas. The **Ikedaya Inn** was the site of a famous armed clash known as "the Ikedaya Incident" in 1864 between the Shinsengumi and some revolutionary-minded former samurai of various clans.

P. 28   *"Myrrh? Are you planning on embalming someone?"* Tobe's original groan here is "Mu…" *Mu* is a monthly magazine focusing on occult subjects, like UFO cover-ups, astrology, and ESP. Hikigaya obviously makes the connection.

P. 28   **"…the rage was about to give me an awakening…"** In *Dragon Ball*, Saiyans awaken to their powers due to anger.

P. 28   *"…hearing that from you feels so unsettling. What's up?"* In the Japanese, he's quoting lyrics from the opening theme of the anime *Kill Me Baby*: *"Doushita no wasa wasa."* It's a play on words, where *wasa wasa* both means an unsettling feeling and also sounds like "what's up, what's up?" And *doushita no* means "what's up?"

P. 31   **"Why *do* they always have to stick multiple commercial breaks in these moments?"** Japanese variety shows on TV are known for dragging out minor revelations, often through commercial breaks, in an attempt to keep the audience in suspense.

P. 35   **Pierre Littbarski** is a German soccer manager and former player who played in JEF United Chiba, a soccer club.

P. 35   **"…you teach me, and I'll teach you…"** From the English *Pokémon* theme song. The original Japanese line here was a reference to the original Japanese Team Rocket speech, which is quite different from the English one: "If someone asks you something, the world's mercy is to answer."

P. 36   *"Phew~. I'm tired (lol)."* is the first line of a long *Madoka* copypasta. The writer is tired because he put all this effort into writing the copypasta, apparently.

P. 38   *"...what exactly do you want me to rock? This town? Your world? Around the clock?"* This was an obscure joke based on associations with the word *yoroshiku* (which, in this case, would translate to something like "glad to be working with you"), referencing the 1980s car-racing anime *Yoroshiku Mechadoc* (Hello Mechadoc) and the lyrics of the opening song to *Space Sheriff Gavan*: "Farewell, tears! Hello, courage!"

P. 38   **"...he's so attractive, you can't help but say *Whoa!*"** This is a reference to "Uho! Hot guy!" a line from the infamous meme-king *bara* manga *Kuso Miso Technique* of *yaranaika* (why don't we just do it) fame. In Japanese, *ii otoko* can mean both "good guy" and "hot guy."

Chapter 3 ··· **Kakeru Tobe** is just hopelessly shallow.

P. 42   **"...know thine enemy, know thyself, and you'll give up on a hundred battles."** The actual saying is "Know thine enemy, know thyself, and you will never lose, in a hundred battles."

P. 43   **"...maybe if you got a Shiny one and put it on your head, the masses would flock to you."** Shiny Pokemon are extremely rare recolors of Pokemon.

P. 44   **"He was unquestionably a background NPC."** In Japanese, this line is half in English, with "mob of the" in English, making it clear it's a reference to the Mob of the Dead mode in *Call of Duty*, which retains its English name in the Japanese edition.

P. 45   **"...is it the rotting that makes her Ebina?"** *Rot* here refers to the word *fujoshi*, which literally means "rotten woman" and is translated in this series as "slash fangirl."

P. 46   **"...I was mentally betting on Super Hitoshi."** This is a reference to the TV quiz show *Hitachi Sekai Fushigi Hakken* (Hitachi world mysterious discoveries). It involves betting on one of a few dolls, the normal ones called Hitoshi-kun, with one called Super Hitoshi-kun. You're less likely to win when betting on Super Hitoshi-kun.

P. 46   **"Oh man, I'm *uriouscay* as *ellhay* about that."** In the Japanese, Tobe is using "Shokotan-go," a manner of speaking made up by the celebrity Shouko Nakagawa.

P. 47   **"I hear there are more attractive, outgoing types at those sorts of events than you would think."** Hachiman means BL fan comic events, which are held for various fandoms, mostly in the Tokyo area, pretty much every weekend. ***801-chan*** refers to *Tonari no 801-chan*, a manga about a *yaoi* fangirl, and ***Genshiken*** is about otaku culture in general but also fangirls specifically.

P. 48   **"If you want to shoot the general, first, give up."** The actual saying is "If you want to shoot the general, first, shoot his horse."

P. 51   **"Divine resignation in the darkest of times."** The actual saying is "Divine supplication only in dark times," referring to people who only show piety when something bad happens.

P. 52   ***"How to Get a Girl in Four Days."*** The movie is called *How to Lose a Guy in Ten Days*, a romantic comedy.

P. 54   *"I bet she'd be good at mah-jongg."* Hikigaya is most certainly talking about the mah-jongg manga *Saki* by Ritz Kobayashi.

Chapter 4 ⋯ At the end of the day, **Hina Ebina** is rotten?

P. 57   **"We're producing, Producer!"** This is an *Idolmaster* meme based off Haruka Amami's line "It's (Tokyo) Dome! The Dome!!" The pattern "Producer-san! It's ___! ___!" is used to emphasize whatever you're excited about.

P. 58   *"A Man's Journey Alone: The Kyoto Arc* or *The Ten Warrior Conspiracy Arc* or *Trust and Betrayal."* Aside from the "man's journey alone" bit, these are all *Rurouni Kenshin* references: to an arc of the anime/manga, one of the PS1 games, and one of the OVAs, respectively.

P. 58   **"Just call me Flip Turner."** Flip Turner is the English name for Tokunosuke Hyori in *Yu-Gi-Oh! ZEXAL*. His deck revolves around Flip Effect monsters. The original joke here was a wordplay between Hachiman skipping pages and the nonsense catchphrase of Yuuma Tsukumo, the protagonist of *ZEXAL*, which is *Kattobingu da ze, ore!* dubbed as "feeling the flow."

P. 58   *"Stop the romance!"* "Romantic ga Tomaranai" (The romance doesn't stop) is a 1985 pop song by the band C-C-B. They perform the song while wearing wedding dresses.

P. 58   **Arashiyama** is a popular tourist area in northwest Kyoto city, while **Toufuku-ji Temple** is a large Zen temple in southeastern Kyoto. Both are staple spots for seeing the landscape and fall leaves. **Fushimi Inari Shrine** is a very popular shrine dedicated to Inari, god of rice. The shrine is most famous for its long row of red torii gates.

P. 60   **"'Hey,' I responded, reminiscent of a certain NHK character."** Hikigaya says *domo*, which is also the name of the NHK mascot, Domo-kun.

P. 61   **"This will ruin the love triangle!!"** The Japanese here says "Triangle Heart" instead of "love triangle," a reference to the *eroge* better known for being the source of the far-more-popular spin-off *Magical Lyrical Girl Nanoha*.

P. 61   **"We were completely dumbfounded. Not just astounded or confounded but dumbfounded... We had found all the dumb there was to find."** The Japanese wordplay here was on a phrase meaning "speechless" and similar-sounding words referring to five- and seven-lined poems. The word, pronounced *zekku*, is then followed by the line "If you write it as ZECK, it sounds kind of like a band manga," in reference to the manga *BECK* by Harold Sakuishi.

P. 61   **"Guh-heh-heh-heh-heh..."** In Japanese, Ebina laughs like *fu-fu-fu*, with the *fu*s written with the character "rotten" from the word *fujoshi* (slash fangirl). Replacing *fu* syllables with the "rotten" character is a common sort of wordplay among *fujoshi*.

P. 63   **"...I want you to take them all at once, right to the bottom...of your heart."** The word Ebina uses here is *sasoiuke*, which is typically used in BL circles to refer to a bottom who initiates sex.

P. 63   **"This was the feeling of overwhelming despair you get when there are still two more transformations left."** This is a reference to Freiza's transformation power in *Dragon Ball*.

P. 63   **"You're a fail bottom."** Fail bottom / *hetare uke* isn't a term that's actually used, because *ukes* are often sort of incompetent by nature, so this is double emphasizing Hachiman's loserdom. *Hetare seme* describes a guy who tries to be a top but isn't very good at it.

P. 66   **"Is there any love there?"** is a famous line from the 1993 TV drama *Hitotsu no Yane no Shita* (Under one roof).

P. 68   **"Crawling with love, I might hope."** *Crawling with Love* is the English subtitle for *Nyaruko: Crawling with Love*, by Manta Aisora. The Japanese joke here was a pun on the word *juuoumujun* (meaning "everywhere") and Juuou Kaishin-geki (Beast King Critical Hit), the special attack move of Crocodine from the manga *Dragon Quest: Dai no Daibouken*.

P. 68   *Nama yatsuhashi* are mochi-based sweets with various fillings that are a local specialty in Kyoto. They look like little flat dumplings.

Chapter 5 ⋯ As you can see, **Yui Yuigahama** is doing her best.

P. 71   *"'Sup! I'm Hachiman! I'm goin' to Tokyo!"* The first two greetings are a reference to an iconic line from *Dragon Ball* from Goku, using his particular country-bumpkin manner of speech. The last sentence is *Ora Tokyo sa iku da*, which is the name of a song by the artist Yoshi Ikuzou, a name which is itself a pun meaning "Okay, let's go!"

P. 73   **"I was swept along by the crowds so much, I started wondering if someone was going to occasionally scold me from afar for changing."** This is a reference to the lyrics of the pop song "Sotsugyou Shashin" (Graduation photo) by Yumi Matsutouya: "Sometimes you scold me from afar as I change, swept along by the crowds. You are my youth itself."

P. 73   **"Even in this crowded station, I'll be what I am, a solitary (Hachi) man."** This is a line from the Neil Diamond song "Solitary Man." In Japanese, here Hikigaya describes the station as Hacchi Bocchi Station, a pun on *Hotch Potch Station*, the name of a children's educational show with puppets that ran from 1995 to 2005, and his own name and the word *loner* (*bocchi*).

P. 73 **Mount Kurama**, near Kyoto, is the site of Kurama Temple, and it's said to be where the *tengu* taught swordsmanship to Minamoto no Yoshitsune, a military commander of the Heian and Kamakura periods and one of the most famous samurai in Japanese history.

P. 75 **"Time to activate my shadow skill."** *Shadow Skill* is the name of a 1990s fantasy-action manga and anime. Within the context of the anime, "shadow skills" are a focus on kicks and footwork, though.

P. 75 **"Encounters in Space!"** This is referencing the PS2 game *Mobile Suit Gundam: Encounters in Space*.

P. 79 **"What a nice day for a trip!"** "Ii Hi no Tabidachi" is the name of a 1978 ballad by Momoe Yamaguchi, and it was adopted by Japanese National Railways as a slogan encouraging people to travel.

P. 86 **Nio** are two wrathful, muscular guardians of the Buddha whose statues stand guard at the entrance of many temples in Japan.

P. 90 **"I wondered if this was a Pokémon talking…"** As in, the Pokémon Ditto. In Japanese, Ebina says *da ne* (yeah), with the Pokémon in question being Fushigidane (Bulbasaur).

P. 91 ***"…that's what you do at a shrine."*** In this scene, Hachiman and Yui are in a Buddhist temple, so Yui is mixing up traditions. When at a Shinto shrine, the proper way to pray is to put money in the offertory box, ring the bell, bow twice, clap your hands in prayer twice, and then bow once more.

P. 93 **Daikokuten** (Great God of Darkness) is one of the seven lucky gods and often portrayed with a black face. He's a god of commerce and prosperity, and he usually carries a bag of goods.

P. 93   The **iron geta** (traditional sandals) in Kiyomizu-dera Temple are very heavy, and it's said that managing to walk while wearing them brings good fortune.

P. 97   **"Gaia must have been whispering at him to shine more."** This is a play on the slogan from the fashion magazine *Men's Knuckle*, which has been memeified and parodied many times.

P. 97   **"...kinda like that show where you get a million yen if you can perform some difficult stunt."** *If You Can Do This, You Get a Million Yen*, also known as *Sports Bakka*, is a TV game show that involved various physical challenges somewhat like *Takeshi's Castle* (and starred many of the same people).

P. 100   *"It's a-me, Wario."* This is a reference to a Wario spin-off manga called *Ore Dayo! Wario Dayo!* (It's me! It's Wario!) by Yuki Sawada. In Japanese, Mario and Wario don't talk with the fake Italian accent, making this bit a little less strange.

P. 101   *Shochu* is a distilled spirit most commonly made from sweet potato, barley, or rice.

Chapter 6 ⋯ Surreptitiously, **Yukino Yukinoshita** goes out to town at night.

P. 103   **King Crimson** is a Stand power in *Jojo's Bizarre Adventure* that can erase time.

P. 104   **"...rambling about *pon* and *kan* and *ponkan*."** *Pon* and *kan* are terms used when playing mah-jongg, and Ponkan is the artist who illustrates these light novels.

P. 104 *"I'm not that sort of pervert or a prince, though…"* This is a reference to the title of the light novel series *Hentai Prince and the Stony Cat*.

P. 105 **"…in the casual sort of way that Isono invites Nakajima."** These are little kids from the long-running newspaper comic *Sazae-san*. Isono is constantly inviting Nakajima to play baseball or soccer with him.

P. 105 **"Listen, Hachiemon. They're so mean!"** Zaimokuza is imitating Nobita, the protagonist of the children's anime *Doraemon*. Nobita often whines to his friend Doraemon, looking for help.

P. 105 *"Don't say it like it's* **Crayon Kingdom."** *The Dream Crayon Kingdom* is an anime for small children. The opening theme song includes the nonsense lyrics *mmm paka paka. Dokapon Kingdom* is a PS2 RPG–board game hybrid that takes four players.

P. 105 **Momotetsu** is short for Momotaro Densetsu, a series of board game–style video games revolving around trains and transportation. Much like Monopoly, it can bring out the worst in people.

P. 106 *"Shut up with your r-r-r-r-reverse; do you think it's time to d-d-d-d-duel or something?"* The original joke here was a wordplay on the Yuuji Oda pop song "Somebody Tonight," which includes a portion that goes "never, never, never, never," which, slurred and incorrectly pronounced, sounds vaguely like *riba, riba, riba, riba* (*riba* = reverse).

P. 107 *"Dirty as I expected, Zaimokuza, dirty."* This is a play on a quote from a notorious *FFXI* player Buronto: "Dirty as expected, ninja, dirty." Buronto is the source of many memes, such as *Kore de katsuru* (With this, I can win!), a meme that has appeared in these novels before.

P. 108 *Tsumo* is when you win in mah-jongg with a concealed hand from a tile you drew rather than taking a tile from someone else. It's a rather early-game sort of win.

P. 110   **Gagaga** is the name of the imprint this series is published under in Japanese.

P. 114   *Hayama* **arrows** are lucky charms shaped like arrows; they're rather bulky and delicate items to be bringing home in a backpack.

P. 117, 118   **Musashi Miyamoto** is possibly the most famous swordsman in Japanese history, and it's said he fought over a hundred duels and never lost. He's perhaps best known for authoring *The Book of Five Rings*, which is about combat and philosophy. The **Yoshioka** style is a school of sword-fighting martial arts.

P. 118   **"Taxis are fast. Faster than Salamander."** This is a reference to the SNES-era Square RPG *Bahamut Lagoon*. The heroine, Yoyo, says, "It's faster than Salamander!" when she rides on the dragon belonging to the general of the enemy forces, comparing it with Salamander, the dragon belonging to the protagonist. The line has been latched on to as a joke.

P. 118   **"Yes, Tenkaippin. Not Dera-beppin."** He's referring to *Deluxe Beppin* (Deluxe beauty), an adult magazine.

P. 119   **"...gazing at the storefront of Tenichi with sincere passion."** Tenichi is a nickname for Tenkaippin.

P. 125   **"C'mon to Kamogawa Sea World!"** This is an aquarium in Chiba that coincidentally has the same name as an area in Kyoto. *C'mon to Kamogawa Sea World* is their advertising slogan.

Chapter 7 ⋯ Unexpectedly, **Yumiko Miura** is actually paying attention.

P. 127   **Yoshiwara Street** was a designated zone for male and female prostitutes in Edo (the old name for Tokyo) during the Tokugawa period.

P. 129   *Oiran* were prostitutes and entertainers, generally distinct from geisha in that geisha were not technically prostitutes (though it was common for them to sleep with clients for various reasons). Over time, *oiran* came to be more elaborately made-up and more exclusive than geisha, who tend to be dressed in a more restrained way. While geisha still exist, *oiran* do not, since prostitution was made illegal in 1958.

P. 131   **"...screaming *Sooooi! Soi! Sooooi!...*"** The cry of "Soi!" is a meme that originated with the gag manga *Pyu to Fuku! Jaguar* (Make It Toot, Jaguar). It doesn't mean anything.

P. 134   **"His pretty smile was curing me with the glittering force of all the stars. It made my heart pound, bringing the feelings inside me to a new stage."** This is just a string of Precure references, from *Smile Pretty Cure!* to *Doki-Doki Precure* (localized as *Glitter Force Doki-Doki*) to *Pretty Cure All-Stars* and *All Stars: New Stage*.

P. 134   **"I glanced at the shop and saw Ebina rapt and panting at the Shinsengumi goods..."** There is a phenomenon of *rekijo* in Japan, young women with a particular interest in Japanese history, and tourist shops go out of their way to appeal to these types with their merchandise. In the same way you might see the romance section of an American bookstore crowded with Regency-period romances, Meiji-period historical dramas, manga, and novels featuring the Shinsengumi are so popular, it's a cliche that girls are only in it for the handsome men and BL potential.

P. 135   **"Mentally cackling..."** He's using a particular type of laughter, *kue-kue-kue*, a reference to the gag manga *Ah! Hana no Ouendan* (Oh! The Flower Cheer Squad). The main character laughs like this.

P. 135   **"*She's kind of housewifely...* She was being pretty strict about money..."** Traditionally speaking, family finances are the wife's duty in a Japanese household, and the stingy wife refusing to let her husband spend money on things is a centuries-old stereotype.

P. 135 **"I'm the fun-money alchemist."** Referring to *Fullmetal Alchemist*. In Japanese, this was *kogane no renkinjutsu* (pocket change alchemy).

P. 137 **"Or if it's *Conan*, it means someone will die."** Hachiman is referring to the anime/manga *Detective Conan*. Literally hundreds of the episodes involve locked-room murder mysteries.

P. 138 **"I have an established reputation for playing defense."** This is yet another reference to a line from the basketball manga *Slam Dunk* that has since become a meme: "Ikegami, who has an established reputation for playing defense."

P. 140 **"...*Tsurezuregusa*, which often shows up in textbooks."** *Tsurezuregusa*, also known as *Essays in Idleness*, are a prominent piece of twelfth-century literature by the monk Yoshida Kenkou with heavy Buddhist themes.

P. 141 **Ryouan-ji** and **Tenryuu-ji Temples** both contain the character for "dragon," while **Konkai Koumyou-ji** and **Kyouou Gokoku-ji Temples** really just have alliteration and length. **Adashino Nenbutsu-ji Temple** is mainly notable because *adashi* is an unusual reading for the character used. Adashino is the name of the district of Kyoto where the temple is located, and *nenbutsu* (or *nembutsu*) is a particular type of Buddhist invocation.

P. 146 *Manga **Nihon Mukashibanashi*** (*Manga Japanese Folk Tales*) is a series of animated shorts from the 1970s featuring classic fairy tales like "Momotaro" and "Tsukihime." Many scenes in the show involve bowls of rice piled abnormally high, such that a "folk-tale serving" has become shorthand to mean a "giant serving of rice."

P. 146 *Sunday GX*, a magazine in the *Shonen Sunday* line, is the manga-serialization magazine that the *Oregairu* manga runs in.

Chapter 8 ··· Even so, **Hayato Hayama** can't make a choice.

P. 154 **"There's a lot of stuff in Nagoya besides that, like *tenmusu* and the Mountain café and stuff."** *Tenmusu* is *onigiri*/rice balls with shrimp tempura filling. Mountain is the name of a famous café in Nagoya that serves inventive desserts.

P. 154 **"And people from Nagoya end their sentences with *mya*, so perhaps Yukinoshita thinks they're felines."** This is slightly exaggerated for comic effect. Nagoya dialect involves ending sentences with *ya* rather than the northern copula *da*. Sometimes, this results in *mya*-like sounds for certain words.

P. 155 The **Bakumatsu years** refers to the final years of the Tokugawa period (before 1868). It was a time of great political upheaval, when Japan opened its borders after hundreds of years of isolation from the world, and it's the subject of a lot of popular fiction.

P. 155 **"...Honnou-ji Temple is deeply disappointing..."** Honnou-ji Temple is famous for being the site where Oda Nobunaga (the notoriously brutal wartime general) committed seppuku, surrounded by the forces of the traitor Mitsuhide Akechi. This scene has been replicated in a lot of pop culture. However, the real temple was burned down, and it was rebuilt in another location, and on the site of Nobunaga's demise there is now nothing more than a stone monument. It really is very disappointing.

P. 161 *Ema* are little pieces of wood with a horse on one side and a wish written on the other. They're hung up on stands at shrines.

P. 163   **"...Yuigahama had tamed a wild fox squirrel."** Hachiman is referencing a scene early in *Nausicaa of the Valley of Wind* in which Nausicaa
tames a wild fox squirrel. It bites her finger, and she chants at it, "There's
nothing to be scared of, nothing to be scared of," until it ends up licking
her finger.

P. 165   **"I was feeling kind of on edge myself, although I'm always on the
edges of any social situation, really."** In Japanese, he says, "I was feeling kind of nervous enough that I think I could have killed some mos-
quitoes," a pun on nervous (*kinchou*) and Kincho, a brand of insect spray.

Chapter 9 ⋯ **His and her** confessions will reach no one.

P. 182   **"Because I'm rotten."** The word Ebina uses here has a bunch of different meanings that are basically impossible to convey at once in English.
It can mean perverted, especially in the sense of a *fujoshi* (literally "rotten woman") who likes m/m fiction. It can also mean rotten in the
sense of depraved, something that has lost its purity and is spiritually
degraded. Hikigaya is often described in these terms.

Bonus track! The girls will rock you. ♡

P. 188   **"Like not having to use conditioner, or how it's got moisturizer
in it, or how foaming it up turns it into a duck."** Merit is the brand
name for a line of hair products.

P. 194   **"You know the old wisdom. *Article the first: Softness of* menma
*is to be valued. Article the second: Sincerely revere the three
treasures—noodles, broth, and toppings.*"** This is a parody of Prince
Shoutoku Taishi's Seventeen Article Constitution written in the *Nihon
Shoki* in AD 604. The real articles are: 1) Harmony is to be valued, and
the avoidance of wanton opposition to be honored. 2) Sincerely revere

the three treasures: the Buddha, dharma (his teaching), and sangha (Buddhist community).

P. 196   **"Just who the hell do you think I am?!"** Kamina's iconic line from *Tengen Toppa Gurren Lagann*.

P. 197   *"Why so reckless? Are you Botchan?"* Botchan is the titular protagonist of a Natsume Soseki novel. The very first line of the book describes him as reckless. Botchan is generally translated as "Young Master."

P. 199   *Okonomiyaki* is something like a savory pancake, usually with pork and cabbage in it, but you can put anything you like in it. *Monjayaki* uses basically the same ingredients and set-up (they're both served on a flat grill on the customer's table), but *monjayaki* is a more liquid, scrambled version.

P. 201   **"Burrraaah!"** This particular yell is a reference to Cell in *Dragonball Z*, and also to his voice actor, Norio Wakamoto, who is famous for doing such yells.

P. 201   **"Prostrate thyself before me!"** "Prostrate thyself before me" is a line most associated with *Mito Koumon*, a super-long-running historical drama that ran from 1969 to 2011, about Tokugawa Mitsukuni, a retired vice-shogun who roams Japan.

P. 201   **"Is that your Solomon Style?"** *Solomon-ryuu* (Solomon style) is the name of an educational/documentary TV show.

P. 203   **"…it started with the climax."** This is a reference to the catchphrase of the protagonist of *Kamen Rider Den-O*, Ryotaro Nogami: "From start to finish, I'm always at a climax!"

P. 204   **"Put the two together, and they're Twenty Million Powers."** Twenty Million Powers is the name of a tag team in *Kinnikuman/Ultimate Muscle*.

P. 204 **"But mixing black and black just gets you more black... It's just like Gin said, really..."** Gin is a villain from *Detective Conan*, the member of the Black Organization who made Shinichi swallow APTX 4869 to turn him into a kid.

P. 205 **"Yuigahama stared into thin air with a cute little noise and thought back."** The noise here is *hoeee*, Sakura's characteristic moe noise in *Cardcaptor Sakura*.

P. 209 **"So this is the Tenchi-matou! Defense, Attack, and Magic all in one stance!"** The Tenchi-matou stance is the ultimate stance used by Vearn, the villain of the manga *Dragon Quest: Dai no Daibouken* (Dai's great adventure). It's supposed to counter any and all attacks.

P. 210 **"The dream situation... Bandai, the company that brings good times!"** Bandai-Namco's corporate slogan is *Dreams, fun, and inspiration*, while premerger, Bandai's corporate slogan was *Dreams and creation*. Both of them sound rather like "dreamy situation."

P. 211 The **Yamanote Line** is the loop train line in downtown Tokyo. It's an alternate name for the game they're about to play because "stations on the Yamanote Line" are a common subject for the game.

P. 212 **"That's way too basic... You could turn that into a programming language."** The original joke here is "That's more ZAQ than the opening of *Sasami-san*," a pun on *zakkuri* (rough, sketchy, basic) and ZAQ, the band that does the opening of *Sasami-san@ganbaranai*.

P. 216 **"Your sense of humor is pitch-black! Are you the coffee sisters?"** In the original, Hikigaya asks if they're gum, a reference to Lotte Black Black caffeinated gum.

P. 217 **"...this is bait!"** In the original, this was a reference to an ASCII-art character originating on 4chan. English speakers would know him exclusively as Pedobear, but on 2ch, he was used as a response to posts that were "fishing" for attention. Thus, his iconic poses include running toward the "bait" and his mouth being caught.

P. 217   **"It's great when *Wataru* and stuff is on."** *Mashin Hero Wataru* is a 1980s kids super-robot anime.

P. 218   **"...on weekends, after Super Hero Time..."** Super Hero Time is a weekend time slot for *tokusatsu/sentai* shows.

P. 220   ***"My Classmates and Acquaintances Fight Too Much!"*** This is a parody of the light-novel series *My Girlfriend and Childhood Friend Fight Too Much*, also known as *Oreshura*.

P. 220   **"Cat and dog fight, ready, go!"** This is a parody of "Gundam fight, ready, go!" from *G-Gundam*.

P. 220   **"Ah! Hikki, you like Chiiba-kun, and he's a dog!"** Chiiba-kun is the prefectural mascot of Chiba prefecture. He's a strange-shaped red dog with a pointed nose, designed after the shape of Chiba.

P. 221   **"Welcome to the Underground..."** This is something that's "whispered into the ears" of people who access 2ch for the first time.

P. 222   **"In the name of the moon, they'll punish you!"** Referring to the catchphrase of Usagi Tsukino, the heroine of *Sailor Moon*. Her first name means "bunny."

P. 222   **"And there'll be more fan service, too!"** Misato says this during nearly every next-episode preview in *Evangelion*.

P. 223 "Ngh! The ultimate three-way choice between cool, passion, and cute..." Cool, passion, and cute are categories of idols in the Idolmaster games.

P. 227 "Love live!" Love Live is a major multimedia franchise based on the theme of cute idol stars.

P. 227 "I-is there a regulation length for modified electric glow sticks?!" Zaimokuza is talking about a little hack that fans of idols do that involves replacing the light for an electric glow stick with a stronger bulb. It's typical to wave glow sticks of a certain color at idol concerts, as an idol will have a theme color. Idol fan clubs will regulate various things about audience participation, including the type of glow sticks used and fan chants.

Afterword

P. 231 "How about Supreme Kai?" Supreme Kai is a rank for certain individuals with godly powers in *Dragonball Z*.